DETERMINATION

The Life of

Eugene & Elizabeth

By Marie E. Rickwood

FriesenPress

One Printers Way
Altona, MB R0G 0B0
Canada

www.friesenpress.com

ISBN

978-1-03-916724-7 (Hardcover)
978-1-03-916723-0 (Paperback)
978-1-03-916725-4 (eBook)

1. *FICTION, BIOGRAPHICAL*

Distributed to the trade by The Ingram Book Company

Table of Contents

This book is dedicated to Dr. Dennis Waechter,

the youngest offspring of Eugene and Elizabeth

who passed away on April 18th, 2022,

the year this book was written.

Determination must fuel hope and desire if success is to be realized.

Marie Rickwood

Acknowledgements

Thanks to my children: Rory, Michelle, Derek, Kellee, Roanne and Jill for their inspiration and encouragement especially my daughter, Kellee for designing the cover and providing the many beautiful pictures, and to my son Derek for his technical support. Also, a special thanks to my husband, Val Fenton for his invaluable input regarding the operation of a farm.

I am also grateful to my seven brothers and sisters: Georgina, Milton, Mervin, Alvin, Celine, Roland, and Dennis. My collaboration with them over the years provided valuable information for writing this story of our parents, Eugene, and Elizabeth Waechter.

Forward

Wouldn't it be amazing if one could have a special screen in the home where a time frame could be inputted for us to look back on our ancestors? Even more amazing if we could, at the same time, also learn about their character, their strengths and weakness, successes, talents and how they handled failures. More importantly what diseases they may have had so we could prepare ourselves for the possibility of inheriting them.

To know something about the people that came before us helps to establish a full identity of oneself. Some of us know very little about our ancestors, some have not met their own grandparents. Many people have a genealogy chart giving names and dates, very few have life stories. It was with this lodged solidly in my mind that I decided to write the story of my parents, Eugene, and Elizabeth Waechter to provide their many descendants with an insight into their character.

The genre of this book is fictional based on fact. The fiction portion gives their story some colour while the most important incidents bring out the facts. Enjoy the read!

Chapter One

In the dim morning light, two altar servers from St. Peter's Cathedral, protected with earmuffs, scampered up the belfry's dusty staircase, pushing and jostling each other to reach the top. Each wanted to be first so that he could ride the rope across the belfry and ring the bell. But the shorter of the two, the less likely, won the race. With both hands gripping the rope in a fit of laughter, he kicked off the rafters and squealed, "Yippee," as he rode the long swing clear across the expanse. Had he looked down, he would have noticed the little mouse he'd disturbed, scurrying along a beam to get out of the way.

The familiar, haunting sound of the big, iron bell carried its message on the wind to every corner of the little town of London, Ontario. Many inhabitants jumped quickly out of bed to prepare for the Holy Mass, it announced, while a few others, groggy with slumber, turned lazily over and, before falling back to sleep, patted their guilty conscience with a weak promise to attend next Sunday.

It's 1924, twenty-year-old Eugene Waechter from Walkerton, Ontario, was lying in his bunk, waiting to hear that bell. Yes, he was waiting for the echoing sound to reach his ears. At this moment, its ring hung in the air like a call to freedom. He'd lain awake all night in the sparsely furnished dorm, staring at the ceiling, deep in calculating thought about how he would make his escape from St. Peter's Seminarian College. What would his father say when the deacon informed him of his departure? Would he be angry? Would his father come looking for him? Whatever the result, Eugene had to escape this seminarian life, a life he'd pretended to want, but it was a lie he'd been living these past three months, and it was carving a giant hole in his conscience.

His mother, Cecelia, died when he was three and a half years old. All he could remember about his mother was her gentleness, her big, warm, gray eyes, and the scent of flowers about her. He loved her perfume and could recall it on demand. There was nothing the doctors, with their limited medicines, could have done to save her life when the poison from an infected tooth traveled through her bloodstream. She was only thirty-three years old when she died, leaving her husband and five children in complete devastation. Her death was also a shock to the entire German community of Walkerton, Ontario.

Eugene had learned his father John Waechter had been heartsick and desperate after his wife Cecelia had died. John hadn't known how to overcome his sorrow or fill the gap her absence had caused. They had been married for fifteen years. She had been a committed wife and mother whose vast expertise in managing a household was sorely missed. She had carried the pedigree from a family that strived for success and achieved it. Her father was the first Reeve of the district, and two of her brothers, both medical doctors, had immigrated to Shakopee, Minnesota, to open a clinic. To replace Cecelia was impossible; however, a substitute was necessary, and so he married a spinster from up the road.

Eugene had missed his mother. He had expected to see her in the morning when he woke. He had wanted to see her cooking at the stove. He had wanted to feel her gentle touch when she combed his hair. Why did she have to leave? Where did she go?

The home was hollow without her. He would stick his head out his bedroom window and call, "Mom, Mom, Mom!"

John Waechter felt music was essential in a child's life, and he thought it might be a diversion that would help Eugene. His father, Stephen, had always sung *Alouette* and other French songs that he had carried from his childhood, all learned from his ancestral grandmother, Ann-Marie LaCroix who made music an integral part of the family's life.

The love of music was carried down the line. John hired a music teacher to give violin, trumpet, and piano lessons. Of all the children, Eugene had the most outstanding aptitude for music. He would later become one of the best trumpet players in the area, but trumpet playing wasn't something from which one could make a living. As the years went by and the children grew, it was clear that Clem, the eldest, would be the farmer to follow in his father's footsteps and someday take over the farm. Antoinette, next in line, had a religious nature, so she would enter the convent. The two younger girls, Rose, and Nora, seemed destined for marriage; this was the conclusion of a concerned father.

But Eugene, his handsome Eugene, floundered. It was Eugene who posed the greatest worry. He didn't have his feet on the ground somehow, didn't have a purpose in life, didn't have any direction. For this reason, John Waechter spoke on the phone with the rector of St. Peter's Seminary and told him about his predicament with his youngest offspring.

"Quite often, Mr. Waechter," stated the rector, "young men receive their calling once here. We have a lad who came in as a rangy-tang hoodlum who had broken the law several times. Today, religious life has transformed him into a pious, happy man who heads the new seminarians' theological training."

That was all John Waechter needed to hear. He packed Eugene's things and delivered him to the seminary along with a cheque for two hundred dollars. Eugene sat pensively beside his father on the train for the long ride to London, Ontario. They hardly spoke. The rhythmic spinning of the train wheels on the steel tracks kept time with his thoughts. All he could think of was he would now have a change of scene, now he wouldn't have to hear the voice of that stepmother again nor be under the iron thumb of his father. Today he would be putting all those things behind him. He would be starting a new life.

That day, the church bell seemed to ring more loudly than ever. Eugene jumped out of bed. He glanced out the window and saw the shadows of night-time lifting as dawn took hold. The church bell always forewarned the freight train's passing. It would be along soon, he'd better hurry. He was lucky it always slowed down when passing the seminary, having a conductor who thought the fast rattle of the train might disturb the prayers within.

He dressed and slipped the note he'd written to the rector under his pillow, just a short note that read:

> Dear Father O'Malley,
>
> Please inform my father that I have gone to Alberta to work in the harvest. The priesthood is not for me.
>
> Eugene Waechter.

Unnoticed, he stepped into the rear of the long line of seminarians silently marching off to chapel. The smell of candles and incense followed them as they walked down the long hallway, down the stairs, and out the door. As they walked across the courtyard, Eugene broke ranks again unnoticed and scampered down the hill. He snatched up the duffel bag he'd stowed the night before beneath the low, outstretched branches of the seminary's landmark, a giant,

Douglas fir tree, and made his way towards the tracks. Eugene sat on the bank panting, his heart thumping as he caught his breath. He cocked his head. He heard a low rumble in the distance; the tracks were in use, and the train was on its way. He thought about the leap he was about to make into the moving boxcar while holding his duffel bag. He hoped the doorway would be wide enough and that he wouldn't misjudge and fall beneath the wheels. He glanced at the tracks, glinting under the morning sunlight, and shuddered at the thought. Just then, a rooster crowed, reminding him of the family farm where he had grown up. He thought about the past several weeks in the seminary, living amidst the whispers, the distant chanting, and silent footsteps; Every day, Eugene had heard a voice in his head saying: "This life is not for you. You have to get out of here." So, when he wasn't involved with the daily routine, he'd lain on his bunk, pondering his dilemma. He pondered so often he'd memorized every groove and curve of the plaster on the ceiling. Catholicism would always be at the core of his existence, but he wouldn't be a fanatic about it and did not want to be a priest. He wanted a wife and a family to call his own.

Luckily, riding free on a freight train was a common practice. Eugene couldn't help but consider it a good omen how, one morning while he had been strolling across the seminary's lawn, a newspaper had fallen off a milk wagon and blown over to his feet. It reported the need for men in Heisler, Alberta, to help with threshing. That was all Eugene needed to begin hatching his escape. He knew it would take three days to get there. He had a small stash of money from the last few dances back home where he'd performed with his trumpet. If he were careful, the money would sustain him until he received the first paycheque.

Now Eugene saw billowing steam in the distance. The roar of the train's engine and the groan of its wheels grew louder and louder. His mouth went dry while the morning breeze cooled his brow where perspiration had formed. And there it was, a giant, black beast puffing steam. He was relieved to see it had slowed to a snail's pace. He grabbed his heavy duffel bag with his cherished trumpet shifting inside. He watched for an open doorway. He saw one, took a deep breath, and leaped.

***

Heisler, Alberta, predominately Catholic, was a German community of hardworking people. Their ingenuity on how to live off the land served them well. Wheat was their mainstay. They grew it by the bushel to sell at the elevator in Heisler, always hoping for a sustainable price. And they planted extensive gardens of vegetables to preserve for the winter. In addition, they raised their beef, pork, and chickens and harvested honey from the many hives situated around the farm.

The women preserved all the produce from the gardens and everything else that came within their hands, including wild strawberries, cranberries, chokecherries, and blueberries which they found growing in abundance in the woodlands and grassy knolls. When the berries were at their peak of ripeness, the women quickly transformed them into fruit, jams, and jellies, a common practice for that part of Alberta. There were no empty spaces on the shelves in their cellars; all were loaded, sealer by a sealer, to ensure an adequate supply for the long winter months ahead. There was always an ample supply of sauerkraut fermenting in large crocks with a stone weighing the cabbage down into the brine. Pork hocks stewed in this kraut was a favorite meal.

Eugene was tired, hungry, and haggard from several days of little sleep. The food he'd been able to pick up at stations along the way was meager. So, when he stumbled into Heisler's Co-op Store, his rumpled clothes were crusty with boxcar dust, his dark, curly hair had fallen past his ears, and his black stubble of a beard made his large gray eyes even larger. His appearance was enough to scare any barber!

As he slowly made his way over the oiled, wooden floors towards the back of the store, he saw a small, gray-haired man standing on a stool behind the counter, putting tobacco cans high up on a shelf. He passed a meridional of farm tools hanging from the ceiling and saw a collection of farm equipment and mechanical tools on the shelves and in barrels. He saw halters, bridals, reigns, shovels and picks, lanterns, coal oil, and gas lamps. Then, standing next to the latest butter churn on display, he saw rolls of oilcloth in all colors and designs ready to be sold by the piece for covering kitchen tables. And the last thing he saw was a box filled with flycatcher ribbons that no farm wife would want to be without.

"Hello, my name is Eugene Waechter, he stammered. I understand there's a need for men to help with the harvest." The words fell out of his mouth in pieces.

The store clerk stepped down off the stool, turned around, and looked aghast at the haggard, travel-worn man before him, but before he could respond, Eugene spoke again, but more clearly now that he had his second wind, "I've come on a freight train from Walkerton,

Ontario." He wasn't expecting him to know where that was. The store clerk didn't conceal his surprise as he shook Eugene's hand.

"All the way from Ontario! By golly, you must have had quite the ride! I'm pleased to meet you; I'm Joseph Schmeltzer. Well, you've come to the right place. There's plenty of work here. This year it's a bumper crop, the best in history, with just the right amount of sun and rain at the right time! The Meyers farm, three miles south of here, is desperate for men to help with the threshing, and they offer room and board." He paused, then added as an afterthought. "Mrs. Meyers is the best cook in town. You can't miss their place. Their name is on the roof of their barn."

"That's good to hear," replied Eugene, as relief washed over him. But, before he could ask where he could get a horse, Joseph continued as though reading his mind, "Sam across the street at the livery stable has extra horses. You could borrow one as long as you keep it well-fed."

Eugene thanked him in German, knowing he would understand with a name like Schmeltzer. He was right. Joseph appreciated hearing a stranger speak his language. He was beaming when he responded in German, telling him he was welcome. Eugene left and walked back out the door. He hurried across the street with a fresh spring to his step. His fatigue slowly began to ebb.

He was relieved! Everything was going his way! He couldn't have felt more grateful as he rode his borrowed horse down the narrow main street. He was surprised at the small size of the town. He noticed three horses tied to hitching posts outside the small hotel; two were hitched to democrats and the other to a small, two-wheel cart.

Also, in line on the street and looking very much out of place was a Model T Ford. Watkins, a company that provided over four hundred household items to the community, had its name emblazoned on its door. Eugene's family in Ontario used their camphor salve to treat colds. They also purchased their large tin of cinnamon for the delicious buns that came out of their oven every week.

At the edge of town, a Catholic Church stood tall and stately. Eugene gave a long-exhausted sigh, "Everything here is so much like back home!" he marveled aloud. "Including the German language."

Although there was a nagging worry about his future, he smiled as he shook the reins and said, "Giddy-up." He had to say it twice to bring his stodgy horse into a trot, sending three magpies pecking along on the ground into flight. He was anxious to reach his destination. He gazed across at the long stretch of land with its fields of golden wheat, heavy with ripe kernels, swaying in the breeze. He marveled at the landscape's flatness, the absence of hills, and how the distant earth melted into the horizon, interlocking the golden wheat with the pale-blue sky.

Chapter Two

Three days later, the Thomas' home, four miles south of town, like most days was in a flurry of activity. Today they were busy canning. There was a multitude of sealers to wash, mostly the two-quart size. And they needed to be sterilized – a double boiler sat on top of the cookstove for this very purpose. Today there would be much canning accomplished, and everyone would participate. There were eight children in the family. Rosella, eleven, was the youngest. They all knew how to work. Ludvina and Elizabeth were busy scraping carrots and chucking peas. Their older sister had married the year before.

Lawrence, the third son, had just returned from town, where he had bought several cases of canning sealers from the Co-op Store for his mother. He spoke excitedly, "I've got some interesting news," he sang out, a grin dancing on his face. But Lawrence

15

wasn't in a hurry to divulge his news quickly; he just kept smiling. Oh, how he was enjoying himself! Ludvina and Elizabeth were all ears.

"You don't have to look so smug just cuz you know something we don't," said Elizabeth.

"Yeh," said Ludvina, "What's your news this time?"

"Let me hear, pretty please, then maybe I'll tell you," replied Lawrence.

Then Ma Thomas walked into the room. She was a petite woman with dark auburn hair gathered back in a bun. Her sparkling eyes were flashing as she gazed about. A milk pail filled to the top with small beets was in her hand. Moving quickly, she set it down on the floor near the table.

"Are you teasing the girls again, Lawrence?"

"Who me?" He gave his best look of innocence. His mother's laughter filled the room.

"Lawrence has some news, Mom, and he wants us to beg him to tell us."

"Now, I'm curious too. What is it, Son?"

"Okay, anything for you, Mom." Lawrence's eyes were shining.

"There's a new man in town. He's traveled over two thousand miles to get here – all the way from Ontario."

"Ontario!" gasped the girls.

"Yes, all the way from Ontario, he's here to help with the harvest. He also speaks German. His name is Eugene Waechter. And something more that's hard to believe. He rode the freight train the whole distance. And he's in his early twenties, as far as Sam could tell.

"I'm surprised you didn't find out how many pancakes he ate for breakfast," Elizabeth said with a laugh. "I wonder if he'll be at the dance tomorrow night," she continued, barely able to conceal her excitement.

"Okay, children, let's get on with the canning. You know we need at least three hundred quarts of vegetables put down to carry us through the winter. I want you to boil these beets and slice them into the sealers. Keep some of the tender leaves for our dinner tonight. Dad loves them. The other kids can help too. I have to leave." She called out to her other son, practicing his violin at the other end of the room. "Nicholas, please go out and saddle up Blazes. She's the best horse for the long ride. And, oh, by the way, make sure she's well-watered."

"Where are you going, Mom?" asked Ludvina.

"I'm going to help Mrs. Schmidt. When I was in the garden, their farmhand came by to tell me she's in labor. He just left. There he goes now." She pointed out the window.

"Do you have to go?" pleaded Elizabeth, who noticed her mother looking weary. "You've already delivered a baby this week."

"Yes, I do, my dear. She needs me. She has no one else to help her." She raised her eyebrows and gestured, showing the palms of her hands. "I'm all she's got."

A few minutes later, Elizabeth gazed out the window to see her mother leading her horse called Blazes across the yard to the woodpile. She saw her mother fasten her black bag onto the saddle. She knew it contained all the things her mother needed for the delivery: sterile cords in a small sealer, one to tie the navel and a finer cord and needle in case a suture was needed, and a bottle of dried opium from which she made tea for desperate cases to help with pain. Also contained in her bag was a basic layette she had painstakingly made by hand from the boy's out-grown, long-john underwear.

She stepped onto the chopping block, swung herself up and into the saddle, grabbed the reins, and clucked the giddy-up.

Elizabeth's heart swelled as she watched her mother trot Blazes out of the yard and then break into a fast gallop down the road, leaving a puff of dust behind her. She is such a wonderful woman! Always helping others. Being so kind to everyone! She gives so much of herself to this family and the community! She has instilled in each of us a faith no one can take away! By golly, I'm fortunate to have such a mother! Yesiree! I'm lucky! By golly!

***

Eugene walked along the field among the recently bound sheaves. He scanned the distance to his right and saw a team of four workhorses slowly pulling a binder while the familiar, earthy smell of freshly cut wheat, mixed with dust, hung heavy in the air, a scent that represented the rewards for their hard work. Eugene picked up two sheaves by their twine and stood them up, one to the other, to begin the eight-sheaf stook, a shelter under which field mice would soon gather. Fellow workers, a short distance away, repeated the action. He learned the stook would stand for several days to completely dry before being hauled by horse and wagon to the threshing machine, a giant beast of a machine that separated the wheat from the straw. Then, when the hopper was full, it would pump the golden kernels into the granary. The harvesting process was similar back home in Ontario. But here in Alberta, harvesting was accomplished on a grander scale.

Yesterday, a fellow worker told him about a new machine called 'the combine.' It was a self-propelled threshing machine that eliminated all the other actions. And it could be operated by one man. One tractor could pull the smaller ones. This sounded very exciting to Eugene.

Although it felt like much longer, this was only his third day on the job, and each day he marveled at the size of Meyer's farm and the crop they were harvesting. He had never seen such a bountiful crop or such expanse of flat land producing it. His father's farm back in Ontario was half the size.

The Meyers had given him a warm welcome and addressed all his creature comforts: a comfortable bed, a place to bathe and launder, and always, always nourishing food. Steak and eggs, pancakes, oatmeal porridge, cinnamon buns, and canned berries were offered for breakfast each day to meet the appetites of the twelve hardworking men who occupied the bunkhouse. And they could always, rest assured, there would be a fine dinner of meat, potatoes, vegetables, and pie served to these men at the end of each day. The tantalizing aroma greeted them each morning and welcomed them when they were famished and dog-tired at the end of the day.

"Mighty fine cinnamon buns, Mrs. Meyers," said Eugene in a loud voice as he reached for a second from the large bowl. She swung around from where she was, flipping pancakes at the stove.

"Why, thank you, Eugene. I'm happy you are enjoying them. Have another."

"No, thank you. I'm on my second now, they're wonderful!" Eugene replied as he stood to take his leave from the table. He could see she was pleased with the compliment just as he intended. S

Nick Thomas also stood up and fell into step with Eugene as they walked toward the barn. Today they would take a team out to haul the stooks over to the threshing machine in the west acreage.

"What do you do for excitement around here?" asked Eugene as they walked.

"Right now, the biggest excitement is the harvest, of course, but, hey, tomorrow night there's a dance in the community hall, and it's always a capacity crowd. All the gals in the community show up, including my two sisters."

"Do they have red hair like yours?"

Nick laughed. "All of the Thomas' have red hair. We take after our mother. She has dark auburn, as do my sisters. The others have the same as mine. I hate the red hair and all these damn freckles even more. And I wish I could shed a few pounds. My genes come from my father, but my mother, on the other hand, is just a little bit of a woman. But don't let that fool you, she might be small, but she's definitely mighty!" His smile widened.

Eugene glanced at this new friend who had made him feel so welcome. Nick was short and rotund and had a friendly, round, freckled face, one that was always smiling or just about to. And, yes, his hair was red, more orange than red, like the colour of carrots. He wore it all slicked back in the pompadour style of the day. But it was his personality that took center stage–pleasant, jovial, and kind. Eugene thought he'd hate to have hair that colour but instead said, "Nothing wrong with being unique,

Nick. But tell me, do you have a temper to go with this red hair of yours?" He flashed a smile.

"Ya! Ya betcha! You better watch out!" Nick shook his fist in the air and laughed.

"You'll have me running back to Ontario," quipped Eugene. "By the way, what kind of music is there for this dance tomorrow night?"

Two other guys and I have a little combo. We play at dances around this community and others. John Meyers is on the piano. Hans Rempel is on the drum. And I play the fiddle." He puffed out his chest.

"What, no trumpet?" exclaimed Eugene.

"We would love to have a trumpet. There just isn't anyone around here that plays it."

"There is now," stated Eugene, with a broad smile and twinkling eyes.

"There is? And who would that be?"

"You're looking at him."

"Wow! You play the trumpet! Would you be willing to join us?"

"There would be nothing I'd enjoy more! But I must warn you: I do not read music. I only play by ear. And I've been known to steal the show."

"We're all in the same boat. We pick up the tune and the beat, and away we go with the fiddler stealing the show." They both laughed.

"Suits me just fine, Nick. Saturday night should prove interesting. But first, I must press up my suit. It got wrinkled all to hell in my duffel bag."

Their conversation took them to the barn. They hitched a horse to a wagon and set out on their day's work ahead.

***

A brilliant harvest moon hung low in the prairie sky, casting a golden glow so bright it was like the dawning of the morning sun. People had tied their horses and buggies to hitching posts along the main street, the church, and past the local cemetery. A horsey smell lay heavy in the air while the hum of conversation followed the people as they filed through the wide-open door of the community hall.

Inside benches lined both sidewalls. In the adjacent room, similar benches sat before tables covered with oilcloth. At the far end was a cookstove with a full wood box. On top of the cookstove sat two twelve-cup coffee pots and a squat tea kettle.

Women were busily making roast beef and deviled egg sandwiches at a side table. They worked on an assembly line, one slicing, another buttering the slabs of homemade bread, another slicing roast beef to go on top, while yet another lady at the end of the line dobbed on some German mustard and sliced the sandwich in half before layering them on a large platter. The simplicity of the food Eugene knew would never diminish its excellence of flavor. The ladies had arranged many butter tarts on cookie sheets, a welcome addition to the sweets.

At Meyer's farm, Eugene was excited about this first social event he was attending. The weeks he'd spent in the seminary had been devoid of excitement, so he was ready. Mrs. Meyers had set up the ironing board near the cookstove where flat irons were heating for him to press his pin-striped suit and round-collared shirt. He had also spent considerable time on his appearance lingering in his bath in the galvanized tub, carefully shaving and combing his unruly, black hair. When he'd finished dressing, he looked in the mirror and said aloud, "You're a darn good-looking man, Eugene Waechter." Then, with renewed confidence, he grabbed the case that held his treasured trumpet and set out the door.

After tying his horse at the designated place at the back, he walked gingerly into the hall. Nick was waiting on the stage and greeted him warmly. They sat on the stage chatting while awaiting the arrival of Hans and John. Their instruments were on a side table near the piano. The stage would have looked empty without the old Steinway piano donated by a resident many years earlier. Age had given its surface a rich patina and yellowed its keys but had not lessened the richness and quality of its tone.

As the people came through the front doors, they were quick to notice the new musician on stage. They looked him up and down: his dark, curly hair; his handsome, strong face; and stylish brown suit. They saw his trumpet, buffed up to its best shine, held now in his hand. But then, had they looked at his feet, they would have seen the woollen winter socks he wore in his spats for the lack of summer ones. Eugene had hoped no one would notice. The womenfolk did.

"What sort of music do you play here for the folks of Heisler?" asked Eugene.

"We play some of the old German waltzes, which are very popular," replied Nick. "We also play schottisches, foxtrots, the French minuet, the Charleston, and occasionally, a jitterbug. The jitterbug is popular with the younger folk these days,"

Just then, Hans came in carrying his drums. He was breathless when he said, "Sorry I'm late. I'd been here sooner, but I had to pull a calf this afternoon. It was the heifer's first. John rode up right behind me." He turned toward the door, "There he is now."

John, a tall, slender man wearing a straw fedora, stepped up onto the stage and rolled back the lid of the Steinway, exposing the yellowed keys. He tapped the middle C to be sure it still worked. Both men were surprised to see a stranger on stage and more so to see a trumpet on the table. Nick quickly made the introductions.

"You must be the man from Ontario," said John. Eugene smiled and nodded, thinking how fast news does travel.

"There wasn't time for us to have a practice, so we'll just have to do our best," stated Nick. He felt proud to have expanded his musical ensemble. "Let's start with a waltz. It'll be nice to have a wind instrument added to our sound. How about, *You, You Are My True Loved One*? He repeated it in German, *Du, Du Bist Mein Waher Ge Liebter Mensch*. Will you be alright with that, Eugene?"

"Yes, I know that song. I'll be simply fine following along."

"See that little blond that just came in." He pointed towards the door. "That's my girlfriend, Verona. We've been dating since, well, forever."

"Wow! Good for you, you old lady killer!" laughed Eugene.

"I've never heard that before. It must be an Ontario expression."

The hall was quickly filling. First, many couples came through the door, some with their teenage children, followed by several single young men. Then, a bevy of young women streamed through and made their way to the side benches. They wore their flapper dresses and forehead bands, called *bandeaus*, with either a bow or flower attached at the side. They wore pump-style shoes with a strap across the instep, and they were itching to kick up a storm dancing the Charleston. At that precise moment, Eugene's hungry eyes made him fully realize why he'd left the Seminary.

He saw two matronly women sitting together at the far end of the hall. He couldn't be sure about their hair color from this distance, but he speculated they must be Nick's sisters. He was about to ask him when John, at the piano, clapped for attention. He hit the middle C and counted *one, two, three,* and the music began on the count of four.

Eugene pursed his lips, raised his trumpet, and blew. Joy filled him. Then, as his instrument's crisp, unmistakable sound mixed in with the others on stage, he became one with his trumpet, the melody, and fellow musicians.

Young men—dressed in their best with their hair slicked back in the popular pompadour style crossed the floor to find a partner. Soon, the floor was swaying as it filled with dancers when their feet found their rhythm upon it. Smiling couples swirled past the stage. Eugene looked at the sea of strange faces different from the dances back home, where he knew everyone. He knew it would take time to become familiar.

One lady smiled when she glided by, and her eyes sparkled each time she met his glance. He found himself waiting to see her again. He didn't have to wait long; she was on the floor with different partners. He took his trumpet from his mouth, smiled, and winked at her when she passed by again. She flushed. It caused him to lose his place in the song momentarily. He promised himself when they had a break, he would seek her out. Once again, he was glad he hadn't become a priest.

Before they played the next dance, Nick raised his voice and asked the crowd to grab their partners for the traditional supper waltz; this was a misnomer as everyone knew it was just a lunch. It was, however, a chance for people to visit and catch up on all the news. And it allowed Eugene to meet this lady.

"You did very well, Eugene," stated Nick. John and Hans agreed. "I think the trumpet has made an enormous difference to our overall sound," said Nick. "Let's get some grub. Playing for the dances always makes me hungry. The food here is plentiful and very well prepared. And I'll be able to introduce you to my sisters and other family friends."

Eugene looked around the room but did not see the lady that had caught his eye. He felt disappointed; it all changed when Nick said, "Here come my sisters now." Lo and behold, one was the 'very one' Eugene had hoped to meet. They walked over to their table and sat down.

"Eugene, I'd like you to meet my sister, Ludvina, and this is Elizabeth, my other one."

"Please to meet you, Ludvina," said Eugene. His eyes were sparkling when he said, "And you too, Lizzie."

Oh, how she hated that nickname, Lizzie. She had to hear it all through her school days and to this day from family and relatives. But coming from this handsome man from Ontario? It was like music to her ears. She looked at his large, gray eyes that seemed to devour her, his black hair that wouldn't stay combed back only to curl on his forehead. She thought he was the most handsome man she'd ever seen . . . and to think he'd winked at her.

Her heart quickened when she murmured, "Hello, Eugene."

Eugene studied both sisters, and, yes, they did have red hair. Not the red/orange shade like Nick had but rather a deep auburn, chestnut color. Ludvina was bigger than Elizabeth and had a rounder face, but Elizabeth was where his gaze rested. Something about her eyes and how sweetly she smiled held his attention, making him want to know her better.

"I hear you have traveled from Ontario," she ventured.

He held her gaze for a few seconds before answering.

"The long trip was well worth it," he said, smiling mischievously as though there was more to his words.

Elizabeth hoped the insinuation was real and not just her imagination. The short repartee suddenly struck her funny. She giggled and then broke into laughter. The sound was music to Eugene's ears better than any note he'd ever played on his trumpet. It made him laugh as well. Something special passed between them at that moment. Others in their company wondered what the big joke was. Conversation buzzed throughout the room like a hive of bees as everyone enjoyed their lunch. Little talk passed between Eugene and Elizabeth, but they had eyes for no one else.

Nick turned to Eugene and said, "I'd like to take you around and introduce you to some of our close friends before we start playing again."

"That would be nice," replied Eugene as they both stood up.

Back on stage, Nick started the second session with the lively sound of a Charleston. "It's to wake everyone up and get them back into the mood of dancing," he said. Elizabeth went back to her bench on the side of the hall. She had lost total interest in dancing. When asked to dance, which was often, she just went through the motions while trying unsuccessfully to keep her eyes off Eugene on the stage.

At the close of the evening, the opportunity for a solo trumpet piece presented itself. Eugene stood up. The people stopped dancing to listen and watch the new musician. He held his elbow high and played an old German favourite: *Du, du bist mein geliebter Mensch*. His crisp, clear notes resounded through the room. The talent he possessed was evident, and his showmanship matched it. Elizabeth was mesmerized and proud at the same time. When he finished, he received a round of applause. He smiled, looked around the room with his eyes resting on the smiling face of Lizzie. He nodded in appreciation before sitting down.

News that this man had ridden the rails all the way from Ontario traveled through the small town of Heisler like a snowball rolling down a hill. Each one hundred and ten people in the hall swiftly knew Eugene's name, where he was from, and how he had arrived. They knew he spoke German and where he was working, and tonight they learned one more thing. He was a talented trumpet player!

When Eugene walked into the church that first Sunday morning in Heisler, Alberta, he sat at the back of the church and could immediately smell candles and incense. But it was the sight of the tabernacle on the alter that rushed in thoughts of the seminary and all it entailed. He also thought about his home in Walkerton and wondered if the deacon had advised his father of his departure and how his father was feeling about it. Would he be disappointed? Would he be angry? He wrestled with these thoughts for a few minutes, then pushed them out of his mind and concentrated on the congregation entering the church. He saw the elderly, the young, and an older adult in a wheelchair. He saw small children holding the hand of their parents with little feet scampering to keep up. They were so sweet! He wondered if he would recognize some of the folk he'd been introduced to the night before. He did. Their faces were familiar, but their names escaped him. They did not see him sitting so inconspicuously in the back row. Then he saw Nick enter with a small entourage of nine people.

He quickly noticed that they all had red hair and thought, this must be the Thomas family. The parents, he assumed, were these two: a petite, older woman, and a short, stocky older man. Eugene watched to see if Elizabeth was with them as they filed in. She was. She came in last. He watched her genuflect and piously cross herself before entering the pew. 'Her conviction must be strong, stronger than mine' he thought.

After mass, everyone congregated outside. Eugene meandered over to Nick and the Thomas family. He enjoyed their surprise at seeing him.

"I see you survived the dance last night," said Nick.

"You, as well," replied Eugene, smiling.

"I'd like you to meet the rest of my family. Here is Mom and Dad, and over there are brothers Lawrence, Matt, and Julius. They're talking to the Meyer boys. My eldest sister, Mary, isn't here. She moved to Edmonton when she married Karl Kapler last year. And, oh, this little cutie is my sister, Rosella. She's the youngest." She smiled up at Eugene with a shiny, freckled face.

Eugene turned to Elizabeth. "You are looking so pretty today, Lizzie." She blushed, happy she'd decided to wear her favorite, blue-flowered dress. "Thank you, Eugene," she murmured.

Before the conversation could progress further, Mrs. Thomas interjected. "Eugene, being new in town and all and away from your family, how would you like to come and join us for Sunday supper?"

"That's very nice of you, Mrs. Thomas. I would enjoy that."

"Great! Come any time in the afternoon. We always have our supper around five. We can play some cards after. *Bid whist* is what we play. Are you familiar with that game?"

"That's all we ever play back home. It surprises me. We're two thousand miles apart, yet there are many similarities between Walkerton and Heisler."

He glanced at his watch. "I best be on my way." He walked towards his horse with a final glance at Elizabeth, then turned around and returned.

"I'm not exactly sure where your farm is."

Pa Thomas spoke up, "It's four miles east from the Meyers. You can't miss it. You'll see a barn with 'Thomas' painted on the roof."

"Thanks, I'll find it," he said.

Names on top of barns must be the trend here, he thought.

Some day I will have a barn of my own with my name on it for all to see!

Chapter Three

As Eugene rode into the yard of the Thomas' farm, he noticed it was small in comparison to that of the Meyers. A large dog rushed out barking and racing around Eugene's horse as he approached the yard. Eugene held the reins tight as he reared up.

"Whoa, whoa," he shouted to calm his horse, but it wasn't until Nick came out of the house and whistled to the dog that Eugene's gelding settled down. Before dismounting, he gazed around. Everything once again was familiar: a log barn with a roof of straw, a corralled stack of hay, two granaries, a woodpile with a large chopping block with an ax stuck precariously on top, an icehouse, a well with a rope attached to a bucket, a large tripod of logs where animals hung after butchering. He also saw cattle and horses grazing out in the field and a flock of chickens pecking their way around the yard. As he'd approached alongside the home, he had spied a healthy vegetable garden the size of an acre. He saw patches of cabbages, potatoes, corn, pole beans, carrots, and a small assembly of other vegetables, all growing in profusion and ready to be harvested the second time. He was impressed.

The home, a wooden frame with its wrap-around verandah, seemed too small for the family that occupied it. Nick met Eugene at the door and invited him in. He looked around, appraising the home. The kitchen, obviously the hub of the house, was large and contained all the necessities of daily life: a rectangular table covered with floral-printed oilcloth and white-painted benches alongside. At each end sat hand-made wooden chairs, also painted white. At the far end of the kitchen stood a cream separator. Next to the door, a lineup of hooks held jackets of all sizes and some straw hats. On the other side was a wash-stand with a basin and bucket of freshwater ready for a quick hand wash. A wooden-framed mirror hung overhead.

Of course, the main item of the kitchen was the wood cook-stove and its house-warming partner, a Quebec heater at the other end of the room. The polished cookstove held a warming oven over the top, a reservoir for water attached to its side, and a wooden box filled to the brim with chopped wood sat behind it. An aroma emanated from the oven; something delicious was roasting.

There were shelves on two walls with curtains attached; these shelves held all the dishes, pots, and pans needed for the food preparation. Next to it stood a sideboard with two coal-oil lamps at one end and a cloth concealing something beneath at the other end. The floor, covered with linoleum, had a trap door that led down into the storage cellar, while a staircase led to the upstairs bedrooms adjacent to the Quebec heater.

Eugene was impressed that everything in the home was in order and spotlessly clean despite its eight inhabitants. His final observance was a glass-covered picture of the Last Supper that hung directly over the table, reminding everyone who ate at this table to be thankful. It was a welcome sight.

"Where is everyone?" asked Eugene, who'd expected to see a houseful.

"Mom and Dad are visiting a lady whose baby mother delivered yesterday, just to check up on her and make sure the babe is feeding well. They call it latching on. The boys are doing their chores in the barn. My eldest sister, Mary, lives nearby in

Edmonton. She married Karl Kapler a couple of years ago, and my little sister, Rosella, is playing with her dolls on the grass behind the house. I'm not sure what Elizabeth and Ludvina are up to right now. They couldn't have heard you arrive, or they would have joined us. They might be upstairs. I know they were looking forward to your visit!"

And so, they were. Upon hearing two male voices talking downstairs, soft thumping sound coming down on the staircase brought Elizabeth and Ludvina into their presence.

"Well, if it isn't the trumpet player!" exclaimed Elizabeth with a warm smile. "It's good to see you again, Eugene. Welcome to our home."

"Thank you, Lizzie. It's good to see you again also." His wink left her flustered.

Finally, she stammered, "I must get the potatoes peeled for dinner. Ludvina, please get some lettuce and carrots from the garden."

Elizabeth walked over to the stove, pushed in more wood, and then shut the door quickly before flying sparks could escape.

The girls set about preparing dinner for everyone. A few minutes later, their parents arrived home. Ma Thomas appeared elated as she walked through the door. She nodded her hello to Eugene while Mr. Thomas shook his hand. "Welcome," he said.

"My, what a lovely baby the Schmidt's had," Ma Thomas said. "Lots of hair, and if the scale was right, he weighed in over eight pounds! I've just visited with them, and he's nursing well. So come along, Eugene, sit outside on the verandah with Mr. Thomas and me while the girls get the dinner on."

They moved out to the verandah. Eugene would have preferred to stay in the kitchen. He had enjoyed watching Elizabeth move about so efficiently. After stoking the stove, she'd set the pots of potatoes and carrots on the stove to cook, then she opened the oven and checked the beef roast, which was sitting on a bed of caramelizing onions. Elizabeth removed it from the pan when determining it was done. Then she placed it on a large cookie sheet to rest before carving. Finally, she reserved the juices in the pan for the gravy. Her naturalness in the kitchen had pleased him.

The verandah faced the south side of the property and looked over an expanse of wheat fields that spread to the horizon. Soon their crop would be harvested, and the threshing crew would descend upon the Thomas farm, and the Thomas women would be cooking up a storm to feed them three times a day.

"Were you born in Ontario, Eugene?" asked Pa Thomas as they seated themselves.

"Yes, in a town by the name of Walkerton. A mite larger than Heisler?"

"And your father?

"My father was also born in that area, as was my grandfather."

"That makes you a third-generation Canadian. Do you know where your great grandfather was born?"

Eugene felt like asking, "What is this, the Spanish Inquisition?" instead, he cleared his throat and said," Yes, he was born in Alsace, Lorraine, France, to a German father and a French Mother. When my ancestors came to Canada, they married German women. So, our French heritage has long been in the past but not forgotten."

"Were you raised as Catholic?" asked Ma Thomas. "I realize you were in church on Sunday, but I didn't notice if you went up to receive communion."

"Yes, I was raised as Catholic. I have a sister who's a nun and a cousin who's a priest."

'That should impress them,' he thought. 'But the last thing they need to know is why I left Ontario. They don't need to know about the seminary.'

Ma Thomas had been quick to observe the attraction between Eugene and Elizabeth. It pleased her more than impressed her. Being of the same faith however, removed a major complication should the attraction progress.

Just then, Elizabeth interrupted their conversation to announce that dinner was served. Other members of the family had gathered around the table. Eugene noticed Ma Thomas had set his place next to Elizabeth, which added to his pleasure. He hoped it was deliberate.

A mountain-high platter of sliced roast beef and a gigantic bowl of mashed potatoes with fresh parsley on top was centering the table. Also, in the center of the table was a jug of gravy, a tray of thickly sliced bread, and a bowl of creamery butter along with a clear, glass bowl of leaf lettuce seasoned with vinegar and a pinch of sugar. Two blueberry pies for dessert sat on the sideboard under a cloth. They were going to be a tasty treat to finish the meal.

When everyone was seated, Ma Thomas clapped her hands. "Now, I want you all to bow your heads, cross yourselves, and be attentive as we thank the good Lord for this food."

One could hear a pin drop.

"In the name of the Father, the Son, and the Holy Ghost, bless us, oh Lord, and these Thy gifts which we are about to receive from the bounty through Christ, our Lord. Amen."

After saying grace, Pa Thomas passed the bowls from one to the other, and with ten people sitting around the table, it didn't take long for them to empty. They ate heartily and chatted about current events: the war raging in Europe and how it was affecting the local economy and finished in a lighter tone: the successful harvest now at its peak.

Towards the end of the meal, Eugene nudged Elizabeth and whispered, "Can we take a walk after?"

She replied, "Uh-huh!" Her heart quickened.

"You can show me around the farm. I'd love to take a closer look at the garden."

"I'd love that, too," replied Elizabeth. "I'd also like to show you our frisky new calf that was born in July.

By the way, I hope you've had enough to eat."

"Sure did. It was delicious! You're a good cook, Lizzie Thomas."

His large gray eyes smiled down at her. He noticed an auburn curl fallen on her forehead and wanted to sweep it aside.

"Uh-huh," she replied again, at a loss for words.

Eugene lay in his bed that night with the sight and voice of Lizzie running through his mind. He loved everything about her: the way she moved, the sound of her voice, the color of her hair, the sparkle of her eyes, and her natural way of communicating, especially the "Uh-huh" she would say to agree. 'Am I falling in love?' he asked himself. It's not a question, Eugene Waechter. But how can it be? You barely know the girl.

Meanwhile, Elizabeth lay in bed thinking about Eugene four miles away. She couldn't get him off her mind. She loved his face, big eyes, curly black hair, and the timbre of his voice. But she didn't know him yet. She'd only just met him. But then, today, when they went for a walk, she did find out more about him. He loved children. He loved music, and he was very interested in the garden and how they took care of the soil. He also showed interest in the milking cows in the barn, and he had petted the new calf. She was sure there was more to learn about him. But the question uppermost in her mind right now was where would he be after the harvest? Would he be going back to Ontario? If not, where will he work? All these questions and more ran through her head like cattle on a stampede.

When they parted, he had thanked her mother for the invitation and, much to Elizabeth's delight, he whispered, "I'll see you next Sunday." But the one question in the epicenter of her thoughts was: 'Is this what falling in love feels like?'

And he saw her all the next Sundays that remained in the harvest season. He would attend Mass and after was that tenth person at the Thomas table. It also became a ritual for him and Lizzie to walk after supper. They would walk around the farm, talk, laugh, genuinely enjoying each other's company. This evening it was a balmy night. The moon hung low in the sky. Leaves fluttered on the birch trees at the edge of the thicket where they strolled, catching just enough of the fading sunlight to show their pale undersides. Elizabeth brushed her hair away from her face.

"That was a wonderful dinner," said Eugene breaking the silence. "Were you the cook?"

"We all participated, my sisters and me. My mother taught us at an early age to cook and bake. Uh-huh, she did. One does the meat, another the vegetables. Today, I had it easy. I only made the gravy."

Eugene smiled and reached for her hand and squeezed it. "That was the best part,"

She felt her face flush and her heart skip a beat. She looked at Eugene's smiling face, so handsome he was with those large grey eyes with their smutty black lashes and unruly, curly, black hair. She had refrained from asking him about his life in Walkerton, but tonight she could no longer contain her curiosity.

"How many siblings do you have? Mother said you have a sister in the convent. Are there any others?"

Eugene smiled, knowing he had been the subject of discussion. "Yes, I have three sisters and one brother. I'm the youngest.

"Are any married?

"My two sisters and brother are all married. My brother is a farmer, and my two sisters also married farmers; they all live in the Walkerton area. The eldest, Antoinette, is in the Notre Dame Convent in Watertown, Ontario. Her religious name is Sister St. Antonio. Yes, I told your parents this when I first came to dinner."

Elizabeth's smiled. Her bright, sparkling eyes showed a keen interest in his life; this spurred Eugene on as memories of his childhood in Ontario flooded in.

"My mother died when I was three. She had an infected tooth, and it took her life. I don't remember her exactly. I have a feeling of her tenderness and the flowery scent about her. After she died, my father told me I ran from room to room, even stuck my head out of the window and called her."

Elizabeth brimming over, patted his hand, which he immediately grabbed and squeezed.

"Did your father remarry?" asked Elizabeth.

"Yes, shortly after my mother died. He married a neighboring spinster. He said he needed a woman in the home to take care of the family and the household."

"What was she like?"

Elizabeth noticed his eyes cloud over when she asked the question. Eugene was silent for a few moments, then he blurted, "She smelled like sauerkraut!"

Elizabeth stifled a giggle. Eugene continued.

"She was mean to me, not to my siblings, only me. She took all her frustrations out on me, but never in front of my father. My father was aware of the discord, but the blame was placed on me because she was so sweet to the others, and they liked her. I know things would have been different had my mother lived."

"I'm sure it would have," said Elizabeth. "Uh-huh, I'm sure of that." She patted his hand again and asked, "What brought you to Heisler?"

"To keep peace in the home, my father decided the best place for me would be in college, connected with a seminary. He hoped I'd become a priest. I think I can answer your question, Lizzie, my dear, in three statements: I wanted to get as far away from my stepmother as quickly as possible. I didn't want to be a priest. And I wanted to see the West and find you." He winked, and once again, Elizabeth blushed.

"Now, tell me a little about yourself and your family,"

"There isn't much to tell," replied Elizabeth. "You know all about my brothers and sisters."

"What about your parents. Where are they from? Have they always lived in Heisler?

"Oh, no, my parents were Americans. When I was eight years old, our family moved from White Lake, South Dakota, and settled here in Heisler. My Uncle Henry, Dad's brother, came also. He had married my mother's sister, Mary Schroeder. Before all of that, my father immigrated from Cologne, Germany. He came to the states with his mother and brothers after his father had died. Shortly after my parents were married, they went to California, hoping to get rich when the gold rush was on. Of course, they didn't, but my mother received her training as a midwife there."

"I see," said Eugene, putting his arm around her shoulders.

***

Eugene continued to play his trumpet at the Saturday night dances. He begged off playing halfway through the evening so he could dance with his Lizzie. The love bug had bitten . . . and bitten hard! Then, when lunch was being served, they sat side by side, unaware of all others. Elizabeth's throat constricted when she thought about saying goodbye to Eugene. He'd become her whole life. Her whole existence! However, both knew the time was running out when they would have to say goodbye.

And Eugene knew he had nothing to offer Elizabeth. He knew he had to earn money to buy some land in the Heisler area before he could propose marriage. Each day he went into the Co-op

Store and checked out the jobs the store owner displayed on the bulletin board but to no avail. Going back to Walkerton and leaving Elizabeth behind filled him with despair. When he had given up all hope, he decided to check once more. Finally, there was a job posted. He was filled with excitement when he read:

HELP WANTED

Park Shipping Company desperately wants able-bodied men to work as laborers building ships in Juneau, Alaska. Top wages, room and board, and travel expenses are provided. Send your response to the above company, Juneau, Alaska, and mark your envelope "Application."

Eugene hurried across the street to the post office to send his application letter. To his utmost surprise, within a week, he had his response in the form of a telegram sent to the Co-op Store. It read: *Please advise Eugene Waechter employment awaits him in Juneau.*

He was overjoyed!

He hurried to the Co-op Store and purchased a local paper to see if there was any land for sale in the Heisler area. The Alberta

Government was selling quarter sections—some not too far from the Thomas Farm with prices ranging from fifty to one hundred dollars. First, Eugene visited the municipal office. He wanted to ensure that he could hold the land for up to two years with a deposit. The deposit and train fare took all his savings from his work at Meyers. Fortunately, he would receive compensation for his travel expense upon arrival. Next, he placed a deposit on a piece of property. It had a barn, one granary, a chicken coop, an outdoor toilet, a well, and a small two-bedroom home. He was elated! Now he could propose to Lizzie!

Today, Sunday, would be his last day in Heisler. He paid special attention to his grooming before going to church. He sat by Elizabeth and held her hand all during Mass. When Mass was over, he turned to Elizabeth and said, "I won't be able to come over until after dinner today. I have some things I have to deal with."

Dinner wasn't the same for Elizabeth without Eugene. She didn't feel like eating. When dinner was over, she helped wash up the dishes. Then she sat on the verandah, watching the road. Time passed, and her heart was heavy, but she finally saw a lone rider in the distance, coming down the road. She ran to meet him. When he alighted from his horse, he said, "Let's go to a nice quiet place where we can sit and talk."

"I know the perfect spot," said Elizabeth. "We used to play there when we were kids."

They walked across the field and to the edge of a small grove of trees that faced the house.

"Here it is," said Elizabeth. Under the cover of some tall birches were two stumps joined by a large plank on top. "Ludvina and I would bring our dolls here and play for hours. We used to dance on this plank. It was left-over wood when Dad built the granary."

"How did you ever bring this heavy thing across the field?"

"My brothers hitched old Nellie to the stone boat, and she did it for us girls."

"I see," smiled Eugene. "That would do it all right."

She hoisted herself onto the plank, and Eugene joined her. He put his arm around her shoulders. She rested her head against his.

A soft wind blew across the field, fluttering her auburn hair, while the rustling leaves of the birches overhead gave a swooshing sound. They were quiet for some time, just enjoying their closeness. Finally, Eugene spoke, "I bought some land, sweetheart."

She sat straight up and lifted her head from his shoulder, "You did . . . what! Where?" Her voice bubbled over with hope and excitement.

"About three miles from here . . . that's where we will live."

She jumped up, "Where *we'll* live? Oh, Eugene!

"I want to marry you, Lizzie darling, if you'll have me. Will you be my wife?" He stood up and gathered her into his arms.

"Uh-huh, uh-huh," she uttered, her eyes shining like two beacons. Eugene kissed her tenderly, and before she could say anything further, he kissed her with a deep intensity that made her melt in his arms.

"But I have to leave for a spell and earn some money before we get married," he continued, catching his breath. "We both knew this was going to have to happen. We knew when the harvest was over that I'd have to leave. It's wound down now. We must be apart for a while. I have to leave to earn some money."

Her eyes were brimming over when she looked at him and asked, "When?"

"I leave tomorrow morning. The time will pass, you'll see. I promise to write to you every day, Lizzie darling. Then, when I return, we can have a wedding and begin our life together."

She saw the determination in his large, gray eyes and checked a sob. She couldn't have been happier, a life together, marriage to this remarkable man. It was a mix of joy and sorrow like nothing she'd ever experienced before! She would have to pray, pray hard, and say her rosary every night that she would see him again, that he would keep his promise, and that she could survive the wait. But he had to leave. She decided at once not to tell the family about the proposal.

A full moon amidst a cluster of stars lit the entire evening sky. It shone down on them as they walked, hand in hand, slowly back to the house and his waiting horse. She kept blowing him kisses as he slowly walked his horse out of the yard. Then, when he was out of sight, she realized that she had a lump in her throat the size of a boulder!

Chapter Four

Eugene arrived in Juneau, Alaska, before the first snowfall with a new purpose in life and full of determination to start earning money. It was a town with 3,000 people, most of whom were workers in the gold mine and shipbuilding industry and others who had come to find their fortunes panning for gold. Compared to the farm country of Heisler, the difference in the atmosphere was stark; here, there was enthusiasm in the air as miners and prospectors filled the streets. "They're walking five feet off the ground, so delusional," thought Eugene.

Eugene realized, after his arrival, that he could also have worked in a gold mine but being above ground and doing carpentry was more to his liking. The bunkhouse provided was near the dry dock, where construction of a large freighter was in progress. Eugene was a ready and willing worker, quickly recognizing what the employer expected of him. After being on the job for a few days, he shared innovative ideas with the foreman, who appreciated his intelligence.

Measurement and numbers were Eugene's forte. He became head sawyer in charge of cutting to precise measurement the lengths and widths of lumber needed for the ship's construction. The pay increase for the position was well beyond anything he could have imagined. He lay in bed calculating how much he could save and how soon he might be able to return to Lizzie. Every evening, he wrote her a letter describing his day on the job and other facts about Juneau.

Back in Heisler, Elizabeth was pining for him. She did not attend any of the dances and waited each day to get his letter. She was soothed for only a few hours when she finally received one. Ma Thomas had become concerned about her daughter. She decided it was time to have a heart-to-heart. She knocked on her bedroom door and entered after hearing a muffled, "Come in."

Elizabeth was lying on her bed saying her rosary, Eugene's latest letter across her chest. A stack of his other letters was on her night table, letters she read over several times.

"Your father and I are very worried about you, my dear daughter. You have disconnected yourself from your family. You have lost weight because you are eating like a little bird. You must shake yourself out of this melancholy."

"It isn't melancholy, Ma. I'm lonely for Eugene."

"I know you are, my dear, but you also must face reality. You don't know this man. You have only been in his company for a few weeks. I'm not saying he's not a good man, Elizabeth. We just don't know him. We don't know why he left Ontario or how serious his intentions are. Only time will tell."

Elizabeth started to sob. "But I love him, Ma. I love him!" She could barely get the words out.

"Well, my dear, I will pray for you. That's all I can say. You must pray too. I see you are. She nodded towards the rosary. And you must keep busy to steer your mind in a different direction. I need you now in the kitchen. This week, I've delivered two babies, which has put me behind with the canning. Ludvina and Rosella are working overtime. So many vegetables need canning, and we all must go out and pick the last of the wild berries. Blueberries are ripening. Blackberries are hanging ripe, ready to drop. The chokecherries need picking. We need fruit for the winter months. Please, Elizabeth, come and give Ma a hand. I need you."

The plea for help from the mother she loved received Elizabeth's attention. She got up from the bed and followed her mother down the stairs to the kitchen. She decided her mother was right. She would keep busy; she would work hard as humanly as possible while waiting for Eugene. They canned all the vegetables and put down several jars of fruit and many more of jam, packing the shelves in the cellar to the brim. In addition, the bins were filled with potatoes, turnips, carrots, and parsnips. The days slowly passed, but alas! Elizabeth had not heard from Eugene for over a week.

She never discussed anything further with her mother. While her mother was not the type of person to say, 'I told you so,' Elizabeth knew she thought it.

Then one day the following week, Brother Nick came into the kitchen where they were busy making dinner. He'd just returned from the post office with a handful of mail.

"No letters for you, Elizabeth," he said teasingly. Once more, her heart crashed to the floor.

"But there is a parcel for you." He pulled a small box out of his bag. It's from Alaska. I wonder who it's from." He was grinning like a Cheshire cat.

"Give it to me," snapped Elizabeth.

"Say, please."

"I don't have to say please to you, you scamp."

She snatched it from his hands and ran upstairs with her heart pounding like a drum. She closed her bedroom door, not intending the bang it caused. Now, she ripped open the parcel. Inside was a small box with another gray velvet box inside. Eugene had also folded a letter down to fit into the box. Slowly she opened the velvet box. She caught her breath. Nestled in the crease was a solitaire diamond set in a band of gold. It sparkled under the rays of sunshine coming through the window. Thrilled beyond measure, she unfolded the letter with shaky hands. It read:

My darling Lizzie,

I haven't written you these past few days as I have been waiting for this ring to arrive. I hope you like it. Now we are officially engaged. We can start planning our wedding. I have been promoted and am making a good wage. As soon as my work is finished, I will be coming home . . . to you in Heisler. I can hardly wait. I think of you all the time, your sparkling eyes, lovely hair, and sweet ways. I love you, Lizzie Thomas.

Eugene

Elizabeth burst into tears of happiness.

Her mother heard her crying and came upstairs to console her. She asked herself, 'Why did that man have to mess with my daughter?'

"Look, Ma, he sent me a diamond. We're engaged! He meant every word he said, and when he comes back, we'll be married. He's bought a quarter-acre a short distance from here. I didn't tell you before because I wasn't sure if you'd be pleased to hear it. Oh, Ma, I'm so happy! Now I can start my hope chest. I want to crochet edgings on pillowcases, make some doilies, and start saving things for my home. Oh, Ma, I'm so happy, so thrilled!"

She hugged her mother, and if she had looked at her mother's face before she turned away, she would have seen a tear of relief roll down her cheek. Everything is going to be wonderful, wonderful for me, thought Lizzie, from now on!

Elizabeth's engagement brought new excitement to the family. It was big news, especially for brother Nick who instantly wore the wings of Cupid; after all, hadn't he introduced them? This wedding was going to be the family's second wedding. The news spread quickly throughout the parish. It was the topic of conversation before the people walked into church and after when congregating outside. Everyone wanted to see Elizabeth Thomas's beautiful ring from that Ontario man. Beaming like the morning star, she proudly stuck out her hand and wiggled her fingers to show them.

Elizabeth showed the visitors who came to their home all her treasures in her hope chest, a lovely pine chest her father had built. He was a man of little words, her father, but his actions spoke loud and clear. Every piece sawed, every nail hammered in, and a swipe of varnish was all done for the love of his daughter. Elizabeth kept adding different things to her chest: doilies, embroidered tablecloths, and whatever she could find that would add to her household. Finally, Ma Thomas contributed a picture of the Last Supper she had ordered from Edmonton. It was a replica of the one hanging over the family's kitchen table.

She spent the spring season planting a garden so that Eugene and she would have their very own sealers of vegetables. And she picked berries and made jam, and from the chokecherries, she made a syrup for pancakes. Her father built more shelves at the far end of the cellar to hold all she canned. Elizabeth pinned a sign overhead that read:

Eugene and Lizzie's Preserves Don't Touch

Elizabeth continued to exchange letters with Eugene every day, and the season passed. Winter's cold welcomed the warmth of Spring. In their communication, they made plans for their wedding. Just family and close friends, Eugene had asked. Elizabeth agreed. Eugene didn't know the date he'd be coming home. It will be when the construction is complete, he'd written. She loved his use of the word 'home.'

***

Over the past year and a half, Eugene had learned much about shipbuilding. Blocks were formed for the central part of the construction. A crane would lift these blocks and deposit them onto the main structure that sat in the dry dock. Then the blocks would be welded into place at the block joints. Finally, jigs had to be used to ensure proper alignment; this process was a guideline that determined productivity.

Having grown up on a farm and have only ever worked on a farm, the building of ships had never entered Eugene's mind. But now, after this experience, he knew his horizons were broadened considerably. He wondered how much more work remained as he looked at the construction progress. Finally, he decided to speak to the foreman.

"Can you give me some idea when my job is over here?" he asked over coffee.

"Well, it's August 1st now, and we have one more block to go. So, I'd say by the first week in September. But we have just signed another contract, and you could work another year and a half if you like."

"While I've enjoyed working here, I have to get back to Alberta. I have a lady there waiting for me. We are planning a wedding."

"Congratulations!"

"Thank you!"

"What kind of work will you do there?"

"I've bought some land, so I'll try my hand at farming. The soil is good. I'll grow some wheat and get some livestock; it should prove interesting." There was something about that statement that made him feel proud.

"Farming, eh? I'd never have guessed it. You're a natural at carpentry."

That night, Eugene wrote to Elizabeth, finally giving the date of his return and asking her to put wedding preparations into motion. Then he mailed a letter to his father. He wrote, "I realize it doesn't give you enough time to attend, and I apologize for this short notice. It couldn't be helped, Dad. Elizabeth and I look forward to having you visit once we are settled." He felt a sense of relief when he dropped it off at the post office along with a letter to his parish in Walkerton for the reading of his bands. In his letter to Elizabeth, he asked her to do the same with her parish in Heisler. The bands had to be read for three consecutive Sundays in both parishes before the wedding.

Elizabeth joyously received the excellent news that Eugene would be home by September 2nd. It put a hum of excitement in the air that evening at the Thomas supper table. The family's conversation was filled with wedding talk when Nick dropped a bombshell right out of the blue!

He declared that he and his long-time girlfriend, Verona, wanted to get married too, just as soon as possible.

It didn't take long for Ma Thomas and Verona's mother to get together to discuss the idea of a double wedding on November 15th, just enough time to have their bands read in each respective parish.

"If they had separate weddings, it would be the same group of people coming to each wedding within the same month," surmised Verona's mother.

Ma Thomas declared, "Why not have a double wedding? It only makes good sense. We can use the church hall and both pitch in with the food. My first thought is a cold plate. You know, a potato salad and a big, fruited ham and such like. We could do some of it the day before," declared Ma Thomas.

Elizabeth was aghast! Never in her wildest dreams did she ever think she'd have to share that special day. It was her day and her day alone. How could her mother suggest such a thing?

"But Ma, it's my special day. I don't want to share it."

Her mother turned to Elizabeth and placed both hands on her shoulders. "You have to remember Elizabeth, dear," she said. "These are challenging times. Verona's family has been struggling financially with her father being ill these past two years. Besides, don't forget, the wedding is also for your brother."

Elizabeth pondered what her mother had said and quickly realized her mother was right. Although the thought left a little nagging, she chastised herself for being selfish. Wasn't Eugene her focus?

Both agreed, as did Nick. Elizabeth knew Eugene would as well. All they wanted to do was get married and get on with their lives. And so, within the month, they were wed. The overcast summer sky did not diminish the excitement of the day. The entire parish came to the church to witness their first double wedding.

The grooms walked in first, one tall with dark hair and wide gray eyes, the other much shorter with red hair and a splattering of freckles. Both were smiling as they walked up the aisle, followed by the groomsmen: Verona's brother, John, and Nick's brother, Lawrence, both feeling especially important indeed, while John, the pianist from Nick's combo, played, *You, You Are*

My True Loved One. They took their places on the right and the left of the communion rail. Following were the maidens of honor: Ludvina and Verona's cousin, Sally, who had traveled with her mother by horse and buggy from Camrose to Heisler. One man from the parish nudged his friend and nodded at Eugene as he walked up the aisle, "That man came from Ontario to steal one of our women!" Although not intended for his ears, Eugene heard it and wouldn't forget.

A few minutes passed. Everyone in the church was anxiously waiting for the brides to enter. They entered. The sun had broken through the clouds and now shone through a stained-glass window creating a kaleidoscope of colors that looked like a fine Persian carpet on the floor. The pianist played a glissando to get everyone's attention, then broke into a loud rendition of, *Here Comes the Bride.* Elizabeth took the lead. She was known for her sparkling eyes, but nothing could compete with this day; they shone like diamonds! She was radiant in a satin chemise trimmed with seed pearls and rhinestones in gatherings of lace that Ma Thomas had ordered from Edmonton. A matching headband crossed her forehead, and a small tulle veil flowed down her back, complimenting her lovely, auburn hair.

Verona was equally lovely in a dress of ivory color that matched her beautiful blond hair. Her lacey chemise accentuated her petite figure. She gazed down the aisle at Nick. He stood there like a wooden soldier with a grin spread across his face.

Somber fathers escorted the brides to the respective grooms, waiting patiently at the altar. When the priest asked, "Who gives these brides into the holy bonds of matrimony?" They'd only practiced once, but their response was a perfectly harmonized, "We do!"

Nick's grin disappeared. He choked up when Verona came to him. Eugene, on the other hand, was smiling broadly. He stepped forward and reached out for Elizabeth as if to say, "I got you now, Lizzie, my darling!"

The mothers of the brides, who typically would have made an entrance just before the wedding party, had slipped into a pew at the back o the church. They had been downstairs in the church hall, working like Trojans, preparing simple food into a tantalizing banquet for fifty guests. In the middle of the buffet table was a large dinner ham decorated with pineapple slices and maraschino cherries. The ham sat on a large board with a knife at its side for the guests to help themselves. Alongside was a massive platter of cold cuts, including head cheese and home-made German sausages. Next to the meats were two large bowls of potato salad that the ladies had garnished with sliced hard-boiled eggs and sprinkled with paprika. Also served were buns fresh from the oven, a garden salad, homemade cottage cheese, green beans with sliced onion covered with sour cream, a variety of pickles, and sliced tomatoes on top of a bed of leaf lettuce. In addition, the desert consisted of a variety of baked pies and cream puffs.

Mrs. Meyers volunteered to bake the three-layer wedding cake; it stood just inside the entrance. She had written the new-lyweds' names on the top layer beneath a miniature statue of a wedding couple. Elizabeth's sister Rosella—dressed in a pink dress Ma Thomas had crocheted—was responsible for overseeing the serving of the wedding cake.

With the Wedding Mass now over, the guests came downstairs to enjoy this ample, delicious buffet. After dinner, designated people from the wedding party and guests proposed several toasts. Then, finally, it was Eugene's turn to speak. Exuding self-confidence, he stood up, cleared his throat, and swept his gaze over the audience.

"Ladies and Gentlemen, as I look around this room, I realize I know so few of you, but I'm hoping time will change that. One thing is sure, on this special day, I'm happy that I decided, all those months ago, to come to Heisler because it is here where I met my wonderful Elizabeth. I want to thank Mr. & Mrs. Thomas for raising this lady who has brought much happiness into my life. When I came from Ontario to steal one of your women, I stole a jewel! And that is for certain!"

He turned to Elizabeth's smiling face and winked. Eugene didn't know if the man who'd made the comment was in the room, but if he were, round about now, he'd be feeling mighty cheap.

The man was in the room listening to Eugene's every word. "Damn it, when I said it, I didn't mean for him to hear me!"

Eugene turned to Ma Thomas and Verona's mother. They were seated together with their husbands.

"Thanks also to the bride's mothers for putting on this wonderful wedding feast!"

Eugene continued, "Elizabeth and I plan to live here in Heisler. I've purchased a little farm next to the Thomas'. We plan to raise a family here, God willing. Thank you all for coming, and I hope you enjoy the rest of the afternoon.

***

They got married on a shoestring; this was a common phrase for any couple in the area who married with little money. And Eugene and Elizabeth's shoestring was very, very short indeed! They had the house and the land, but little money left.

Eugene used the plank they'd sat on when proposing to Elizabeth and built a large, sturdy kitchen table that she promptly covered with cheerfully printed oilcloth. When the neighborhood found out he was a carpenter, several pieces of wood were donated, from which he built kitchen chairs and shelving for the sealers of canned food. And much to Elizabeth's delight, Eugene made a crib and a highchair, just in case. They ordered a new mattress from Eaton's catalogue for the bed frame Eugene built, and in addition, they ordered basic linens. And sitting in the corner of their little, two-bedroom home was Elizabeth's pride and joy: the pine hope chest her father had built for her.

At a farm sale, Eugene purchased a kitchen stove complete with an over-head warming oven and side reservoir along with two coal-oil lamps and a lantern. He also purchased the vital farm machinery: plow, disc, and harrow to prepare land for seed.

Ma and Pa Thomas's wedding gift was a cream separator and five young heifers that would be ready for breeding in the spring. Until they had milk of their own, Ma Thomas saved milk and cream for them. Elizabeth shook the cream in a sealer for lack of a butter churn until it turned into butter, which she tinted with little carrot juice so that it wouldn't look like lard.

And so, they started their married life, gathering all their needs to build a little farm. There were many tasks to accomplish, including fencing around the quarter section. Eugene borrowed horses to complete the plowing that would be followed in the spring with discing and harrowing in preparation for planting. Eugene also had to fall enough trees for firewood for Alberta's long, cold winter ahead. He spent hours chopping, splitting, and stacking the wood beside the house. "It helps to insulate," he told Elizabeth. Eugene was a proud, self-reliant man, when Elizabeth's brothers offered to help with everything, he accepted on the proviso, he could reciprocate in any way they may need him in the future.

The Christmas season came and went while the longing for spring crowded their thoughts and conversation. Elizabeth was dreaming of having the best vegetable garden in all of Heisler.

Eugene spoke of the crops he would plant–hay, corn, and alfalfa for silage, primarily wheat.

Every Saturday evening, they played bid whist with Nick and Verona, and every Sunday morning, their attendance at Mass was a common sight. It became a ritual for them to pray before and after every meal. They both knew the after prayer in German, and thus they would say it in the familiar language they heard as children. Elizabeth had long since been in the habit of saying her rosary every night before falling asleep. The sharing of their faith had become an intricate part of their married life. When the money they had spent so frugally was running low, they prayed every night, asking God to help them get through.

Chapter Five

The family welcomed a bright sunny day after the morning's heavy snowfall. When Eugene returned from the post office with a letter postmarked Walkerton, he knew it must be from his father. He decided to wait until he got home to open it in the presence of Elizabeth.

"I could smell those out in the yard," he said upon entering the kitchen, his face rosy from the cold. A blast of cold air following him in. Before taking off his coat and snowy boots, which would leave a puddle on the floor, he slid a letter from the front pocket of his jacket. Elizabeth was at the stove, taking cinnamon buns out of the oven.

"You can have one while they're hot."

"Sounds like a good idea, but I want to open this letter I got from Dad before I do." He showed it to her, then tore it open and began reading aloud:

Dear Eugene,

Son, you are full of surprises. I was surprised when the Deacon wrote me of your departure from St. Peter's, and then I was surprised to hear your bands read in church a day before receiving your letter.

I have sold the section of land across the river and am dividing the proceeds equally among my five children. Hence your share is enclosed plus a tad extra as a wedding gift. I know you will find a good use for it now. I trust you have chosen well for a wife and that you will always have the same love and respect for her that I had for your mother. God rest her soul. I am anxious to meet this Elizabeth of yours. I wish you happiness always.

Love,

Your Dad.

Eugene looked back in the envelope, and sure enough, a cheque lay in all its beauty. His hands were shaking slightly when he unfolded it. He gasped when he saw the amount . . . two thousand dollars! It was a fortune!

He looked at Lizzie and laughed aloud, "Well, I'll be a son of a gun! Now we can get all the livestock and chickens we need! We'll be able to sell cream! And I need horses, at least two to work the fields!" He was speaking rapidly. "This is an answer to our prayers! Two thousand smackeroos! That's not chicken feed!" He gave the cheque a little slap before putting it into his wallet.

Elizabeth smiled and said, "Now I can buy all the garden seed I want. I'm going to have the biggest garden this side of the Rockies! Eugene laughed at her enthusiasm. Filled with glee, they hugged, and then she looked into his eyes.

"I have something to tell you, Eugene," said Elizabeth, her face flushed with anticipation. "I've been waiting to tell you but didn't want to do it till the time was right." But then, she bit her lip, "I, I think I'm with child! I think I'm going to have a baby, Eugene! I wasn't sure before, but this morning I felt sick to my stomach; now I'm certain!"

"A baby!" His tone rose an octave. "That's wonderful news, sweetheart, wonderful! A baby!" He whispered, "Our baby, yours and mine, Lizzie! Good news comes to us all at once!"

"Uh-huh!" replied Elizabeth breathlessly.

He hugged her, and she closed her eyes. She felt the warmth of his lips as he kissed her forehead. She took a hanky from under her sleeve and wiped the tears from her eyes. She was smiling when she set two saucers and two knives and a little crock of butter upon the table—the table Eugene had built out of those planks. She took the coffee pot from the back of the stove and poured two steaming mugs to the brim. Then, she broke off two oven-warm cinnamon buns from the cluster on the breadboard and placed one on each saucer.

They sat down to eat, both silently savoring their double-good fortune. Never had cinnamon buns tasted as good as they did this day!

Eight and half months later, on September 15th, Eugene came home early from working on the neighbors' threshing crew to check on Elizabeth.

"I'm happy to see you, dear," said Elizabeth. "My water has broken, and the pains have started. You need to go and get

Mother. I think you better hurry!" she proclaimed in a voice two octaves higher. Eugene was out the door in a flash. He whistled for their faithful horse, named Silver, and with a slap on his flank, galloped the two miles up the road to the Thomas. When Ma Thomas saw Eugene galloping into the yard, she knew right away and dropped everything she was doing, grabbed her birthing valise, threw on her coat, climbed up behind Eugene, and flew down the road at a fast gallop.

Meanwhile, Elizabeth lay on their bed waiting for each pain to arrive, one a little stronger than the other, and when it reached its peak, she held her breath until it receded. "Oh, please hurry, Mother," she murmured aloud. "Jesus, Mary, and Joseph pray for me" Again and again, the pains came, stronger and stronger. She was moaning, and her hair was wet from perspiration when the door was flung open, and Eugene and her mother hurried to her bedside. The half-hour taken for their return had seemed like an eternity. Ma Thomas flew into action, exercising her midwifery skills–doing what she had done so many times in the past. She checked to see how far Elizabeth was dilated. Then she opened her birthing valise and removed a sealer containing a sterile cord.

Elizabeth, surprisingly, was close to delivery. Mighty quick for a first baby, she thought.

"I want you to breath slowly with each pain, Elizabeth dear. Just think of the sweet, little person trying to come into the world. It's hard on them, too, you know," said Ma Thomas. She swiped a cool cloth across her daughter's forehead. Meanwhile, Eugene paced the floor from the bedroom to kitchen, from kitchen to bedroom.

Finally, he sat down at the kitchen table, a cup of coffee in front of him and a cigarette in the ashtray, desperately wishing he could do something to help. But unfortunately, all that he heard from the other room was the ticking of the clock, Elizabeth's moaning, and the soft murmuring of Ma Thomas. He thought about his mother and how she would have experienced the same agony. And he thought about the child, his very own child, and how sweet it would be, especially if it looked like Lizzie and had her eyes and auburn hair.

Then, he heard his mother-in-law's raised voice, "Good girl, we are almost there! With your next pain, I want you to push, push hard. That's it, push again, Elizabeth, push again." Eugene sat teary-eyed, both hands covering his face. Then he heard a sound from the bedroom that was so precious, fresh, and clear: a baby's cry. It was like music and sweeter than any note he could ever raise on his trumpet.

He breathed a sigh of relief, stood up, wiped his eyes on his sleeve, and entered the bedroom. What he saw gladdened his heart. There was Lizzie, a smile on her face and her eyes shining like two stars. The reason for her smile came quickly to his attention. A beautiful, chubby baby girl was lying across Elizabeth's chest. She was all pink and pretty. 'She's a miracle,' thought Eugene.

"By golly, we did it, Eugene. She's simply incredible! Look how tiny her fingers and toes are!

Eugene nodded, overcome with joy. He whispered, "So we have our little Georgina!"

Eugene could not take his eyes from the newborn, thinking, 'What a miracle! She's so perfect! It's a mighty big name for someone so small! They had chosen the name over breakfast that very morning.

"I have a wife, but now I also have a family," his words filled the silence in the room.

With that thought, responsibility came crashing down on his shoulders. Ma Thomas, busily cleaning up, reached for Georgina to give her first bath.

"Eugene, I will stay over tonight to make sure she latches on and starts nursing. The first fluid is the colostrum, which builds her immunity. The milk will be here in a couple of days. I want Elizabeth to eat a bowl of cream-of-wheat every morning. That will give her good nurse milk," said Ma Thomas.

"You bet; I'll make the porridge every morning for her." He smiled at Lizzie, kissed her forehead, then started for the spare bedroom where he would sleep. He stopped halfway. "I, we, cannot thank you enough for what you have just done for us."

"Yes, thank you, Mom," said Elizabeth.

"You're most welcome," said Ma Thomas, chuckling. "I have a personal stake in this delivery. She is my first grandchild." Then, smiling, she gazed lovingly down at the squirming newborn in her arms.

***

The full flush of winter was upon them. White was every-where, across the fields, on top of buildings, smothering the woodpile, stacked neatly atop the fence posts; it sparkled across the land like a large, white blanket. At night the temperature would dip down to a crackling thirty below. Finally, after several months of frigid weather, the Waechter's welcomed Spring's thaw with open arms despite the slush and mud. They knew the bright, sunny days ahead would make short shrift of the mess. They also knew they could do the planting they dreamed of all winter. Springtime was exciting. Eugene seeded the fields, and Elizabeth planted her garden. Georgina sat in a cardboard box, shaking a rattle, and watching her mother's every move. She giggled when Elizabeth shook the package of seeds in front of her face. She was a happy baby, healthy and easily amused. Eugene placed her on his shoulders and introduced her to all the animals on the farm. By the time she was ten months old, she could mimic every animal. When asked what sound a cow makes, she would wrinkle up her nose, say 'moo,' then giggle.

Eugene had ridden into Heisler to buy some flour. Before doing that, he picked up the latest edition of *the Edmonton Journal*, which carried the dark story of the stock market crash. The headlines in large, bright red letters declared STOCK MARKET CRASHES. He brought the newspaper home and sat down at the kitchen table to read it. The year was 1929. The paper spoke of dark days ahead. He thought about the excellent crop they'd had last fall and the one just sown with anticipation for the same. Heaven Forbid! If there was any worry about the Alberta economy, it was small. Surely this news wouldn't affect Heisler.

But the men of the congregation, who met after church, were telling a different story. They spoke of hard times ahead, prices going up, and the value of their wheat sale going down. They were right. By 1932 commodity prices plummeted, ironically due to oversupply. Huge surpluses created by South America glutted the world markets, dropping the price of wheat in half for both Alberta and Saskatchewan farmers.

Joseph Schmeltzer from the Co-op Store affirmed what the men said in downtown Heisler and added his comments: "Most of my wholesale purchases have gone up twenty percent and, as much as I hate doing it, I have to pass this cost onto my customers or close the store."

He grimaced and took a sip of his coffee.

***

Life went on for Eugene and Elizabeth as the lean years slowly peeled away. Even though times were hard, each day brought new experiences and joys to their married life. And each year brought the biggest joy of all, a new child. Before long, Georgina had three healthy little brothers: Milton, Mervin, and Alvin–all popular names of the times.

Despite the rise in prices at the store and the decline in wheat revenue, they managed to make a living. They increased their livestock. Now there was milk for the family and cream to sell. Elizabeth continued to preserve everything for the winter just as her mother had done. Nothing was wasted. Coupled with the cream cheques, the sale of wheat carried them through the year, albeit barely. They fed their children and took them to church every Sunday, dressed up in their best bib and tucker.

***

Once again, they were expecting another child. Georgina was keeping her little brothers in tow. As young as she was, she was helpful to Elizabeth in many ways. She folded diapers, emptied the chamber pot, and amused her little brothers, who were hoping for a little sister in the Spring, while Elizabeth and Eugene just prayed for another healthy child.

At first, Eugene was oblivious to what was happening, but with the topic of bad times continually discussed by the men after Mass and with wheat prices dropping, Eugene had to sit up and take notice. He could see there was no possibility of things turning around. The decline in wheat prices didn't have the short duration he'd anticipated.

The Depression had snuck in like a thief in the night. Panic hit Eugene full force. He could think of little else but the Depression as he walked over the frozen earth from the barn to the house. He stopped at the woodpile and split some kindling. Earlier, he'd fed the chickens, milked the cows, fed the animals, and he'd shoveled manure out of the gutter in the barn. He continued to the house with an armful of wood.

Something had been heavy on his mind for months causing worry and regret. There was something he neglected to share with Elizabeth. Weren't married couples supposed to be upfront and straight with each other? How could he hurt a woman such as Lizzie? 'I must tell her!' he thought. The problem isn't going away!

Like always, when he walked through the door, his four little children ran to greet him with open arms, screaming, "Daddy, Daddy!" He'd hug them, call each other by name, and tussle their hair.

Elizabeth stood by the cream separator, a wave of auburn hair falling over her cheek as she cranked the handle, its centrifugal force shooting cream out of one spout and skim milk out the other. She put the balance of skim milk to beneficial use in pancakes, gravies, and soups. She always returned a little cream into the skim milk jug so the children could benefit from the fat.

The homey smell of wood burning enveloped the small home. The bread was rising beneath a cloth in a large, granite basin, adding the heady aroma of yeast to the mix. Eugene sat down at the kitchen table and rolled himself a cigarette. Elizabeth joined him.

"Good yield of cream this morning," Elizabeth said with a smile. "The cows are producing well." She poured two cups of coffee; it was their last serving of coffee, coffee now being so hard to get.

It would have been a delightful, tranquil moment if not for the black cloud in Eugene's sky. He drew his hands across his face in despair.

"Goodness me, Eugene, whatever is the matter?"

When his eyes met hers, she saw the worry in their depths. And Eugene saw the sparkle in hers disappear as she held his gaze, waiting for his response.

They heard the children's laughter coming from the other room where they were playing. Then, at last, Eugene spoke. "As you know, Lizzie, the price we get for our grain has dropped. But unfortunately, it's been dropping for the past two years. I'd hoped it would've been better this past harvest, but the price was down again."

"Yes, I know, but we're doing all right. There's food on the table, and we have feed for the animals."

"Lizzie, there's more that needs paying than the food. For example, the taxes!

"The taxes . . .but you've always, in the past, managed to cover them from the grain revenue."

"That's true, Lizzie, up to two years ago. I'm so sorry. I should have told you."

"What! You haven't paid the taxes for two years! Why didn't you tell me? How could you let it slide for two years without telling me, Eugene? How could you? Married people are supposed to share in everything. Don't you know that?

"I kept thinking the next year would be better, and I'd catch up, but it didn't get better, only worse. Other farmers are in the same boat. I've been worried about it and worried about upsetting you. You have your hands full with the children!"

She raised both palms, a frightened and hurt look on her face! "What in heaven's name is going to happen now?"

"We'll stay here until we have to move. That's all we can do, Lizzie," he lamented. That's all we can do! I'm sorry, Lizzie, I should have told you from the onset. We're just going to have to make the best of it! Come here."

He stood up and stretched out his arms. She rose and walked into his embrace. He kissed her forehead, and she closed her eyes while a tear ran down her cheek. Just then, the new life inside her womb fluttered for the first time as if a party to their conversation.

After the evening meal of a hearty stew was finished and the dishes washed, Elizabeth prepared the children for bed. Now washed and diapered, Elizabeth tucked Baby Alvin into bed with a bottle of milk, a treat he'd almost outgrown. Then, Milton and Mervin stood patiently before the washstand, waiting for Mother to wash their faces. Georgina, on the other hand, having put on her nightgown, assumed the responsibility of lining everyone's shoes against the wall, a chore she had invented and in which she took immense pride.

Once the children were asleep, Elizabeth and Eugene played a few hands of rummy. Their earlier conversation was not mentioned. Still, as the minutes slowly ticked by, both knew what was uppermost in each other's minds.

At nine o'clock, Eugene said, "I'm heading off to bed. Morning comes early." He stood up, banked the heater and the cookstove with wood then went into the bedroom.

"I'll be along shortly," said Elizabeth. She sat at the table for a few minutes thinking over the day that had just passed. At that moment, Elizabeth recalled how her mother had told her to ask for God's help if ever she were troubled. Well, now she was indeed troubled! Would they not have a home? Would the children suffer? Where would this new baby be born? Could she trust Eugene in the future? Her heart was heavy. She glanced up at the shelf where she had a wooden box of little treasures. One such treasure was a rosary her mother had given her. She reached up and took it down. Her routine every night was to pray her rosary in bed, but now she decided to say it here right at the kitchen table.

She had silently made the sign of the cross and just finished the Apostle's Creed when she heard the kitchen door squeak open.

A brilliant light streamed in. She gasped while her heart fluttered with fear. But then, a figure slowly began to form in the epicenter of the light. And there, stood Jesus with his cross over his shoulders. There was no doubt. It was Him. He looked just like all His depictions. His voice was soft yet firm as He slowly spoke:

"Do not be afraid, Elizabeth. I have come to give you courage. There will be tough times ahead. You must bear your cross just like I have born mine. But, in the end, you will be fine."

Then He turned and walked out through the doorway, the door closing gently behind Him without a sound.

Elizabeth put both hands on her cheeks, trying to understand what she had just seen and heard, then she hurried into the bedroom and shook Eugene.

"Eugene, wake up, wake up!"

His voice was heavy with sleep. He opened his eyes, "What's the matter? For goodness sakes, what is it?"

"Oh Eugene, I saw Jesus! He just came into the kitchen! He walked right through the kitchen door!" She was panting, and her eyes were wild. "Jesus just came into our home, Eugene! Jesus came into our home!"

"Lizzie, go back to bed. You've been dreaming!"

She responded breathlessly, "No, no, I wasn't dreaming. I hadn't gone to bed yet. I was sitting at the kitchen table saying my rosary when the door opened, and in came Jesus carrying a cross over His shoulders! He told me there would be tough times ahead and, and that I would have to carry my cross just as He carried His!"

She caught her breath.

"Come to bed, Lizzie. You've had a grueling day," soothed Eugene. Then, as he walked into the kitchen to blow out the lamp, he thought, 'It's the worry about losing the farm that's making her hallucinate. My poor Lizzie!'

Elizabeth, donning her nightgown with trembling hands, thought: 'He didn't believe one word I said, not one, single word.

It doesn't matter, though; I know it is true.' She whispered aloud, "I know it's true, Lord!"

The following day dawned with a bright blue sky. The heavy November frost proclaimed snow was not far away. Having finished all his morning chores, Eugene saddled Silver for a trip into town. His first stop was at the Co-op Store, where he would pick up the mail and *the Edmonton Journal*. He also enjoyed visiting Joseph Schmeltzer, who had all the world's news.

"Good morning, Joseph," said Eugene. "Hard at it again, I see."

Joseph stepped down from a chair where he'd placed new coal oil lamps on a high shelf. He turned. "Oh, it's you, Eugene. I didn't quite recognize the voice. How's everything with you?

"Not bad and not good either. I was disappointed with the drop in wheat. I thought it would get better. This is the third year in a row that it's dropped." He had no sooner said it than he wished he hadn't. No one must suspect he hadn't paid his taxes.

"It's the depression, Eugene. Everyone's in the same boat. You aren't the only one. John Meyers was here ahead of you today. He doesn't know how he'll feed his family this winter. Then again, his wife wasn't much of a canner. I'm going hand to mouth myself. Sales have dropped right off."

"That's too bad," Eugene replied.

His thoughts were on his family and what would happen to them in the future. He didn't want to talk to Joseph any longer today. He was tired of listening to the woes of the world. Lately, there wasn't anything but bad news all around.

"Is there mail for me?" he asked.

Joseph turned and checked the cubicles. "Let me see." He reached into the bag and pulled out one letter. He handed it to Eugene, who tucked it into his jacket pocket without looking at it.

"I'm heading off to the grocery store to get Lizzie some yeast and flour."

He made his purchase at the store, picked up the paper, and headed back home in a full gallop. The biting cold air across his face helped to clear his thoughts. His face was pink when he entered the coziness of his home. The little boys greeted him with their usual exuberance. Georgina was helping her mother roll out noodles to add to the pot of chicken broth bubbling on the stove. He tossed the paper on the table and exclaimed, "Sure smells good, Lizzie!"

She smiled in response.

Then, his eyes hit upon the headlines of the paper on the table:

HOMESTEAD LANDS ARE AVAILABLE NORTHEAST OF EDMONTON.

He sat down to read it. The article stated how the Canadian Homestead Act would give one quarter-section of land free to any male farmer who agreed to cultivate forty acres and build a permanent dwelling within three years. The only cost to the farmer would be a one-dollar administration fee. Once the farmer had met the initial homestead requirements, he could purchase an additional quarter-section for another ten dollars. Applications were available at any postal outlet. Excited, Eugene read it over several times. It was the answer to their problem! Strange, he hadn't noticed anything posted by Joseph at the co-op. Perhaps Joseph hadn't received the notification as yet.

"Lizzie, this is the answer to our dilemma. I know we have to start over, but we're young. We can do it. There are a lot of trees there, I've heard. I can build us a nice log house."

"I'll miss all my family here, Eugene, Mother, and all."

"I know you'll miss all your folks, but your family is right here in this house, Lizzie. We have to do what we have to do. We don't have any other choice."

She thought about her vision and its meaning, then replied, "I know you're right. I have to get used to the idea. There are a lot of plans to make." She patted his hand. He was ever so grateful for her acquiescence.

"Yes, there's a lot to think about in the days ahead. But first, I have to get my application in. So, I'll ride into town tomorrow to see if I can get one," stated Eugene

"Was there any mail today?" asked Elizabeth.

"Oh, yes, I've forgotten. There's a letter here in my jacket."

Chapter Six

The letter from the municipal offices of Forestburg stated that *due to two years of unpaid taxes, unfortunately, the municipality regrets informing the family of Eugene Waechter that they must vacate the premises located at 22128, Range Rd 6. by July 1, 1933.* Eugene read the letter twice, then covered his face with both hands. Shocked at seeing him do that, Lizzie quickly asked, "What's wrong, Eugene?"

"We have to vacate by the first of July next year." He passed the letter over to her to read.

"Oh no! she exclaimed. "But it's no shock, Eugene. We were expecting it!"

"But now it's a reality. When I bought this farm, I never dreamt that I would lose it in a few years! It's like getting our feet kicked right out from under us! They looked at each with eyes filled with despair.

Then Eugene continued, "I guess that seals it; we're heading north. I'll get the papers tomorrow, fill out the homestead land application in Alberta, and mail it. Then we'll just have to wait."

"We have much to think about and discuss, Eugene, but first, let's have our lunch. Children, come to the table - noodle soup, your favorite!" Oblivious to their parents' great worry, they came running.

Eugene was out of breath when he tied Silver up outside the co-op. To his astonishment, several horses were lined up at the store. It looked like he wasn't the only man to pick up an application for the homestead land. Joseph must have been right when he said many others are in the same boat.

Eugene filled out his application on the spot and gave it to Joseph for the mailbag. He passed a group of men in a deep discussion about homesteading on his way out the door. He was in no mood to join in, so he spurred his horse to full gallop home.

Again, Elizabeth poured two cups of coffee. Finally, they sat down to talk about what it would mean to leave the farm.

"How do we travel, and what do we take with us?" was Elizabeth's first question.

"I was thinking about that when riding home from the co-op. This is how I see it, dear: We travel with a covered wagon and team of horses. We bring two milking cows, a half dozen laying hens, and a tent to live in until I get the house built."

Elizabeth looked at him, trying to comprehend what it would be like living in a tent with the newborn baby they expected in the spring. But then, her thoughts quickly travelled to food and how she would feed the family. "How will I do the cooking?"

"We can build campfires along the way and bring our kitchen stove to use once we arrive at our destination. Luckily, it's not large. It will fit in the utility trailer attached to the wagon."

"We can have a yard sale for all the stuff we can't bring," stated Elizabeth.

"Ya," said Eugene, "and what doesn't sell, we can give to your family."

Elizabeth smiled. "Let's make it an adventure. The children will enjoy that."

They sat for a few minutes sipping their coffee, then Eugene broke the silence. "I wonder how long it will be before I hear back from the people at the Canadian Homestead Act. I'm anxious to know what land they'll assign us."

"And I wonder if there will be a Catholic Church there," said Elizabeth.

Two weeks later to the day, they had their answer. One-quarter of a section was theirs in *St. Lina, Alberta,* a predominately French hamlet within the county of St. Paul, fifty miles from Cold Lake. Hurray and Alleluia!

Eugene spread the small and tattered Alberta map out on the kitchen table. He'd brought the map from Ontario, but he hadn't looked at it in years. He could hear Elizabeth scolding the boys outside the door.

"You boys know better than to run around outside and not look where you're stepping. Animals don't have a toilet like you do. You slipped in it and fell. Now, look at your mess, and Momma has to clean you up. Off with your clothes! They're going to take some scrubbing! Phoo, stinky! stinky!"

The little gaffers looked up at their mother's face with guilty eyes.

The exchange made Eugene smile as he looked at the map and marked their trip to St. Lina. He figured it would take them about a week, but he would know better once he worked out the mileage. He was also anxious to talk to the men after church on Sunday. Now when they spoke of homesteading, he could say he already had his land–that would surprise the lot of them. But first, he and Lizzie had to make a family trip over to the Thomas' to tell them. Heaven, forbid they hear the news second-hand! Tomorrow after chores would be a good time.

The next day, a clear fall day greeted them as they all climbed into the buggy to ride over to the folks. The children were always excited to see their grandparents, and they loved the attention from their aunts and uncles when ever they met. However, Eugene, felt apprehensive, knowing this close-knit family would not be pleased with the news they were about to hear.

Ma Thomas came out the door and into the yard with her arms outstretched. The children ran to her for their hugs.

"This is a pleasant surprise. Come on in. There's coffee left from breakfast, a little watered down because I have to stretch it. I also have a batch of cookies coming out of the oven. One would think I knew you were coming." She smiled and led the way into the house, her heavy skirt swirling as she moved. A sweet, vanilla aroma filled the warm air of the kitchen as they entered.

Georgina slid onto the bench by the table, and her brothers followed, except for Alvin, who sat on his mother's lap. At eighteen months old, it was the safest place for him. Their Gramma placed a tray of cookies in the center of the table. "Don't touch them. They're hot!" she said. "Just wait a few minutes." Elizabeth prevented Little Alvin from grabbing one. Milton and Mervin sat on their hands impatiently, waiting while Georgina sat like the proverbial big sister, pretending not to be anxious. Finally, when Ma Thomas had finished pouring each a glass of milk, she announced the cookies had cooled. They now could take one. Four disappeared off the tray in short order.

"You'd think I never feed them," said Elizabeth. "What do you say, children?"

A harmonized echo of 'thank you' followed.

Pa Thomas, the consummate quiet man, sat at the far end of the table smiling at his beloved grandchildren as he watched their little hands reaching.

"Nick and Verona were here yesterday, ventured Ma Thomas. "They're expecting another baby just ahead of you. My, oh, my! The grandchildren are coming fast and furious!"

Elizabeth smiled at the news she wasn't the only one expecting and said, "That's wonderful!"

All the while Eugene sat pensively sipping his coffee. He was trying to decide how to tell them his news, he finally said, "I have good news and I have bad news. What do you want to hear first?"

"Bad news first," said Pa Thomas from across the table unusually loud.

Eugene dashed a quick glance at Elizabeth who was staring at an oil-cloth pattern on the table.

His voice was husky when he said, "I haven't had the money to pay the taxes on our farm. So, we are being evicted."

Elizabeth quickly chimed in, "It wasn't Eugene's fault. He's been working hard. As you know, wheat prices have been down." She looked at him lovingly.

"You're not alone. There's a big struggle all across the land," declared Ma Thomas. "When do you have to leave?"

"We have until the first of July next year."

"Christmas is just around the corner. July will come quickly," said Ma Thomas. She looked at Elizabeth, tearing up, so she continued, "You're not alone," she repeated. "So many in our parish have the same struggle. Times are tough. The depression has hit everyone hard. Nick and Verona are struggling too – things are terrible in Killam."

Ma Thomas knew how to take the edge off things.

Eugene had always liked his mother-in-law, but, at this moment, he liked her even more.

"There was a long line-up at the co-op a couple of weeks ago," he said. "It stretched halfway down the street and past the livery stable."

"Why were they lined up there? Did Joe have a big sale on?"

"No, they were lined up to get applications for homestead land. So that brings me to the good news. We have been given a quarter section of land under the Homestead Act."

"Where?" came the question from the quiet man across the table.

Eugene looked at his father-in-law and replied, "St. Lina, twenty miles from St. Paul and 154 miles from here."

Elizabeth handed Alvin to Eugene, stood up, and hugged her parents. Ma Thomas was the first to speak: "Of course, we'll miss you. We'll really miss you!" She touched Elizabeth's arm. "But you must do what you must do, my dear. We'll get to see each other often, I'm sure. I hear talk they're putting in more train lines."

"We should be heading home," said Eugene, standing up. "There's much to do, much to calculate and think about. I'll have to have a farm auction in the spring and send the word to other parishes. I hope there's some around for the buying. Mind you, we'll take what we can with us."

"Eugene says I can take my kitchen stove. I'm happy about that. It's a great little stove, heats up quickly, and has a great oven and reservoir," said Elizabeth.

"It has a great little cook using it," said Eugene, making Elizabeth blush.

Finally, when Eugene declared it was time to leave the children, having their fill of cookies and milk, slid out from the bench, anxious to leave their containment.

On the drive home, Eugene thought about the Thomas family, how close-knit they were, and how it would be hard for Lizzie to leave. He was also thinking about the men's coffee *klatch* after Mass on Sunday. He was anxious to hear what they all had to say about the depression, especially homesteading. Undoubtedly, they would have many opinions and comments to make. So many of them were in the lineup at Joe's.

He was right. The following Sunday, they were seated around an eight-foot table having coffee from the large, mottled-blue granite coffee pot on the cookstove in the church hall. They spoke of the tough times, the effect the depression was having on everyone, and the Homestead Act and what it offered. Such comments followed:

"What happens if we don't get the forty acres cleared that they're asking for? What then? I've been hanging onto my application."

"Forty acres isn't that much. Some of the lands will be treeless at the start. I wish I could pick out the land and deal with them on my terms."

"How do they select the land to give us? So I'm holding my application, too, until I get some answers."

"Houses will have to be built out of logs, as will all the other outbuildings."

"I don't know if it's a good idea to apply for this land. I'll move to Edmonton and try to get work there."

"I hate the city, all the crowds. I don't think I could last one month in the city. I've always lived on a farm where the air is fresh, as is the food, and stars fill the sky."

"You're a sentimental old cuss, aren't you?"

"You're very quiet, Eugene. What do you think about this homesteading business?" asked Joseph.

"I don't see where any of us have an alternative. Times aren't going to be getting any better. If some of us aren't in a desperate situation now, we soon will be. I've read people are starving in Germany, our ancestorial land. There may even be another world war on the horizon."

"Have you sent in your application, Eugene?"

"You bet I did! I not only sent it in, but I also already have my land in the hamlet of St. Lina. It's located twenty miles from St. Paul, Alberta. I take possession July 1st, next year."

He enjoyed the surprised looks on their faces and thought now they wouldn't be such skeptics. He stood up from the table and put his cup in the dishpan of soapy water on the stove. He glanced over to where the ladies sat and caught Lizzie's eye and received her nod, their agreement to leave. Then, he then walked over to the large, empty hall where the children chased each other about. . Memories of the hall, his trumpet playing, and the first sighting of Lizzie came flooding in as though it had happened just yesterday. Soon he would be leaving all this behind when his family relocated to St. Lina. 'So much has happened in these past five years,' he thought. 'Four children and another on its way. And then there was Lizzie, the consummate mother and cook and such an easy-going and good-natured lady. And she was always quick to laugh.' His choice for a wife couldn't have been better!

He thought about the seminary he had left behind in Ontario with absolutely no regrets.

He thought about the seminarians, their repetitive daily routine, and all they were missing in life. He knew they believed their choice to be a higher calling, but it was a calling he hadn't received. 'Oh well, that's that,' he thought. 'Or as it's said in German . . . *das ist, das.*'

Georgina noticed her father in the doorway and hurried over to him, flushed and breathless from running.

"Please round up your brothers," said Eugene, patting her head, "We're heading home."

"Okay, Daddy."

***

Time moved on, albeit slowly. The move to St. Lina was uppermost in their minds, and hardly a day passed that they didn't speak of it. All the while, winter brought the cold, heaps of snow, and the eternal burning of firewood to warm their home. Then, just when they thought it would never end, the air warmed, and the snow began to melt, leaving mud and slush in its wake. It was March. It could very well freeze, and more snow was likely. The prevailing warm weather was just a tease.

Lizzie was drawing near her delivery time, and while she hadn't been sick, her baby's growth was impeded. Finally, Ma Thomas intervened and advised Eugene to take Elizabeth to the nearest hospital just in case she required special medical attention at the time of the delivery. Her pregnancy was barely visible, but Elizabeth maintained the baby was just as active as Alvin, her precious little son, who'd be two in August.

When the expectant delivery date drew near, Eugene gave the children to Ma Thomas for tending, then hitched Silver to the buggy. Bundled up warm and with a heavy quilt wrapped over their knees, they drove to the nearest hospital at a full trot.

The hospital took all the necessary information, and a nurse came with a wheelchair to take Lizzie to her designation while she awaited labor, her rosary clutched in her hands.

That image of Lizzie remained in Eugene's mind the entire trip back to the Thomas home. The children were anxious to see him return and wanted to know where the baby was.

"It will take a little time, kids, but Mom will be back with a little brother or sister for you before you know it."

"I bet you're hungry, Eugene," Ma Thomas said. "I have a full pot of stew for everyone, and I have put dumplings in as I know the children love them."

"Sounds *wunderbar*," said Eugene with a smile of appreciation. "The hospital will make a phone call to Joe at the co-op to tell me about the birth. I'll have to check with him every day. I'm afraid I'll need to eat and run today," he continued as they all sat down. "I have to do the evening chores and bank up the fires in the house. Tomorrow, after morning chores, I'll ride into town to see if anything has happened. Thanks for minding my little brood."

He surveyed the meager surroundings in his home and wished he had more to give Lizzie. It seemed strange to walk into the house without his children there to greet him and without the aroma of either bread baking or something simmering on the stove. But most of all, without Lizzie's sparkling eyes to warm him, the home was lonely, without heart, and without life.

And now, any day now, or right at this moment, his Lizzie was enduring the pains of childbirth. Oh, how he wished he could bear the pain for her! Such is life! And she would be doing it without complaint, just accepting it and looking at it as her sense of duty, just as was expected of her.

Please, let tomorrow bring the good news!

Morning dawned bright and sunny, shining through the bedroom window like a beacon and waking Eugene from his fretful sleep. He hurried through the morning chores, then shook the reigns to make Silver lope into a full gallop down the snow-covered road into Heisler. No one was in the store, only Joe, who greeted him cheerfully. "What can I do for you this fine, sunny morning?" he asked, beaming his biggest smile.

"Did you, by any chance, get a call from the Forestburg Hospital?" asked Eugene hopefully. "They will be calling you when Lizzie gives birth."

"Ah, Eugene, I'm sorry, there's not been a call. The phone hasn't rung in two days."

"Okay, thanks anyway. I'll keep checking in with you. As you can imagine, we're all anxious." Then, filled with disappointment at no news about Lizzie, he slowly turned and left the store.

For the next ten days, Eugene's life became a fearful, routine blur comprised of spending time at the Thomas', tending to the chores, banking the fire, and riding in to see Joe. By the eleventh day, when there was no news, Eugene was frantic. He sat with his coffee cup in front of him at the Thomas', untouched.

"I'm going to the hospital," he declared. "It's over ten days! I'm worried. She may have died for all I know."

His big eyes were moist as he looked up at Ma Thomas. The active noise of the children upstairs was in sharp contrast to the somber hush amongst the family members who sat around the table. She placed her hand on his shoulder.

"The baby will come when it's ready, Eugene. Sometimes these things take longer than expected. She'll be just fine. You'll see."

"I have to see what's going on at that hospital. I have to go and see Lizzie."

"I'll do your chores for you while you're gone," offered Lizzie's brother, Lawrence.

"Thank you, I'd appreciate that," replied Eugene as he prepared to leave the table.

"Just a moment," said Ma Thomas. "Before you go, let's all bow our heads and say the Lord's Prayer for the safe delivery of this new life coming into the world: In the name of the father, the Son and the Holy Ghost, Our Father who art in heaven . . ."

They didn't notice that five-year-old Georgina had snuck down the stairs as they prayed. She sat on the bottom step, her face in her hands, quietly sobbing.

Eugene fed and watered Silver for the long ride into Forestburg. He was a lonely rider peeling off the miles. The horses' hooves made a rhythmic rat-a-tat-tat sound as they came in contact with the hard-packed, snow-covered road. The flat white land stretched on and on until finally disappearing into the horizon. In the distance of this prairie landscape, a small grove of willow trees reached their branches up to the sunlight to nourish their budding branches.

It was March 14th, 1933, when Eugene walked up to the reception desk. The employee who sat there looked bored as she doodled on a scrap of paper. Eugene inquired about his wife, with a face flushed pink from the hard, cold ride.

"I'm here to see my wife, Elizabeth Waechter, pronounced 'waiter,'" stated Eugene, then added, "She's having a baby."

'Some people should not be behind a desk serving the public,' thought Eugene. 'There she is. She hasn't even looked at me, and she's chewing gum to boot!'

The receptionist picked up the wall phone and cranked two rings.

"There's a man here wanting to see Elizabeth Waechter," she said, stumbling over the last name.

Eugene's anxious mood made him impatient and short-tempered, and he quickly corrected her, "It's 'Waiter,'" he said, thinking, 'she's deaf, too.'

"Sure, I'll hold," she said into the phone with it stuck to her ear.

The seconds passing were like hours to Eugene, whose patience was running thinner than the wings on a housefly.

Finally, the receptionist, obviously having been asked a question, said, "I'll check." She took a small filing box off the shelf and, while humming, flipped through it. "No," she finally said. "She hasn't checked out."

Eugene wasn't going to wait around any longer. He turned and made his way to the staircase and went up, taking two steps at a time with the receptionist shouting at him from down below.

"Hey, mister, you can't go there. Stop! You can't go there."

But he was up to the labor room on the second level of the hospital well ahead of her. There, he encountered a nurse at her station.

"You're not supposed to be up here, sir," said the nurse on duty.

"I'm looking for my wife. I brought her here over ten days ago. I want to see her," he demanded breathlessly.

"I just told Mabel on the downstairs phone that your wife is not on this floor."

"What is the matter with you people? Can't you keep track of your patients? You don't deserve to be working in a hospital. I keep better track of my animals on my farm. I'm going to report you to the police. I'm worried about my wife! She's expecting a baby! What have you done with her? You, you knuckleheads!"

"Who's a knucklehead?" The voice came from behind; Eugene swung around, coming face to face with a doctor.

"They can't tell me where my wife is," declared Eugene, his eyes wide and unblinking. "I brought her here ten days ago to have her baby."

"If it is Elizabeth Waechter, you are looking for, I just delivered her baby about an hour ago. She should be in her room by now." He raised his thumb to indicate one floor up.

"Thank God! How is she? And how is the baby?"

"They're both fine. The baby is tiny, weighing in at four pounds, but healthy. Go upstairs. You'll be able to see them both. By the way, I'm Doctor Schwartz.

"Thank you, Doctor, thank you!" Eugene shook the doctor's hand vigorously and then swiftly left for the stairs.

The doctor called him back. "We have to monitor her weight, Mr. Waechter, and keep her in the hospital for about a week before she can be discharged."

"I see, much appreciated," replied Eugene as he hurried toward the stairs.

He came to the nursery first and saw several newborns tucked in their bassinets. He scanned the names at the top of their bassinets, and then he saw it:

Baby Waechter – SPECIAL ATTENTION REQUIRED.

Her delicate pink skin matched her pink blanket. She had a smattering of dark hair. Although her eyes were closed, Eugene could tell they were large. Overall, she had the sweetest of countenance! Oh yes, she was one little beauty!

Just then, a nurse walked by.

Eugene stopped her and asked, "What is meant by special attention?"

"All babies that weigh in under five pounds have to be monitored and fed more often," she replied. "Once they're five pounds, they can go home."

"I see," replied Eugene. After checking for the room number on the desk, he found Elizabeth. She was sitting up in bed drinking a glass of orange juice. She smiled at him and set her glass down. He hugged her.

"I've been so worried about you, darling!"

"By golly, Eugene, I've done it again! Did you see her? She's beautiful! She's tiny, but I'll make sure she nurses well. I know I'll have to feed her more often. I know she'll thrive. I'll eat lots of cream-of-wheat porridge. Ma has said many times that's the best! Waiting to go into labor was the hard part. I didn't think she'd ever be born, but my water broke last night.

"What will we call this tiny girl of ours?" asked Eugene.

"I've been thinking about it. A French nun taught at our school when I was in grade five. I liked her. She was gentle, always smiling, and an outstanding teacher. Her name was Celine. Let's call our new little girl Celine," declared Elizabeth.

"I think that's a great idea. And, as you know, Lizzie, there's French in my background. It isn't all German. So, it would be nice to have a name in the family to reflect that."

"I miss the other children," said Lizzie. "I feel like I've been away for months. By the time I get home, it will be over two weeks. It sure is nice of Ma to look after the family."

"Yes, your mother is a wonderful woman! She's been doing so much for us, tending to the children's needs. Georgina has been sad. I know she'll feel better when I get home and tell her she has a little sister now. The boys are having fun with the family. Ma has been potty-training little Alvin. He seems to be catching on quickly. But, for some reason, he didn't eat much of his supper last night."

"I wish I could stay longer, Lizzie dear, but I must get back. Silver is tied up outside. I need to feed and water him before I head home. I'm anxious to tell the children about Celine. They will be so happy, especially Georgina. I plan to bring the children when we come to bring you both home. I know they'll be happy to hear that."

She nodded her "Uh-huh," with eyes shining brightly like beacons in the night.

He leaned over from the bed's edge, where he'd been seated, and kissed her.

Chapter Seven

There was much fodder for Eugene's thoughts on the ride back to Heisler. He couldn't get the image of the new baby girl out of his mind, so tiny yet so perfect. But then, he thought of Alvin when he was born. He, too, had been small, weighing only five pounds, yet he was strong. 'But this new baby girl, Baby Celine, weighs only four pounds, my God, only four pounds!' 'Just like a delicate little flower!' Eugene thought.

As the horses' hooves beat the road, many things, ideas, and plans swarmed like buzzing bees through Eugene's mind.

'Elizabeth looked good! She is such a trooper! She looked so beautiful in bed with her sparkling eyes. The children will be happy to see her. I know, like me, they've missed her. It has been the hardest on little Alvin. He seems to have lost his appetite.'

It'll help if I make a chart so the kids can scratch off the dates. It will help them pass the days without their mother. It will be nice for the children to come with me when I bring Lizzie home. It's best if Alvin stays behind with Gramma Thomas. She has been so good to us! Lizzie's younger sister have been helpful with the kids! And Lawrence has been just excellent at doing my chores for me! There's no way anyone could ever fault the Thomas family.

I'll have to get the ball rolling on selling farm equipment and livestock. Then, I can use the money for grubstaking at our new settlement in St. Lina. It's a good thing I saved some of the money Dad gave me. I could have paid the taxes with it, but that would only have prolonged the agony. It felt better having it in the bank, and now I need it. Thank you, Lord.

I'm happy there's a barn, chicken coop, and a well on the quarter section I received. It stated that in the letter I received from the government. I sure hope they're not mistaken. It's going to be exciting to see the place and get established. Building a log house will be challenging, but I can do it if anyone can. One thing I'm good at is carpentry and butchering. I'm glad to have worked in a butcher shop in Ontario. I learned a lot from that experience, and now it's paying off. I don't hear from the folks back East often, except at Christmas. Then again, they don't hear from me either. When I get home, I will sit down and write a long letter back East and tell them about the new baby. I can't help thinking about the new baby and the other wonderful little kiddies we have. I'm so fortunate! Celine, Celine, I have to get used to that French name. I like it. It sounds soft and pretty at the same time. Suits the little darling!'

He came to the bend in the road three miles from his destination with those thoughts and others. Those last miles seemed to stretch on forever. Finally, he arrived at Thomas' home. He tethered Silver at the hitching post and gave him a bucket of water before walking into the house, tired but incredibly happy, indeed!

The scream of "Daddy's home!" echoed throughout the house as the children ran to greet him. After the hugs, Eugene said, "I have news for you. I have good news."

The excitement captured the attention of the household.

Georgina, Milton, and Mervin slid in on the bench behind the table except for Alvin, who was napping.

"You have a little sister. She was born early this morning."

"Hurray, "said Georgina gleefully, "At last, I have a little sister!"

Milton and Mervin clapped their hands.

"We all must take good care of her. You're too young to remember Alvin when he was first born, so this is a new experience for you. Her name is Celine. She will eat and sleep a lot. She's very, very tiny," said Eugene.

Milton asked, "Can she poop?" He immediately felt a jab from Georgina. Mervin giggled with his hands over his mouth.

Eugene laughed, "But of course, she can, silly boy, and you will change her diapers." Seeing the total shock on Milton's face, he patted his head and chuckled, "Just joking, son."

"They will be coming home in six days. I want you to be good children for Gramma and help Mom where you can when she gets home. She'll be tired for a few days. You can all come with me when we go to get them," said Eugene. Gramma can take care of Alvin. Eugene smiled his thank you to Ma Thomas across the room. He's a bit young for the trip. We can scratch off the days on the calendar–you can take turns. Georgina, you're the eldest. You can go first."

Eugene paused, looked at each in turn, and continued, "Time will go by fast. You'll see."

The four children gleefully clapped their hands in unison. His words were as much a comfort to himself as they were to his children!

Two months later, Baby Celine was baptized in St. Martin's Catholic Church, just as her siblings had been and where her parents had been married. Unfortunately, Lizzie did not produce nurse milk for Celine. Eugene picked out his healthiest milking cow, and Celine only had milk from that same cow. They deluded it with water, and Lizzie fed her often. She grew slowly but was bright and a good sleeper. She smiled with all the stimulation around her, often bringing joy and entertainment to the family. When she smiled for the first time, everyone laughed at the cuteness.

***

Spring's warmth gave chase t to winter's snow and the month of May brought the sun that dried up the slush and mud of the season. Now, all the family could think of was their departure from Heisler to St. Lina.

Ma Thomas answered the door at Eugene's knock. She invited him in, but Eugene spoke before she could say anything. "I plan to ride into St. Lina and build a log house on the homestead property before I bring the family. I think it will take two or three weeks. Then I'll come back for them."

Before saying anything further, Pa Thomas, the man of few words, spoke up, "Lawrence can move in with Lizzie to help with the chores and other things while you're away."

"Did I hear my name spoken?" asked Lawrence coming in from the other room.

"Yes, you did," said Ma Thomas. "Would you be willing to move in with Lizzie for a couple of weeks while Eugene's away building their log house in St. Lina?"

"Of course, I'd be willing. What are brothers for? When are you leaving?"

"Day after tomorrow," replied Eugene.

"I'll come over early in the morning and do the chores so you can get a head start. You have quite a ride ahead of you."

"I know, thanks, friend. I plan to camp along the way and get there as fast as possible. I'll only stop when I have to."

Riding back home, Eugene was elated. Finally, finally, everything was going his way. Now he could leave, and with Lawrence there, he wouldn't be worrying about the family.

"I hope things will go as well when I get to my destination," he said aloud.

It was 1934 and early morning when a bedraggled Eugene rode into the hamlet called St. Lina. He did not know what to expect or where he would find the resources to complete his mission of building his home. Eugene also didn't know how quickly he could locate his new property from the map given to him by the municipality. A Catholic church centered the village with a co-op store directly across from it. He saw two nuns leaving the church and entering the building beside it, which he presumed was the convent house.

Further on, he reached a crossroads. He could see a school to the right, and across from the school was a Red and White Grocery Store with the name Lozeau's printed over the door. Directly ahead was a post office. He turned his horse to the left for the two-mile ride to what presumably was his new homestead. The map pointed out that his property would be to the left of that first intersection, the right of which would be the road to Lac La Biche, sixty miles in the distance.

Yes, the map was right!

Eugene walked the horse slowly onto the property. Sure enough, there was the barn, the chicken coop, the well, and even a small woodpile. How convenient!

"This is it! This is my new home!" exclaimed Eugene

Only his horse, the magpies that were flying about, and perhaps a gopher that had come out of it's hole that heard his joyous voice.

He visualized how his log house would be situated right over there. He saw acres of cleared land as far as his eyes could scan. Presumably, someone had lived here in the past and for the land clearing requirements of the Homesteader's Act to be accomplished. Now to build the house, find the logs, and help with the construction. A ride back into town would give him the answers, but first, he had to give his horse water and tether him so he could graze on the tall grass by the well. What a good horse Silver was! 'He is serving me so well,' thought Eugene. He patted the side of Silver's neck.

He spread his sleeping bag on the grass and fell sound asleep.

When he awoke, he decided to try Lozeau's store to buy some food supplies and receive information about building his log house.

"Hello, yours is a new face in town," said Marcel Lozeau. "What can I do for you this bright, sunny day?" The French lilt to his words was barely noticeable.

"My name is Eugene Waechter, pronounced Waiter. I've been travelling for over one hundred miles to take possession of my land at the Lac La Biche intersection."

"I'm Marcel Lozeau, owner of this store. By the way, I know that land well. My friend Eli Maseau owned that land. Poor fella had a heart attack and died. It was weeks before his body was found in his covered wagon." He made a wry face and blew out of the side of his mouth to indicate the stench. Eugene got the message. Marcel continued, "He used to come into this store almost every day, sometimes just to chat."

"That's unfortunate. Well, I don't intend to die. Instead, I plan to build a log house and when that's finished, bring my family here." But the thought of dying on the land lingered for a moment.

"Where are you from?' asked Marcel.

"From Heisler," he replied. Eugene could tell by the look on Marcell's face that he didn't know where that was.

"Can you tell me where I can get some logs and some men to help with construction?" asked Eugene.

"I sure can. A half-mile north of here is my good friend, Leo Tremblay. He has a small log mill in his yard and has been supplying logs as far away as St. Paul."

Marcel knew that was a bit of a stretch but felt it would give Leo a boost, who hadn't had a sale for some time. He continued, "And he will know if fellas are around who'd be happy to give you a hand."

"Thanks, Marcel. I'm heading there right now."

"You can't miss it. Just head north. You'll see his operation from the road."

Eugene rode into the yard of Leo Tremblay. He could see a makeshift sawmill center stage in full display. A large circular saw, its jagged teeth glinting under the sun, was affixed to the center of a long, well-constructed, wooden table. At the front end, there was a feed-in that was adjustable depending upon the thickness of boards, studs, casings, and other specially cut wood. The Tremblay's had piled a mountain of logs high in the yard - someone had been very busy, indeed, sawing them down and dragging them on a skid out of the woods.

Eugene was pleased!

Before Eugene could stop his horse, Leo, a short, muscular man looking like a wrestler, came out of the small house to greet him. Eugene dismounted and walked towards the mill, and Leo joined him there.

"Quite a system you have here!" said Eugene. "Lozeau told me about you. I own the Maseau farm and want to build a house there."

"I know de place well," replied Leo. "I helped him build a barn and chicken coop for de chickens. The poor man died before we could get de house for him built."

His gruff voice carried a definite French accent.

"How big you want de house built?"

"I figure about twenty-five feet by twenty with three bedrooms on the second floor, plaster on the walls, and linoleum on the floors. Also, a cellar for canned foods. I need a couple of good hands to help."

"Dat's no problem, me and my sons will be able to help. But, of course, we expect some money. We do good job."

"Let's talk about the money. How much do you expect? I know you'll keep in mind there's a depression on," Eugene said.

"Do you want me to tell you for de whole ting or dis and dat?

"You tell me," said Eugene.

"Den, let's go for de whole ting."

"All right, the whole kit and caboodle, a finished home ready to move into."

"I need to figure it out. Dat was twenty-five feet by twenty feet, right?"

"Right," replied Eugene.

Leo took a pen and a small booklet out of his pocket. He sat on a chopping block and started calculating.

"Me tinks it can all be done, ready to move into for de small price of five hundred dollars. Dat includes materials and labour."

Eugene was impressed. He had been expecting more, but he wasn't about to let Leo know that.

"Wow, five hundred dollars! That isn't chicken feed! I'll tell you what. I'll think it over tonight. Tomorrow is Sunday. Will you be going to Mass tomorrow? If so, I'll give you my answer then?

"Yes, I'll be there."

"By the way, what time is Mass?"

"Ten o'clock," replied Leo. "See you dere."

After stopping back at Lozeau's store for food supplies, Eugene rode back to his land to examine the construction of the barn and chicken coop. He wanted to check the construction of these buildings, the uniformity and angle of the cuts, and overall general symmetry. In addition, he noted shavings were the insulation between the inside boarded walls and the outside logs, extra protection for the bitterly frigid winter climate of the area; this was a must for the family home. But overall, he could find no fault with the carpentry.

Satisfied, he took the small hatchet and some cooking utensils from his packsack and split some kindling to build a fire. Then, withdrawing some of the food supplies he had lowered in a bucket down the well, he prepared his dinner of bacon, pork and beans, bread, and boiled potatoes. 'What a trip this has been,' he thought as he lay near the fire in his sleeping bag. The last thing he saw in the sky before exhaustion took over was northern lights in hues of green, orange, pink, and blue.

When Eugene walked into church the following day, he had washed, shaved, and put on a clean, wrinkled shirt he'd pulled out of his duffel bag. He came early, sat in a pew at the back, and watched the people come in. It reminded him of when he first arrived in Heisler, everyone was a stranger then, too. First, he was watching for Leo Tremblay. Finally, he saw the short, stocky figure striding up the aisle. He appeared noticeably short next to the three strong-looking young men accompanying him. They must be his sons, he thought. They certainly haven't taken after their father. The mother followed up the rear. She was a petite lady, a good head shorter than her husband. Now Eugene wondered who the sons took after.

After Mass, Eugene and Leo greeted each other outside. They got down to business following the introductions and shaking of hands. Eugene spoke first.

"I would like to hire you to build the house. However, I do have some stipulations," stated Eugene as he preceded to name them by number:

1. You will start tomorrow morning.

2. I'm expecting the home to be sufficiently insulated as well as the window casings and outside doors.

3. I want an eight-by-eight cellar dug with shelving affixed to three walls. The fourth wall should have an escape hatch to the outside; this will enable us to shoot the root

vegetables from the outside right into the bin for storage over the winter.

4. The construction of this home has to be built on a timely basis. I'd like to see it done in two weeks. My wife and children are anxious to join me here.

5. You will supply all materials and labor.

6. In addition, you will build an outhouse.

7. Tomorrow, I will give you one hundred dollars to get started. Then, I will give you another one hundred dollars once the footings are in and the outside walls are built. Then, when finished, I will give you the final payment of three hundred dollars bringing the complete total to five hundred.

After accepting the contract paper, Leo read it over slowly and shook Eugene's hand vigorously in agreement! He was happy that, at last, he was going to earn some money. Now he could pay the grocery bill at Lozeau's store.

"That's a deal, then Leo," said Eugene before walking over to his horse. He felt the spring sun on his shoulders and noticed some parishioners looking his way, no doubt wondering who he was and why they were shaking hands. The Tremblay's smiled broadly when they left the churchyard that Sunday morning in May 1933.

The following day, Eugene had hardly gotten out of his sleeping bag when he heard horses' whinny and pounding feet coming into the yard. The Tremblay's, all four of them, were atop a large pile of logs on a long wagon. The four steeds pulling them were unruly and didn't want to stop. It took several 'whoa' before they were still.

"Good morning," said Eugene as he placed a tea kettle on top of the grill that covered the hot coals in the fire. "I see we are ready to get started."

"The boys will dig de cellar while we lay the footings," said Leo. He pointed to concrete slabs on the wagon that he had on hand. "It will take two of us to carry dem."

"I've paced off the four corners of the house," replied Eugene, "There, there, there, there," pointing to each in turn where he'd placed a wood stick.

It took all their strength to lay the footings in place.

"Der, I'm glad dat's done!" exclaimed Leo.

With their shovels flying, his sons dug the cellar in record time. He continued, "We can spread the earth around; dis gives de floorboards a cushion. It looks like dey have hit hardpan, but dat's okay, be good walls for de cellar. Dey will build de shelves and de bin after de boys are done digging, den, we can go to town with de walls."

Eugene didn't hear a word he'd said. Instead, with pen and paper in hand, he'd sat down on the chopping block to write a quick note to Lizzie:

My Darling Lizzie,

I hope and pray all is well with you and the children and that baby Celine is still thriving. How is Lawrence making out with the chores? You will be happy to know that our new home is being built as we speak, only twenty feet away from where I'm seated. I made an inquiry at the local store and found this carpenter with some strong sons to help. He knows what he is doing, so we should have a well-built and warm home. If all goes well, it should be finished in two weeks, then I'll gallop back to you, and we can prepare to travel back here and start our new life in our brand-new home in a brand-new town. I have purchased a milking cow, several bred heifers, and chickens from a local farmer, delivered when we return. People here are also suffering from the depression. They are happy to get their hands on some cash, which has been to our advantage. I went to Mass on Sunday. The priest spoke a few words in English in his sermon before breaking into French. Most, if not all, of the folks here are homesteaders from Quebec. But, as you know, our Latin Mass never changes, and that's a good thing. I will try to write to you again soon and update you on the construction. As we agreed when I left, Lawrence will be checking with the co-op to fetch your mail. You know you can write back to me general delivery, St. Lina, Alberta. And, oh, yes, there is an excellent spot here for you to plant your vegetable garden. I saw that big box of seeds you have under the bed. So, I must get back to the construction, my dear. They will start laying the logs shortly. Kiss the kiddies for me.

Your loving husband,

Eugene.

"I'm heading into town to mail a letter and will be right back," shouted Eugene as he passed the work crew. Two of the brothers worked in the cellar, while Leo and his other son saw the length of logs and notched them. Eugene thought, 'they sure are hard workers and fast too. I lucked out!' The logs went up, then the trusses, and finally the roof. The days passed.

Ten days later, to Eugene's delight, his home was finished. He took the last walk-through and was more than pleased! The inner walls on the interior had been plastered and covered with whitewash, and the floors sparkled with linoleum on both levels. Leo did the unexpected by lining up shelving adjacent to the kitchen stove. A protective chimney collar of asbestos and iron was placed where the ceiling met the roof. It now was ready to receive the pipes stacked at one end of the kitchen. In addition, he left a considerable amount of scrap wood behind which Eugene could use for furniture. Yes, Eugene was more than pleased.

As the work-weary Tremblay carpenters gathered up their tools and hitched their horses to the wagon, it was time to say goodbye. Eugene handed the final payment of three hundred dollars to Leo and shook hands with him and the hands of his three hard-working sons.

"I need something else done," said Eugene, "and I'm happy to pay you for it. I need the frames made for three double beds. I have the springs and mattresses. I also need a big enough table for eight people and two benches and two chairs."

The table Eugene had built all those years earlier now was too small

"When I arrive back with the family," he continued, "I would like to see the beds in the bedrooms upstairs and the table, benches, and chairs in the kitchen. I will have a kitchen cook-stove on my wagon and mattresses and will need someone to help me unload those things."

"We will be happy to do dat," said Leo in his broken English. They agreed on a price. "Come by and let us know when you are back."

"I cannot thank you enough," said Eugene. "You've done an excellent job here." I want you to take this small token." He reached in his pocket and handed Leo another five dollars. He didn't hesitate to take it, saying, "You didn't have to do that." Eugene winked and said, "That's why I did."

They were chuckling when they climbed into their wagon. When it was a few yards down the driveway, Eugene heard them raucously singing, *"Alouette, gentile Alouette, Alouette, je te plumerai."*

A chorus of howling coyotes off in the distance prevented Eugene from going to sleep that night, but once he did, he slept soundly. After a quick breakfast in the morning, he fed and watered his horse and then doused the fire. As he rode slowly down the road, he was filled with emotions. He was anxious to see his family and bring them here, yet he hated to leave his new farm. Before turning towards town and returning to Heisler, he stopped and took a long look at his new home. It looked beautiful, perfect for the landscape, and located just in the right spot! He took in the other buildings: the barn, the chicken coop, which they sometimes called 'the henhouse,' and the outside toilet, which was situated on the opposite side of the house from the well. He thought about an icehouse he would build. A lake nearby to get ice blocks in the winter gave the perfect solution for keeping food cool in the summer. He also thought about constructing a smokehouse for the curing of ham. And, of course, he thought about the one major building that was missing: the granary. He would rectify that as soon possible. There was so much to think about when starting up a new farm.

Lizzie will be so pleased! In his mind's eye, he could see cattle grazing in the pasture, chickens scratching on the ground around their coop, but best of all, he could see children playing in the yard. Overall, he was happy and excited to bring his family to this, their new home.

'If I keep the horse at an even trot, I should be back in Heisler in four days. I'll check out the stopping points for the family's trip back here; we will know exactly where we'll stop each day. I'll check in with some farms along the way for feed and water for the animals. If all goes well, the trip from Heisler back here with the family should be accomplished in about eight days, give or take.'

"Giddy up," he said with a slap of the reins, and he was off, leaving a ball of dust in his wake. He trotted through the town, past the post office, past St. Helen's Catholic Church, past the co-op, and onto the road that would take him back southwest to Heisler.

He planned to make his first stop at St. Brides and then bed down for the night at Foisy, approximately one-third of the way back to Heisler. The rugged terrain of this part of Alberta made him wonder how the farmers faired. He did not see a lot of flat land like there was around Heisler. Instead, there were sporadic, bushy areas, sloughs surrounded by bulrushes, and a few rock-filled clearings. Further inland from the road, there might be a different impression. He trotted on.

When he reached St. Brides, he dismounted. His stiff legs needed to be walked on a bit to shake out the kinks. He was also thankful that he had the mind to cushion his saddle with the sheepskin, making it easier on his backside. Finally, he tethered his hungry horse near a slough with tall grass, giving him an entire banquet.

A few yards ahead stood a grocery store where he could buy some bread and smoked meat for his trip. He walked through the door, which opened virtually right out onto the road.

"Hello," said Eugene. "I'm just passing through. I need some food supplies and fresh water for my canteen."

"We'll be glad to help you," said the young lady at the counter. "We have smoked ham and freshly baked buns and cinnamon rolls."

She packed up a lunch bag for Eugene and filled his canteen.

He asked, "I'm wondering if there is any place nearby where I could camp with my family for one night? I'm coming back through with them in a couple of weeks."

"We have a lot of space behind the store." I know my parents would be happy to have you stay."

"That's wonderful," replied Eugene. He took out a little booklet from his pocket and marked down *St. Brides, a good stop.*

Eugene traveled on, passing through several other hamlets. He was able to set up more potential stops for the trip back. By the time he reached Daysland, his last stop, the little booklet had come out of his pocket several more times as he marked down stopping points; that gave him great comfort. Here at Daysland, he bought suckers for the children and a chocolate heart for Lizzie. He could hardly wait to get home.

"Giddy-up!"

He put the horse into a fast gallop that continued right into the yard. The children came running out of the house screaming, "Daddy's home, Daddy's home!"

Chapter Eight

Lizzie was hanging clothes out on the line. There was bread rising in the kitchen, and today, of all days, she had a marvelous stew bubbling on the stove. 'Oh, I'm so glad I've got that going,' she thought, her heart tripping at the sight of her husband as he rode into the yard. He must be hungry from his long trip.

When he alighted from his horse, he went to his Lizzie and hugged her.

"How have you been, Lizzie dear? I know it's not been easy for you here alone with the kids. Before she could answer him, the children piled upon their father, demanding his attention. Elizabeth slipped away to get the dinner on the table.

When the beautiful dinner concluded, the children were happy to receive the suckers. Eugene and Elizabeth sat out in the yard with a cup of tea. Celine lay sleeping in a basket beside them. Elizabeth broke the chocolate heart in half and shared it with Eugene. He patted her hand. He had so much to tell her.

"Well, Lizzie dear, our home is built – it's not huge, but it's adequate. It has an upstairs. The floors are linoleum, and the walls are whitewashed. There are three windows on each floor. There will be two stoves heating the place—a Quebec heater at one end, a cookstove at the other. There is a cellar with shelves for all your canning. But, oh, Lizzie, I lucked out! I found a carpenter named Leo Tremblay, who was marvelous, and he had three husky sons helping him. They worked so quickly. I could hardly believe it! The logs went up one after the other in record time."

"Did you meet Mrs. Tremblay? If so, what is she like?" asked Elizabeth.

"She's a short, jolly lady and very friendly. I know you will like her.

"Is there a good spot near the house for my garden?"

"But of course, Lizzy. There are plenty of spots for your garden, as many as you want."

"Oh, one more question. "How far is our farm from St. Lina. I hope the children don't have any trouble getting to school."

"No, it's only a couple of miles. I'm sure there'll be no problem."

He sipped his tea and continued, "It's quite a nice farm! What surprised me most was that the land was already cleared, so I don't have to do that."

He decided not to tell her about the previous owner lying dead on the property for days before being found, at least not right away. He didn't want to spoil the joy of moving into a new home.

"There's even a pile of wood. But mind you, I'll have to add much more to it before winter arrives. It's colder there . . . it's further north! And, oh, yes, I went to Mass. The sermon was in French. Most of the population is French. In Heisler, everyone spoke German, but in St. Lina, it will be different. The French are hardworking and efficient in what they do . . . at least the Tremblay's are for sure. I wish the French side of my ancestry would have carried the language down to me at times like this."

"Lawrence was a tremendous help for me here," declared Lizzie. "He took me out of my world three feet high, but I missed you so much, especially at night with no one to cuddle up to."

He squeezed her hand.

The night before they were to leave for St. Lina, Ma Thomas paid an unexpected visit. She rode her horse into the yard, stopping at the chopping block by the woodpile to alight. Eugene and Lizzie were enjoying a cup of tea after having tucked the children in for the night. They heard the horse come into the yard and were waiting for the rap on the door. Again, it was a surprise to see Ma Thomas.

"Just in time for some tea," said Eugene.

"I planned to arrive once the kids were in bed," said Ma Thomas. "I have something to tell you before you leave Heisler. As you both know, I have been delivering babies in this area for several years. My last count was fifty-six. Mind you. I delivered several more before that in California when Pa and I had headed there for the gold rush. So now that you are leaving, I want to pass some of my knowledge on to you.

She held their rapt attention!

"Elizabeth, you are still a young woman. You can have more children. I know St. Lina is quite a distance from St. Paul, and you could give birth quickly now that you've had several."

She looked at Eugene with a serious eye.

"Eugene, you must know what to do if that happens. Elizabeth, as you've done for the birth of the other children, in the month the baby is due, be sure to have the bed well-covered with oilcloth and a disposable pad. And it is important to have a sterilized cord in a well-sealed jar. Cleanliness is all-important. I cannot stress that enough."

She paused, waiting to hear Elizabeth's, "Uh-huh, Mom." Then she turned to Eugene.

"Eugene, you will have to tend to the baby, but wash your hands thoroughly with soap and rinse well before you do anything. Once the baby is born, clear any mucus in its mouth, pick it up by the heels, and give a gentle slap on the backside. You want to hear it cry. The umbilical cord will be remaining in the mother. You must wait for it to stop pulsating, tie a cord one inch from its stomach, then tie another one inch further and cut between the cords. Wrap the baby in a warm blanket and lay aside. Now, afterbirth must come away from the mother. This is the sack the baby was in. In medical terms, it is called the placenta. A gentle press on Lizzie's stomach should help if it is slow at coming out. There will be fluid and blood, but don't be alarmed. That's natural."

"How do I dispose of all of that?" asked Eugene.

"Burn it," replied Ma Thomas, "that is the best way of disposal."

A few moments of silence followed as they took it all in. Then Ma Thomas stood up. "Now, I must head back home before it gets dark."

"Thanks, Mom," said Elizabeth with a hug.

"I'll walk you to your horse," said Eugene. Once outside, Eugene thanked her for her advice on delivering a baby. "But I hope it doesn't come to that," said Eugene as he helped her up onto her horse.

She chuckled and said, "It more than likely will."

He watched her as she trotted her horse out the yard.

The following days were a hectic time for Eugene. He had managed to sell the plow, disc, other small farm items, and the livestock. He planned to take a cow and some chickens, for milk and eggs along the way.

In preparation for the road trip, Eugene attached three metal arches over the large wagon to support the canvas they would put on to make it into a covered wagon – protection from the rain. He had laid three bed springs crosswise at the rear, supporting three mattresses stacked on top of one another, providing a place for the children to nap. A clothes basket with a pillow nestled in the bottom gave the perfect sleeping place for baby Celine.

Eugene built an additional smaller wagon, and he attached it to the rear of the main one. It contained Lizzie's treasured kitchen stove, the boiler pan filled with pots, pans, and dishes wrapped in toweling, a roll of bedding, and last Lizzie's all-important box of garden seeds. The canvas and a folded tent covered all. And, at the rear was a cage holding the four laying hens. Completing this entourage (and forced to limp along) was their best milking cow, tethered with a rope to the end of the wagon. Finally, two horses, hitched up to the very front, were the superpower that would pull this make-shift caravan with a man, his pregnant wife, four children, and all their paraphernalia one hundred and fifty miles north to their new homestead in St. Lina, Alberta.

The spring sun was warm and shone brightly, casting a warm glow on the caravan in the front yard of Eugene Waechter on that 16th day of May in 1933. What Eugene and Lizzie had been thinking about and planning for months had finally come to fruition. Today they would say goodbye to family and friends in Heisler. The Thomas family came out in full force to bid their farewells. Ma Thomas brought several loaves of homemade bread, the aroma permeating the morning air. Neighboring friends also arrived with sealers of preserves, stews, soups, and vegetables. After stowing these items away in the wagon, Eugene and Lizzie made their rounds of goodbyes.

They were about to leave when Nick and Verona galloped into the yard, their horse's back slick with sweat from its fast run from the neighboring town of Killam.

"Whoa, whoa," said Nick drawing on the reins. Their carrot-top, freckle-faced children, Evelyn and Adrian, sitting in the democrat, were anxious to get down to run and say goodbye to their cousins.

"I'm so glad you're still here. I was afraid we'd missed you!" said Nick breathlessly.

"We were just about to pull out," stated Eugene. "Good to see you. I can't believe all these years have passed since we first met. I'd rather stay here if I had a choice."

"I know. This depression has been hard on everyone. Verona and I have had to let our place go too. We're moving to Lac la Biche. I heard today we received approval for our homestead land. Ma and Pa won't be happy to hear more of us are moving away."

He glanced over at his parents standing with the other family members, unsure if they'd heard.

"You won't be that far from us," he continued. "Lac La Biche is not far from St. Lina. And I'm glad to hear that."

"So am I," said Lizzie with a forlorn expression.

"Do you still have your trumpet?" asked Nick. "Is it buried somewhere in there?" He pointed to the wagon.

"You betcha," said Eugene. "I'm not going to part with that. I remember all the good times we had playing together. Whatever made us stop? We got too busy with the family, you moved away, and when the depression hit, people stayed at home."

"Well, all the best to your family," said Nick.

"Thanks," said Eugene. "And the same to you. We best be on our way. We have a long trip ahead of us. They shook hands, and Lizzie hugged her brother and sister-in-law.

Eugene lifted the children into the wagon one by one; they flapped their little hands like seals to say goodbye. Lastly, he helped a sobbing Lizzie, holding Baby Celine in her arms, up to her seat. Eugene nodded to Pa Thomas but quickly averted his glance from Ma Thomas because she was sobbing too. Oh, how he hated these goodbyes!

The horses were snorting, wanting to go, the chickens were cackling their disagreement at being caged, and the cow bellowed to add to the chorus. Eugene shook hands with everyone once more, then stepped up into the wagon. He slapped the reins shouting, "giddy-up," and they lunched forward. He had to draw hard to rein them in. He held one hand high over his head as a final wave as they moved down the dusty, gravel road leaving the waving crowd behind. Finally, they were on their way, but Lizzie kept waving until her family was out of sight.

They were on their way. Eugene, Lizzie, their two daughters: Georgina and Baby Celine, and three little boys: Milton, Mervin, and Alvin, headed one hundred and fifty miles northeast to St. Lina, Alberta, where the coyotes howl at the moon and the northern lights dance their colors in the evening sky.

***

After ten long days on the road with stops at the predetermined farms along the way, at long last, the hamlet of St. Lina was spread before them.

"There's the church on the right with the convent right beside. The nuns teach at the school," said Eugene. "And to the left is the co-op store. You can buy almost everything there. Lozeau's grocery store is just ahead, and to the left, down the road for two miles, is our new home."

He was anxious to see it again, but he was not nearly as anxious as Lizzie. Her eyes were bright with anticipation. "It's a smaller place than Heisler, but other than that, it looks the same," she declared.

"Here we are!" said Eugene. "Our new home! *Wunderbar!*"

The children hollered, "Hurray! Hurray!" Then they clapped their hands. After all the miles riding over bumpy roads in a wagon, Eugene finally lifted the anxious and weary family down. Once on the ground, they had to stand still for a few moments to get their bearings. But surprisingly, the long journey had not been too hard on them.

"While you're looking around the house, Lizzie, I will put the animals to graze and ride over to the Tremblay's to let them know we've arrived so they can come and help me unload. And I'll stop at Lozeau's store for the groceries you said we needed. I have to hurry before the store closes."

He mounted Silver, one of the pulling horses, and headed down the road.

Silver galloped on. 'I didn't check to see if they built the kitchen furniture and the bed frames,' Eugene thought. 'Oh, well, I'll find out soon enough.'

Lizzie gave him a wave and entered her new home with the children in tow. After one sweeping glance, she thought, 'Is this all there is?' She struggled to hold back the tears. Right now, the last thing she wanted was for the children to see her distress. And she certainly didn't wish for Eugene to find out she was unhappy. With these thoughts, she quickly looked upstairs. The three bedrooms were adequate. Each had a bed frame and a window. The bedroom at the rear was the only one with a door. She assumed it would be theirs. Once back downstairs, while sitting on the bench giving Celine her bottle, she consoled herself with the thought that there must be people in this world who don't even have a roof over their heads.

She thought the room smells like the forest as her eyes came to rest on the newly built table and benches. Everything is spanking new here. The floors are all covered with new linoleum, and the walls are whitewashed, so sparkling white! I like the shelving near the cookstove to store the pots and dishes. I'll buy some pretty oilcloth for this table. And, of course, I will place The Last

Supper picture in the center on the wall over the table. In her mind's eye, she could see that same Last Supper picture on the wall over the table in her childhood home. It had hung there for as long as she could remember. The thought brought her family in Heisler to mind, filling her with nostalgia. When would she see them again? She quickly chastised herself, thinking instead, 'My family is here with Eugene and the children. I can't be clinging to Heisler.'

With Celine cradled in her arms, she turned just in time to grab little Alvin from climbing the stairs, then spoke to the other children, "Listen, children, when your baby sister has finished her bottle, I want you all to help me unload the wagon. Then, I will hand things down to you to place on the table. When we finish that, I will give you a slice of bread with Gramma's strawberry jam you all like."

Elizabeth emptied the boiler pan of its contents little by little. When she had finished putting everything on one of the shelves and the children were eating their bread, they heard the noise of a horse's hooves galloping into the yard. Eugene was back, followed by the two young Tremblay brothers to help unload. Eugene introduced the brothers to Lizzie and handed her the groceries that she then placed on the shelf. He carried the large sack of flour on his shoulder and set it in a corner by the table. She'll need it for baking bread tomorrow. Lizzie was grateful for the fly stickers he'd bought, as many nasty flies were buzzing through the open door.

It took three men to unload the cookstove. It fit nicely in the designated spot. The men installed the pipes, and it was ready to go. Eugene gave his helpers four bits, and Lizzie thanked them before they galloped off. Then she set about polishing her beloved stove, shining up the handles. Oh, how she loved her McClary stove! She gathered up some kindling from the woodpile. Now it was ready to be lit. Anyone riding down the road would see smoke coming out the chimney for the first time. It was a sure sign people were living in the little log house that had stood vacant for the past ten days.

With all the excitement, no one noticed Alvin was missing.

"Where's Alvin?" shouted Lizzie. Her voice was shrill. "He's not out playing with the others!" Everyone started looking.

"Hurry!" They all called out, "Alvin, Alvin, where are you?"

They walked around the farm, looking, behind the woodpile, in the barn, and behind it. They checked upstairs. He was not there. Where could the little two-year-old be? Did he wander off into the woodland a mile away? Eugene ran in that direction, but there was no sign of him. Eugene and Lizzie were beside themselves! They had looked frantically around and around for a full hour and had just started praying aloud when suddenly, Georgina hollered, "Mom, Dad, here he is!"

Alvin was playing with the chickens in the hen house. He was having such a good time! He had a stick in his hand and giggled when the chickens jumped away from him. Lizzie grabbed him, slapped him on the backside then hugged him close to her.

"Don't ever do that again! You had us worried! Stay where we can see you!"

It had been a most exciting and tiresome day. They were exhausted. Lizzie prepared a quick supper, made up the beds, and put the children down. She and Eugene had their usual evening tea and went to bed for their first sleep in the new home in St. Lina, Alberta. With Baby Celine in a basket by her bed, Elizabeth reached for her rosary from under her pillow. Eugene turned from one side to the other, he couldn't sleep. Being the head of a family of seven lay heavily on his mind. Many thoughts were keeping him awake. During the night, his tossing and turning awakened Elizabeth. "

"What's the matter, Eugene? It's not like you not to be sleeping soundly. Is there something troubling you?"

"With Alvin giving us that scare today, I can't help wondering if the farm is a dangerous place for our children. I can't help worrying they won't be safe."

"Eugene, the farm is the safest place for children. Much safer than the city. We'll will establish farm rules tell them repeatedly to be careful and make them aware of what can happen. They'll be fine, simply fine. You'll see."

"I suppose your right, Lizzie."

"Uh-huh," she murmured, then turned over and went back to sleep.

She gave Eugene a measure of consolation, but other thoughts roamed through his head:

'I hope I can make a go of it here. I hope the earth will give a good crop. It looks kind of rocky in places. There seems to be quite a bit of clay. I'll have to build it up. Planting clover and turning under is a good 'summer follow' treatment.

I must get more livestock; best to get young heifers with calf. I'll investigate that tomorrow. And also, find out where there is a farm sale somewhere close where I can get a plow and disc and perhaps a harrow. We could use a washstand. I could build it.'

The children have been such good little gaffers. I can still hear little Mervin when we picked up Lizzie from the hospital, thanking the doctor for his baby sister. For a three-year-old to do that is remarkable. I don't think Lizzie likes the house that much. I think it's too rustic for her. I'll buy her a lovely cabinet for the kitchen. I know that'll make her happy. And I'll plow a patch behind the house where she can have her garden. She'll love that. It will get allot of sun there.'

A hank of her rich-auburn hair had fallen across her cheek. He carefully moved it back and removed the rosary from her fingers. Earlier, she had fallen into a deep, exhaustive slumber after saying only one decade. The sight of the rosary brought memories of the seminary back to him, something he hadn't thought about in ages. The only responsibilities those seminarians had were light duties and daily prayers. They don't have to worry about where their next meal is coming from or if they have a place for their family to live. They don't have a worry in the world. But they miss so much life has to offer!

He thought about his children again, hoping they would do well in school taught by nuns. Georgina will start next year. He glanced again at Lizzie, sleeping so peacefully beside him. She was a marvelous wife, good with children and good at putting a meal on the table. Nothing could compare to the beautiful bread she bakes. I hope she feels at home here in St. Lina as she did in Heisler. I hope she'll be happy. Then he remembered something. How could he have forgotten? On one of his stops, while traveling from Heisler to St. Lina, he had purchased a little gift for Elizabeth with plans to give it to her when they arrived at their new home. I'll give it to her tomorrow evening at suppertime so the kids can witness it. Yes, that's when I'll do it. He crossed himself, said a short prayer, and fell instantly asleep, unaware of the coyotes howling in the distance.

Eugene was anxious for the day to pass so he could give Lizzie her gift. They kept busy organizing their new household, tending their few animals while the children explored and played in the yard. That evening when they sat down to dinner, Eugene announced, "I want you all to stay at the table when you've finished eating. I have a surprise for your mother."

The children perked right up and started to eat quickly. Georgina leaned over to Milton. "A surprise for mom. I wonder what it is." Elizabeth laughed aloud, then sang out, "Something for me! What can it be!"

When everyone had finished eating, Elizabeth stacked the plates and pushed them to the center of the table, then sat expectedly.

Eugene reached into his pocket, took out a flat box, and handed it to her. She slowly opened it, and there lying on blue velvet was an ivory pendant with two hearts crusted on its center. The long chain of ivory beads was long enough to hang down the front of any one of her dresses.

"It's beautiful!" gasped Elizabeth' "Really beautiful!" Thank you so much, Eugene!"

The happy atmosphere of the children around the table was palpable. They were all smiling and enjoyed looking at it and touching it in turn. Eugene watched with pride, then spoke emphatically, "Your mother deserves a gift. She does so much for everyone: washes our clothes, cooks our meals, and cleans our home. I don't want you kids ever to forget that, and I want you to help her wherever you can."

The look on his face and the tone of his voice would lock his words forever in their memory.

Elizabeth went to bed that night with a new joy in her heart.

Chapter Nine

Early summer on their new farm found Eugene and Elizabeth busy from morning until night. He built an icehouse and two pigsties from scrap wood donated by the Tremblay. She planted a large garden behind the house and filled it with vegetables she would preserve for the winter and, across the way, grew a large field of potatoes that, when harvested, would go down in the cellar through the outside chute.

Building up a new farm takes time; it takes time before there is any cash coming in. Cream cheques were desperately needed and building up a herd of livestock didn't happen overnight. Fortunately, Eugene was able to buy four bred cows at a farm sale that would quickly turn into milking cows. Then there would be money coming in from the sale of their cream, money for flour, yeast, spices, garden seeds, and other small commodities not gleaned from the earth.

As he was about to leave the farm sale, he stopped. Containers of canning sealers sitting on the ground in a large, galvanized tub caught his eye. He tethered his horse and dismounted. He walked over to the owner and found out, he wanted four bits for the lot, tub and all.

"I'll take them," said Eugene before wandering inside the house. There wasn't much to see that his household needed, so he meandered into a second room. Standing in a corner was a pale-blue kitchen cabinet, just what he knew would delight Elizabeth. There were two doors above resting on an area for rolling out dough, with two doors below. One concealed shelving, while the other housed a pull-out bin for flour. All the doors had a motif of flowers in their center. It was perfect!

He returned to the owner to get the price. "Two bucks," stated the owner.

"Will you take a buck and a half," asked Eugene.

"Sold," said the owner.

Eugene was excited about his bargains as he rode home. He was happy about the cattle he'd purchased but more so about the cabinet. He planned to come back the next day with the wagon to transport the cabinet and sealers. He could hitch the cows behind it for the two-mile ride back home. He also planned not to tell Elizabeth about the kitchen cabinet. Instead, he wanted to surprise her when he brought it home.

"Oh, thank you, Eugene," she declared when he told her about the sealers. "I've been concerned there wouldn't be enough. I have planted a big garden, and I hear that blueberries grow in abundance here, and the wild chokecherries make great jelly and syrup for pancakes. I'm going to need plenty of sealers. I already have a good supply of screw tops and rubbers."

They could hear the happy squeals of the children as they played in the yard, music to their ears. Little Celine was sitting up in her basket, playing with, of all things, sealer rings. She was a good-natured baby and easy to please.

"I hope you didn't have to pay too much for the sealers," said Elizabeth. "I know we don't have any money coming in right now."

"Nope, I got a real bargain! Besides, Elizabeth, I still have fifteen hundred dollars left from Dad's money, so we're not broke."

"That's good to hear," said Elizabeth with a wave of relief washing over her face while thinking, 'My man knows how to hang onto a dollar.'

"I must tend to dinner now and get the kids in to wash up. Thank goodness the other kids have kept a close eye on Alvin since the chicken episode. Speaking of chickens, we have chicken and dumplings for supper."

Eugene glanced at the jars of canned chicken and vegetables sitting on the table. It was amazing how she added dumplings and turned them into a meal to feast upon! He also glanced at the large sack of flour sitting in the corner by the table, grateful to know tomorrow it would have a new home in the cabinet. Finally, he glanced at the shelf behind the table and could see the crusty edge of freshly baked bread peeking out from underneath a tea towel.

The following Sunday, the Waechter family was preparing to attend their first Mass. The children were being scrubbed and combed and dressed into their Sunday best. As they turned the corner towards the church, they saw the street lined up with horses and buggies, bringing the smell of barnyard into the air.

"It looks like the entire community attends church," said Eugene. "Oh, look, there's more coming!"

Eugene finally found a spot to tie up nearest the convent. In the community of St. Lina, the highlight of the week was when everyone went to Mass. The priest was extremely popular. Everybody knew him and wanted to shake his hand. He was the community king, and the church, a large white building seemingly too big for the street, was his castle.

They filed into in to the church under watchful eyes, a new family wasn't often in attendance. Finding an empty pew proved difficult, but, finally, they found one near the front directly behind an entire row of nuns in their black and white habits from the Order of The Sisters of the Notre Dame. All eyes were upon them.

Eugene led the way holding Alvin's hand. He stepped back to allow Elizabeth and the children to go first. They genuflected before side-stepping into the pew. When Little Alvin let go of his father's hand and attempted to genuflect, he lost his balance and fell back on his rear. This example of two-year-old sweetness drew a rumbling snicker throughout the church.

The family was familiar with the Latin Mass but not with the sermon, as the priest delivered it entirely in French. However, at the end of the sermon, he offered a few words in English with a strong French accent. He also appealed for money in a pleading way, saying the church had to live too, despite the hard times.

After Mass, the parishioners gathered outside for conversation, and the musical phrasing of the French language filled the air,

"Comment vas-tu ces jours-ci Blanche. J'espère que ta mère va mieux. Avez-vous vu la nouvelle amie entrer. Le petit garçon détail si mignon."

Both ladies laughed when they reflected on the *petit garcon,* who fell back on his bum trying to genuflect.

The priest mixed with the congregation, smiling, and stopping to greet each group. He came over to Eugene's family and welcomed them to the parish. He introduced himself as Fr. Roland Berube. His dark hair, receding from his shining, priestly face, was combed in a pompadour style. When they shook hands, Eugene noted that his hands were as soft as a rabbit's fur compared to his own hardworking, calloused ones.

The men with whom Eugene conversed warned him of the cold winter ahead. "You're going to need plenty of firewood. It can get bitter."

"It can dip down to sixty below at times," said Joe Lozeau. "It'll freeze the arse off a monkey."

Eugene laughed on a couple of fronts at his highly unlikely analogy. Nonetheless, he had a new mission: to gather as much firewood as possible. 'I can bank the cords around the house for extra warmth,' he thought.

Leo Tremblay, who was hurrying to get home, came over for a quick hello and invited them to come and visit anytime. One of them agreed to come by later and give Eugene a hand with the things he'd purchased at the yard sale. Mrs. Tremblay, introduced as Germaine, had a spontaneous laugh. It seemed unbelievable that this petite lady could give birth to such big sons. Also with them was their young teen-age daughter.

Eugene and Elizabeth's first Mass in St. Lina was heart-warming indeed! It was also an eye-opener at the number of the parishioners attending, obviously from miles around.

Later that afternoon, Eugene returned with his purchases and brought the cabinet inside.

"Oh, Eugene, I love it! It's perfect! Now I have a place to the keep the flour!" She nodded at the sack standing in the corner. "All I have to do is pull this out." She reached for the handle on the cabinet and pulled out the large bin that was lined with tin. She opened the doors above the cabinet. "And here I can keep all the dishes. Oh, I'm so pleased, Eugene! And I love the colour blue. It's just like the sky. It brightens up the kitchen. Uh-huh, I'm so pleased!" She turned and gave him a hug saying, "Thank you, thank you so much,"

When she stepped back, her auburn hair seemed to glow beneath the shaft of window light. He gazed into her smiling eyes, thinking it didn't take much to make her happy. But she deserved more, oh, so much more. One day Lizzie . . . one day!

***

The first winter in St. Lina came with such a force that it shocked Eugene and Elizabeth with its severity. Each day arrived well below zero, leaving a blue fog lingering over the crackling snow that winter's wind had blown into various heaps around the land.

"I'm surprised at how much colder it's here compared to Heisler," stated Elizabeth. "Snow is coming down again for the third day." She nodded towards the window.

"I'm happy I cut enough wood and stacked it all around the house. It helps a great deal to keep the house warm," said Eugene.

He watched Lizzie build some pancakes for breakfast. She whipped together milk, eggs, and melted butter in a bowl before adding the flour and leavening. Then, before dropping a spoonful into hot fat in their big cast-iron frying pan, she always added a pinch of nutmeg. The aroma must have awakened the children. One by one, they had arisen and were scampering down the stairs to the table, except for little Alvin, who came last, inching his way down the stairs on his backside. Eugene lifted him into the highchair while Baby Celine propped up in her basket contentedly watched everyone.

They had just finished eating when they heard horse hoofs pounding as they trotted into the yard.

"Who can that be this time of day?" asked Elizabeth.

Eugene wiped the frost off the window and looked out into the yard.

"I can't tell who it is. There's a scarf around his face. We'll know soon enough." Then, after hearing the light rap on the door, he hollered, "Come in."

"Well, if it isn't Father Berube! What a pleasant surprise! What brings you here this snowy morning?"

Hesitant to answer, the priest stood with snow dripping off his clothes onto the mat by the door. He had removed his hat and overcoat, which Elizabeth hung on the hook behind the stove.

"I've come to bless your home," he declared while stepping out of his boots.

"That's wonderful," said Eugene. "We need all the blessings we can get!"

Baby Celine, startled by the stranger in the house, started to fuss, so Elizabeth picked her up and straddled her over her left hip. She glanced over at her other children, who had taken their positions on the staircase. She raised her forefinger over her pursed lips, schussing them to be quiet. Alvin, content in his highchair, watched it all.

Father Berube reached into his overcoat pocket and removed a little box that contained a silver ball on a stick known as the *aspergillum*, a Latin word meaning sprinkle. He reached into his other pocket and removed a small holy water bucket with a handle; he unscrewed the top and commenced: "In the name of the Father, the Son, and the Holy Spirit."

Eugene and Elizabeth, with heads bowed, crossed themselves.

The priest continued: "Peace be to dis house and to all who dwell here, in the name of the Lord. When Christ took flesh through the Blessed Virgin Mary, he made his home wit us. Let us now pray that he will enter dis home and bless it wit his presence. May he always be here among us; may he nurture our love for each other, share in our joys, comfort us in our sorrows. Inspired by dese teachings and example, let us seek to make our home, before all else, a dwelling place of love, diffusing far and wide the goodness of Christ."

With that, he moved from one corner to the other. He dipped the *aspergillum* into the holy water and murmured Latin words of blessing while raising his hand and shaking a sprinkle.

When he had finished, he asked everyone to say the Lord's Prayer.

The priest had done his job. He had accomplished what he had come to do. He turned to put on his coat when Elizabeth interjected.

"You must have a cup of tea. I have some still hot from breakfast. And I have cinnamon buns. Would you stay and have some? I can give you a half dozen to take home as well."

The children listened intently, hoping he would stay. Having someone in their new home was a novelty.

"*Merci,* dat, dat sounds wonderful, dat will hit de spot!" said Father Berube, patting his stomach.

Eugene stood back thinking that the home he had built for his family was now blessed. A strong spiritual feeling washed over him and gladdened his heart!

***

And so, the days melted into months and the months into years. The children grew so fast that their parents could hardly keep up with them. They often spoke of the day the priest came to bless their home and how Alvin banged on his highchair tray until the priest shared part of his cinnamon bun with him. Next season Alvin would be starting school, and Celine wasn't too far behind him. Georgina, Milton, and Mervin had adjusted to school life. They were picking up some of the French language they heard at school. Like all farm children, they spent considerable time in and around the farm, in the barn watching the milking, collecting eggs from the hen house, and playing tag in the yard. They had a new game called aunty-eye-over, one where they'd throw the ball over the house to someone on the other side. If someone caught the ball, they would dash around the house and toss it at their opponent; hitting them would count as a point. Elizabeth kept cautioning them not to break a window.

Eugene and Elizabeth, who had started as a couple, would soon be a family of eight. The year was 1936, and there was another baby on the way, due in October. The joyful news of a new life quickly erased Eugene's thought that there would be another mouth to feed, especially when he saw how healthy his brood was and how they added unending interest to their lives.

Spring was welcomed after the long cold winter leaving slush and mud around the yard soon to be dried by summer's heat. Elizabeth worked hard to preserve food for the winter, and Eugene harvested the wheat albeit meager.

He had learned early on this homestead land wasn't suitable for growing wheat, with too much clay and many rocks. He had spent hours hauling the rocks off on the stone boat. And when he thought he had completed the job, more would turn up when he plowed. He sowed the land anyway, gladly took what little income he could glean, and was grateful for the alfalfa he grew, which was good feed for the cattle. It was a hand-to-mouth existence. He continued to build up his herd, ever so grateful for the cream cheque they provided, which kept the staple items on the shelves in Lizzie's cabinet.

Everyone in the community rode the same pony, trying to scratch a living and survive the depression. Its onset, caused by the stock market crash, was further complicated by drought in Western Canada. These thoughts were foremost as Eugene walked to the barn to milk the cows feeling the bumps of the frozen ground beneath his gumboots with each step.

Now as he milked the cows, his thoughts turned to Elizabeth. He worried about her and rightly so, the baby was due any day. Milking six cows morning and night meant he would have to be away from the house one and half hours each time before he could return to be at her side.

Elizabeth had been busy this morning; She'd packed the lunch buckets for the children who had left for school, mixed a batch of bread, and had set it to rise. She gave Celine a hunk of dough to roll into little balls for baking in the oven. Later the balls would be buttered, and Celine would carry them around in a tin cup to munch. Elizabeth managed to wash several clothing articles with the scrub board in the washtub, which doubled up as the family bathtub. The soap made from tallow and lye was most effective. She then hung the clothes on the clothesline to dry in the fall sunshine. Still holding the tin cup, Celine followed her mother back into the house. As soon as Elizabeth crossed the threshold, a sharp pain struck her lower abdomen. 'Oh no! Am I going into labor!' she thought. She punched down the bread and put it into tins to rise the second time before putting them in the oven. All the while, Celine was playing on the staircase, lining up her dolls on each step.

She opened a jar of canned chicken and peeled several large potatoes along with the last of the carrots she'd dug up in the garden, which, though frozen, were still good.

"We can have blueberries for dessert,' she decided. 'Eugene should be back in about a half-hour."

When the second pain struck, Elizabeth knew it was time to organize things.

'Oh God, please help me! Please give me the strength to do this!" She went upstairs and padded the bed. She took the jar with the sterilized cord, scissors, and spring scale from the bureau and placed it on the dresser where she had lain a small blanket and diaper. Then she donned her long, flannelette nightgown and called out, "Celine, what are you doing?"

"Playing with my dollies," she replied from the staircase.

"Mommy is resting in bed. Be a good girl. Daddy will be back soon."

"Yes, Mommy," she murmured.

Just then, an excruciating pain gripped her. She was catching her breath when she heard the kitchen door open. 'Thank God Eugene is back!'

"Where's Mommy?" asked Eugene.

"In bed, upstairs," Celine replied.

Eugene hurried up the staircase to Elizabeth. "How are you? Are you in labor? How far apart are the pains?"

"Yes, Eugene. My time has come. The pains are ten minutes apart and strong. I don't think I will be long. We need to give Celine lunch–bread, jam, and a glass of milk, then put her down for her nap. But first, the bread that's rising under the tea towels must be placed in the oven. It will take close to an hour. Once brown, the bread will be done." She paused to catch her breath. She sensed his hesitancy and wished her mother was there to see her through this. And Eugene wished he could fetch a doctor, but that was out of the question. There was no one for miles around and, besides, he couldn't leave Lizzie and Celine alone at a time like this. I must do it! I must!

"Okay, darling. I'll get right to it," he said before descending to the kitchen.

Minutes later, he spoke softly to Celine, "There you are, my little one, have a good sleep." He covered her and all her dolls with the quilt Elizabeth had made, bent down, kissed her forehead, and quietly closed the door.

He returned to Elizabeth, who was now writhing in pain. He stroked her forehead and murmured soothing words. When the pain subsided, Elizabeth said, "Let's say the rosary together. Let's ask God for another healthy child." She took a deep breath. "And let's thank God for his many blessings." Her auburn hair clung to the sides of her face. The pitiful look in her eyes only added to his feelings of compassion mixed with sheer helplessness.

He recalled what Ma Thomas had told him about her mid-wifery experience and instruction: "Attention Eugene, Elizabeth is still a young woman, she will have more children, and you will have to help her in the North Country."

One-half hour later, Eugene tied the cord of a healthy baby boy that he then wrapped in a blanket and suspended on a hook scale. He weighed in at seven pounds on the dot. It was October 5th, 1936. From the first pain to the last had been just over two hours. He kissed her smiling cheek and said, "Thank you, Lizzie darling." Recalling all the invaluable instructions her mother had given them had been put to practical use when this new life joined their household.

Elizabeth, exhausted from childbirth, her body rested quietly in the euphoria of painlessness. She crossed herself, thanked God, and said three Hail Marys, a Glory Be, and one Our Father. When finished, like at all her previous deliveries, she thought, 'What lies ahead for this boy? Will he be healthy and strong like the other kids? What will be his mission in life? Please, Lord, help me raise him to honor you and your son, Jesus.'

Eugene took the bread out of the oven and spilled them out of their tins onto a tea towel on the table before going outside.

He was in the yard with a spade in hand, breaking through the hard crust of frosted earth to bury the afterbirth—not wanting to burn it as Ma Thomas had suggested—when he heard the echoing of children's voices in the distance. The children were coming home from school. He went back into the house to wait for them.

They came in one by one, rosy-cheeked from their two-mile walk, and hung their coats up on hooks next to the washstand. Eugene gathered them around, "You have a new baby brother upstairs. He was born a short while ago. I want you to be really good children and please don't be noisy. Mom is tired and will need a lot of rest. Your little brother is named Roland after our wonderful priest, Father Berube. You can sneak upstairs to see him, but remember, be gentle and don't jump onto the bed."

"Oh, Mom, he's so tiny!" exclaimed Georgina. "Look at his tiny fingers. How can he breathe through such a tiny nose?"

"I think I was better looking when I was first born," chuckled Alvin.

Milton stood back and, true to his quiet nature, didn't utter a word; however, the grin on his face showed he was enjoying the moment. And Mervin, with a smile in his eyes, reached out and held his baby brother's tiny hand, showing the compassionate side of his personality.

Celine, awakened by all the commotion, left her bedroom, crawled up onto the bed, and cuddled up next to her mother. She leaned on one elbow and peered over at the newborn. She was baffled. How could her new little brother be the same size as one of her dolls? 'Maybe Momma will let me put a dress on him,' she thought.

Elizabeth looked down at the baby boy in her arms and declared, "My little Rolly."

Chapter Ten

Life continued in the Waechter household. Like most families during the depression, they struggled to prevent falling into the abyss of poverty. However, during part of that first year, after Roland was born, Eugene had to find work away from home. During the winter, when he was away, Elizabeth experienced difficult episodes all alone on the farm She had to deal with the animals and the children single handed. She missed Eugene! The loneliness she felt was almost unbearable, but her strong faith saw her through those troubling times. She looked forward to the Sundays when they attended the church where she would see other adults and could visit outside after Mass when it wasn't too cold to do so.

Chopping wood, Eugene thought about this homestead land he had been given if only he hadn't promised to develop it. How could a man develop land where earth could not grow wheat successfully? How could land grow much when it had poor drainage consisting mainly of clay and rocks? He spent hours picking rocks off and hauling them away with the stone boat, only to have the rock's surface again after a rainfall. As he walked back into the house, he passed the kitchen window, paused, and looked in at his family seated around the table eating their morning porridge. Rolly was in the highchair, and Lizzie stirred the pot at the stove.

'What a wonderful family I have. I wish I could do more for them,' he thought.

The children grew quickly, especially Rolly who, before long, each morning was sitting in his highchair anxiously waiting for his serving of porridge. He was walking at eleven months and toddled around the yard under the watchful eye of Georgina.

At age nine, Georgina, the eldest, kept her siblings in tow with her large grey eyes and assertive manner. She was a bright girl and prided herself in being her mother's handmaiden. Her contagious laughter filled the room, advertising her sharp sense of humour. She could also squeal equally loud when one of her brothers chased her holding a dead mouse by its tail.

Milton, next in age, had a mitt full of dark-brown curls and vivid-green eyes. He was quiet by nature and brooding but never missed a trick. He loved the outdoors and would spend hours in the small woodland on the property and tell everyone at the supper table all about the different animals he had seen that day. Eugene took him along when checking his trap lines. Fur sales brought in a few pennies from the Hudson Bay Company.

Mervin was next in line, a talkative, slight-of-build boy who always had an opinion on any given subject. He had wavy, brown hair and piercing, hazel eyes. His kind heart was often on display in how he treated his siblings. He had a collection of pennies which he counted daily, and he liked to build and fix things.

Alvin was next. Being short in stature and wearing the nickname of Shorty did not diminish his astute sense of humour. He was a happy little boy, always ready for a joke, and then he'd laugh so hard his face would turn red. He loved to put things together. He was a frequent sight in the yard with a hammer and nails, looking for something to pound.

After Alvin came Celine. She had a round face, hazel eyes, and soft brown curls. With three older brothers and one older sister, she had sat on the 'I'm the youngest throne' for the past three years, which she now forfeited to Rolly. Indeed, a stranger once offered Elizabeth money to buy something for her beautiful, youngest daughter.

Baby Rolly thrived and walked at eleven months old. His large brown eyes dominated his cute face. Even at this early age, he had the appealing ability to roll his eyes when displeased with something or someone. He was a delight to the other children, making them laugh at his antics. Celine, who quickly forgave him for pushing her off the throne, enjoyed him immensely, particularly when she compared him to her dollies.

Eugene taught the way of farm life to the boys. They were taught how to ride a horse, milk a cow, chop wood, and were always in the audience when their father was butchering an animal. While they were too young now for any of these things on their own, they learned by being witnesses. They watched while their father gut a slaughtered animal. He hoisted it up on a large tripod he had built for the occasion. They watched him hang the hams in the smokehouse, helping him stoke the fires that produced the necessary smoke that flavoured the meat. In winter, they watched him dig ice blocks from a frozen lake and bury it in the deep sawdust-filled cavity in the small shed he'd built for summer refrigeration. Milk, butter, and meat would be place in a bucket and lowered into this cavity away from the heat of summer.

And they had watched a calf pulled with rope from a mother cow when a problematic birth was underway. Harvest time was another lesson, one of camaraderie and sharing with neighbouring farmers, as they, in turn, helped each other with the fall harvest. At this time, the children would smell pancakes early in the morning when their mother was cooking breakfast for the threshing crew who had slept in the barn.

All of the things learned were carved into the boys' psyche. It gave them an appreciation of the farming way of life. It gave them knowledge for potential future endeavors.

Likewise, Elizabeth had shown the girls how to bake bread, make tender pastry from rendered pork fat, make soap from tallow and lye, and above all, a smooth gravy from meat drippings. She would also teach them how to make tasty bechamel sauce from butter, cream, and flour. She echoed her favourite saying many times: "What good is a woman if she doesn't have the where-with-all to keep a clean home and put a decent meal on the table?"

And she spoke most fervently at the breakfast table, for it was there where she had everyone's collective attention. And it was there that she could make eye contact with each of her children.

"Listen up, children," she would say in a much louder and clearer voice, "It is essential to live as a Christian if you want true happiness in your life for yourself and your family."

How could they forget that loving face and those most serious words spoken with such eloquence, and sincerity by the person who was the very center of their lives?

St. Lina Catholic School in 1936 was under the direction of the sisters of Notre Dame –French-speaking nuns from Quebec who had dedicated their entire lives to educating the young. It was a two-room schoolhouse with a long foyer down the middle with a classroom on either side, grades one to four on one side with five to nine on the other. All classes were taught in both English and French. The dominant language was French, the native language of ninety-five percent of the classroom. Sr. St. Edward oversaw her staff of six nuns and was known to everyone as Mother Superior. She was also the head of the convent, which lay adjacent to the Church of St. Helen Catholic church two blocks away. There was no hospital or dentist in St. Lina so

Mother Superior, having first aid training, often cared for minor medical and dental needs. She would offer her patients a shot of brandy before pulling a tooth.

The nuns organized a Christmas Concert every winter and picnics every summer. They were the gas that ran the engine of social life for all the community farmers, but the priest always had to give his sanction for any event that was planned.

Some students could walk to school, but it was much too cold during the winter months. A stable on the school property was where the children could tie up their horses during school hours. At this time, the nuns would have lit a wood-burning heater in each classroom. The children brought jars of milk which the nuns poured into a large pot on the stove. They added chocolate syrup and gave the children a warm jar of chocolate milk to warm themselves before the classes began. The children looked forward to this treat.

Classes always started with a prayer, and, on holy days of obligation, the children would be marched in a long file over to the church to attend Mass. Upon entering the church, they lined up in the aisle. They remained there until the lead sister made a snapping sound with a clicker she held in her hand. Then, before entering their respective pews, the nuns taught the children to genuflect in honour of the blessed sacrament that sat upon the altar up ahead. The nuns taught the pupils to kneel before being seated and bow their heads in prayer piously and respectfully much to the admiration of the onlooking parishioners.

Eugene and Elizabeth's children, Georgina, Milton, Mervin, and Alvin, were now in attendance and doing well. They would come home with some French words learned. The children would hear German words they did not understand at home when their parents didn't want them to hear. But English prevailed in the house, the language they all knew. Little Celine, hearing her older siblings tossing out a French word here and there, was anxious to go to school to learn some, too, but now had contented herself playing with her little brother, Rolly.

The days passed, the children were growing, and something else was on the horizon. Eugene and Elizabeth enjoyed quiet time together after the children had gone to bed. He had just finished his favourite evening snack of hot milk poured over bread chunks in a deep bowl. He seasoned it with dollops of butter, salt, and pepper.

"Eugene," said Elizabeth.

"Yes, Lizzie," he said, putting his bowl in the dishpan.

"I think we are having another baby," she replied. "I don't think it. I know it. This morning I felt a wave of nausea. As you know, last month, I stopped breastfeeding Rolly. He was drinking so well from a cup at nine months old; that's what made it possible for me to become with child." She had spoken rapidly, not giving him a chance to respond.

He turned quickly, came to her, and pulled up a chair close to hers. He put his arm around her. "If it is meant to be. It's meant to be. Maybe we'll have a little girl to even things out this time." He told her he loved her in German, *"Ich liebe dich sehr, Lizzie"* He continued to speak of his love for her in German, the language they barely used, but what came in handy when something didn't need to reach the children's ears, but now, at this very moment, it sounded so incredibly special!

"God willing," she replied, glowing.

***

The winter came like a growling tiger, northern winds blew, and blizzards piled snow high, blocking the door. It took all of Eugene's might to open it to the outside, where the land was silent and the air foggy from the cold. The windowpanes were frosted both inside and out. The leaf designs thereon delighted the children. During the cold snap, Eugene slept on a mat on the floor next to the Quebec Heater to keep it stoked with the wood piled high behind it clear up the wall to the ceiling. He kept the cookstove fired up as well, but with the damper partly closed; it would cast sufficient heat for that part of the log house and be ready to cook the hot oatmeal porridge they would eat in the morning. It was a winter that would be known as the coldest in history. The children were bundled up and taken to school in the wagon sleigh pulled by Silver, the family's faithful horse.

There was always meat, preserved vegetables, butter, milk, and eggs; these being the commodities from the farm, but it was cash the family needed to buy the other things: rolled oats, flour, yeast, coffee, tea, coal oil, clothing, and several other items. Eugene had established a trap line and was able to sell a few furs to the Hudson Bay Company. His eldest son, Milton liked to go with his dad to check the lines. But it was the cream cheques that filled the void when the small amount of cash from the fall harvest was depleted. This hand-to-mouth existence had forced

Eugene to take a job off the farm, typical for most farmers in the St. Lina area.

As life continued, Eugene and Elizabeth made friends with the local farmers. Visitors would be expected on Sundays to drop by, and, naturally, they would stay for dinner. Elizabeth was undaunted by having to prepare a meal for extras spontaneously. She knew how to put that extra potato in the pot. The Tremblays, who were so generous with their time and talent when Eugene first came to St. Lina to build his log house, became their card-playing friends. The game of choice was Bid Whist. Once a week, Leo and Germaine would come by in the evening for a game that would last a couple of hours and conclude with a light lunch.

In addition to these visits, the family's primary source of social life was the weekly Mass they faithfully attended. After Mass, they built friendships with other farmers and shared news and ideas about farming, while the women folk shared recipes, candle-making techniques, and a host of other subjects from knitting to quilting. It was common knowledge amongst the farmers that each would be ready and willing to help each other in need.

****

Spring of 1938 arrived with the usual slush and mud, but its nuisance was pushed into the background as the glorious warm air drew buds out on the trees. Songbirds scampered about their branches, serenading each other while building their nests, and there were always the infamous magpies flying about the farm. Since mid-April, the *Farmer's Almanac* had said that the hot weather was here to stay, so Eugene and Elizabeth planted their vegetable garden the first week of May. Elizabeth was grateful to have it done. She knew there would be no time once the new baby arrived.

Eugene was up early in the morning out in the fields, plowing, discing, and harrowing, preparing the soil to sow the wheat. He took lunch with him for his long workday that lasted until sundown.

On May 10, 1938, Elizabeth, heavy with child, had so much energy, even she was surprised. She baked bread, made several pies, scrubbed the linoleum-covered floor muddied by Spring, and even put a wash out on the line. While these things were happening, she had a large pot of stew simmering on the back of the stove. Rolly had been bathed, diapered, and put down for the night. The other children were playing hide and seek around the house. She was placing the loaves of bread beneath the tea towel in the large crock when she felt a snap in her lower abdomen. Her water had broken and came out with a gush down her legs to the floor. She wiped it up and sighed aloud, "Uh, Oh." The long pain that came next took her breath away. She caught her breath when it had ebbed, opened the kitchen door, and shouted, out to the yard, "Georgina, come here quickly!" Georgina!"

Georgina heard her mother's call from the other side of the house and came running.

"The baby is coming. Daddy won't be back until dark. I want you to run over to Mrs. Esslesteins and ask her to come over. I need help. Please hurry."

Ten-year-old Georgina turned on a dime and ran like a jack-rabbit as fast as her little legs could carry her. She ran over the muddy, dirt road to the neighbour's farm one-half mile away. She was panting, muddied, and could hardly speak when she pounded her little fist on their door.

Elizabeth made her way slowly upstairs. First, she checked the readiness of the bed and the jar of sterile cord, scissors, hook scales, and small blanket, just as she had done eighteen months earlier for the birth of Rolly. Then, donning her nightgown, she lay down on the bed and, covering herself with a flannelette sheet, waited for another pain. Despite hearing the children playing outside, she felt alone, anxious, and afraid. What if the neighbor didn't come back with Georgina? What if Eugene didn't get back? Could she do this all alone?

The subsequent pain that struck was earth-shatteringly long. She stifled a scream at its peak and the strong urge to bear down. 'Oh, Lord, please help me through this!'

When the next pain struck, she heard the door downstairs open and close. A voice called out, "Lizzie."

Relief engulfed her! It was Eugene.

"Eugene . . . Eu, Eu, Eugene," she screamed.

He heard the panic in her voice, and he knew. He ran up the stairs, two at a time, to see her writhing on the bed. "I'm here, Lizzie, here to help, but first, I have to wash my hands!" He hurried downstairs to the washstand, lathered his hands, rinsed them quickly, and ran upstairs while drying his hand with a towel. Lizzie was lying very still. A tear rolled down her cheek. Then he heard a muffled little cry from beneath the flannelette sheet. He quickly threw it back. To his astonishment, there, between her legs, was their baby, red-faced and crying loudly.

"Good for you, Lizzie! We have our girl! Oh my, such long, dark hair!"

Elizabeth laughed, "I've not seen such hair on a newborn!" She kept laughing from joy and relief.

He waited for the umbilical cord to stop pulsating, then tied and cut it with the sterile cord . . . just as Ma Thomas had taught him, just as he'd done for Rolly. He laid this new, tiny piece of humanity upon the receiving blanket, tied a knot with the corners, and raised it with the scale. He marveled at the weight and seven inches of long, black hair that hung over his arm.

"Six and a quarter," he stated, a good size and perfect in every way!" He put the babe in Lizzie's arms and attended to the afterbirth.

"Are we still going to call her Marie Elizabeth as planned?" he asked.

"Oh, yes, I've always liked the name Marie, and I want her to have my name and my mother's."

Eugene smiled and said, "She looks like a Marie Elizabeth."

They both could hear the other Waechter children playing outside, running around the yard playing tag, utterly oblivious to the momentous event that had just occurred in the house. Celine was entertaining Rolly with a rubber ball near the woodpile. They were going to be so surprised!

Evelyn called out before leaving her home, "John, I'm going over to the Waechter home to help Elizabeth. She's having her baby." Walking swiftly, Evelyn Esselstein held Georgina's hand tightly, who was sobbing with worry for her mother. "I hope she'll be all right. It's taking us so long to get there." She quickened her steps. Evelyn followed suit, thinking: 'I better not go too fast, the child won't keep up with me.'

Finally, they reached the house and hurried in. Eugene was sitting at the table with the boys; they had just finished their bowl of stew.

"How's Elizabeth?" Evelyn asked.

"Just fine," replied Eugene. "You can go upstairs to see her. I'm taking the boys to the barn with me to do the chores.

To their utmost surprise, Elizabeth lay smiling with Marie in her arms.

"I wasn't expecting to see the birth over; that sure was quick! But my, she's a lovely baby!" said Evelyn, gazing down at the baby. Elizabeth smiled. "I think I'll have to braid that long hair of hers."

Georgina crawled up onto the bed and kissed her mother and her baby sister. "Oh, she's so cute. Look at all the hair!" she declared. "She's so tiny, Mama." It was the same declaration she'd made when Rolly was born.

"I know," said Elizabeth. "She'll grow quickly just like Rolly is doing."

As Lizzie had stated, Marie grew fast, gaining an amazing pound a week. Her tiny body grew strong and plump right before one's eyes, but it took all of Elizabeth's strength to nourish her baby. She awoke each morning exhausted with dark rings beneath her eyes, barely able to get through the day. Eugene was at his wit's end with worry. It tugged at his heartstrings to see the woman he loved, who always had boundless energy, now be reduced to a state of weakness.

"I don't know what I can do about Lizzie's declining health," he told the Tremblays. "She has no energy. I want to take her to see a doctor in St. Paul, but that takes money. I have no extra.

And there will probably be medicine to buy." He drew both hands across his face despairingly.

Leo held Eugene's gaze unblinking, his face serious.

"Mon Dieu, Eugene we pay de taxes, don't we? We give money to de government every year. Sometimes we must ask for some of de money back. I know de boss guy of de municipality. He buys de lumber from me. He lives about two hours from here when de horse trots, less if de horse gallops. I'll go wit you. We'll get some money back to help Elizabeth. Yes, I'll go wit you today, right now."

"It feels like I would be begging. I've never had to beg before," said Eugene with a forlorn expression. "But for Lizzie, I'll do what it takes. I'll keep Georgina home from school tomorrow to help her, and we can go early tomorrow morning. Sure, do appreciate this, Leo."

"I'm happy to help you, my good friend. We are neighbours, and dat's what neighbours do. Someday you may have to help me with someting." He winked.

Eugene would remember that moment for the rest of his life.

Six weeks later, Elizabeth was back to normal. The effects of the magical tonic the doctor had prescribed worked miracles.

Its results were noticeable in only a few days. The children were excited about the new baby. Now there were two for them to marvel at; Rolly was only eighteen months old. Rolly didn't change his disposition because a new baby was in the house. Instead, he was protective of his little sister. He would dance a little jig to make her giggle when she was seated in her highchair. And when she was walking, they were inseparable, playing in and out of the house.

Shortly later, Celine started school, making her feel on par with her older siblings. She also showed strong maternal instincts toward the younger ones, mothering them, and watching what they were doing.

The boys spent time with their father while Georgina continued to be a helping hand for her mother.

The warm summer months made up for the frigid winter. It was a season to watch things grow. The words, 'the garden is up,' were music to everyone's ears, for soon Elizabeth would be filling the home with the tantalizing smell of pickling spices and fresh vegetables bubbling on the stove. Sealers of all her canning lined the shelves in the cellar. The bountiful garden made Eugene build more shelves next to the large bin that held the potatoes. There was fresh food for the family once again!

Chapter Eleven

Elizabeth couldn't stop giggling as she watched Leo and Germaine Tremblay dancing the jitterbug a hundred miles an hour with barely enough room for the twirling right there in front of her cookstove. They had dropped in for a game of cards just as Eugene had taken out his trumpet for polishing. When he began to play a snappy tune, they jumped up from their chairs and started dancing. Elizabeth glanced over at Eugene at the other end of the table. His cheeks were puffed out and he was tapping his foot to the beat. He winked at Elizabeth.

"I didn't know you played the trumpet," said Leo breathlessly after they sat down. I often wish I could play a musical instrument," lamented Leo. "Do you play any others?"

"Yes," replied Eugene. "When you know one wind instrument, it's not difficult, with some practice, to play them all. I also play the violin. I brought this trumpet with me from Ontario years ago. I used to play for dances back East. I was playing for dances in Heisler when I met Lizzie." He gave her a nod and another wink.

"I haven't made this thing toot for a long time," he continued holding it up. It's been sitting in a box under my bed."

"They used to hold dances at the old Sideview school. It's south of here, about three miles. I hear they may be starting them up again if they can find the music. Would you be interested? If you are, I can tell my friend, Robert Magnet, who runs them," said Leo.

"How do they pay the musicians?" asked Eugene.

"They pass a hat around, and your pay is what's in it."

Eugene sat pensively, mulling it over. "I could give it a shot if Lizzie doesn't mind." He turned to smile at her across the table. She nodded her approval.

A few days later when Eugene was chopping alder wood, a man rode into the yard. With a 'whoa,' he stopped his steed alongside Eugene and dismounted.

"Hello, you must be Eugene," he said, smiling. "I'm Robert Magnet. Leo told me you play the trumpet. I've come to talk to you about playing at the Sideview dances. With my wife on the piano and me on the drums, a trumpet would round things off things nicely." He smiled broadly.

At that moment, Eugene recognized him from seeing him at church.

They shook hands. "How do you do, Robert. Yes, I play the trumpet and have played for dances in the past. But it's been a while. We will need to get together to practice, I presume."

"That sounds ideal to me," replied Robert. "If we get a couple of practices in before the dance starts, I think we'll do simply fine. I was thinking of starting the dances a week from Saturday."

"How do you inform the people," asked Eugene.

"I put notices around, in the co-op, post office, and I'll ask the father he'll let me put one in the church's lobby. He may not want to, but there's no harm in asking."

"And of course, there's also word of mouth, especially after the dances get rolling. We'll be so good people flock in just to hear us," laughed Eugene.

Robert chuckled at this remark. "Would tomorrow night work for our first practice? We live three miles south of here. You can't miss it. When you see a barn with a red roof, that will be us."

"I'll see you tomorrow, then around seven after the chores, if that's okay."

"Tomorrow, it is." Robert happily rode off in a fast trot. Eugene watched his horse break into a gallop when he passed through the gate. He picked up his axe and continued chopping the wood with a little more vigor.

'Blowing the old horn will be fun,' he thought. 'Something to look forward to here in St. Lina. I'm not particularly eager to leave Lizzie behind. We can get someone to babysit. Georgina isn't quite old enough to mind the others. I'll ask around after Mass tomorrow. The Tremblays also have a young daughter, perhaps she can come.

***

"Look no further, Eugene. I'm sure our daughter will be happy to babysit for you. It won't cost you anything, just a promise that you'll play your trumpet at her wedding. She's planning to marry her beau next Spring," said Leo. Germaine stood nearby smiling.

They practiced as planned twice before the dance started, and when Saturday arrived, they were as ready as they would ever be. They practiced waltzes, schottisches, and two steps. Amongst the songs were: *I Got Rhythm, Moon Glow, Pennies From Heaven, Wabash Cannonball*, and the new song they heard on the radio, *You Are My Sunshine.*

The dances started with an overflow crowd, mainly because Father Berube had graciously allowed Eugene's notice to be placed in the church; everyone read it. They wanted to hear the parishioner, who originated from Ontario, play his trumpet. Yvette Tremblay, an eighteen-year-old, pleasant young woman, arrived early and immediately took charge of the children. It was a treat for Eugene and Elizabeth to be going out to a social event. The other farmers in the community were also excited to have a chance to hear music, to kick up their heels while enjoying the new spark that had come into their lives.

The first dance saw the Sideview Hall filled to capacity. It had been used as a school a few years back when the municipality could staff it, but this night had remained empty. Horses and buggies surrounded the hall, some tied to hitching posts, and others secured their steeds by placing a rock on the ground over the reins. The hall's small kitchen held a cookstove and some plates, silverware, and cups. A lunch consisting of sandwiches, cookies, and cakes, which the women brought, was served halfway through the evening.

Social mixing was no problem. Everyone danced with each other's partners. Eugene put his trumpet down at the first opportunity and swirled his Lizzie around the floor for one dance. Later Elizabeth waltzed by the music-makers in the arms of Leo, and when she did, Eugene gave her a wink, just as he'd done all those years earlier at the Heisler dance. This night he remembered that defining moment with nostalgia. Elizabeth threw her head back and laughed. She remembered too.

It was a wonderful evening filled with joy and laughter. The music was perfect in every way. They played tunes, some they hadn't practiced, merely by ear but with perfect rhythm from the talented musical trio.

At the end of the evening, Robert Magnet walked up to the front.

"Ladies and gentlemen, did you enjoy the dance tonight?"

Loud applause and cat whistles rang through the hall.

"We will be having a dance every other Saturday." Applause broke at the good news. When it ended, he continued, "I will be passing a hat around for you to show your appreciation for the music. Thanks for coming. We will see you again in two weeks."

Some people started leaving, not wanting to contribute, while others reached into their pockets. Eugene watched them and wondered if they were as broke as he was.

It was eleven-thirty in the evening when Eugene and Elizabeth made their way home in their democrat. The day's warmth hung in the air while the summer moon shone all about. A flick of the reins and a 'giddy-up' spurred Silver into a slow trot. The clippety-clop of his hooves pounding down on the earth-packed road added to the magical ambiance of the evening. Finally, after a few moments, Eugene broke their silence.

"Well, Lizzie, my dear, did you have an enjoyable time tonight?"

"Ya, I certainly did, but those old farmers just don't dance as well as you do, Eugene. During the home waltz, my partner stepped on my toe, my right big toe. I'll check it when I get home. I bet it'll be bruised."

"That's too bad, dear," said Eugene soothingly, his cheeks aching from all the blowing. He opened his mouth wide to stretch them. But, appeased by his sympathy, she continued. "The turnout was better than I thought it would be."

"Yes, that surprised me too."

"Did you have a chance to count the change?"

"Yes, we each made forty-eight cents."

"That's not very much. I guess people are just as hard-up as are."

"I'm not complaining," replied Eugene. "It buys us a sack of flour."

"That's true. Heaven knows we need lots of that," said Elizabeth.

As they pulled into the yard, they could see Yvette through the window holding Baby Marie. They rode past to the front of the house where Yvette had tethered her horse.

"The children were good." said Yvette. "The baby just woke up. I think she must be hungry because she's sucking her fist. I was about to give her the water bottle like you told me to do."

"Thanks a lot, Yvette. It was nice for us to get out together. It's a lovely evening for you to ride back to your home," said Eugene, gesturing towards the window.

Elizabeth thanked her as well. Then, cradling her baby in her arms, she made her way upstairs; there, she diapered her and gave her last nursing for the night, undressed, put on her flannelette nightgown, and checked her toe; it had turned a dark blue.

"*Dummkopf*," she said aloud in German. She could hear Yvette's horse trotting out the yard, thinking. 'Oh, well, it was fun being out where there were people and music. And Eugene played the trumpet so beautifully! I'm proud of him!'

The dances continued for the rest of the summer until the harvest activity stole the farmer's free time for then the men were busy day and night bringing in the wheat, helping each other with threshing, while the women fed them. The women also spent hours upon hours canning summer's bounty from the gardens they had so dutifully nurtured. Over the summer, they also preserved wild strawberries and made pancake syrup from chokecherries. In addition, jars of canned vegetables, chicken, ground beef, and pork lined the shelves in the cellar. Elizabeth was lucky to have raspberries growing in abundance from which she made jam.

There was simply no time for dancing.

As in past years, there wasn't an abundance of wheat to put in the granary. The soil on the Waechter farm was poor and filled with rocks and clay, not rich black soil like in other parts of Alberta. The revenue from the sale of cream was their only source of cash. Eugene knew he would have to find work outside the farm. Many of the other farmers in the St. Lina area and other parts of Alberta had to do likewise. The thought of leaving Lizzie on the farm by herself with the children was extremely uncomfortable, but down the road, he may have to. What else could he do? He would have no choice. They needed money to survive.

Father Berube also needed money. Operating the church and sustaining himself had become an increasing problem. The collection plate these past few months had been sparse. He knew he had to approach the congregation. Oh, how he hated to do that, but he had to. There was no other choice. He looked directly at Eugene and Elizabeth. Eugene had just sung the Latin part of the High Mass, accompanying himself with the violin. He had returned to join Elizabeth in their pew at the front when the priest, after his regular sermon, made his plea in his typical French, then spoke in English.

"Ladies and Gentlemen, I come to a subject I find hard to talk about, but I must. I am finding it most challenging to keep the church operating. I certainly do not want to close it down. I need money to cover the expenses, or I will have to. I don't want to do dat. Our church gives us spiritual strength during dese troubling times. It feeds our soul. We all need our church. Any small contribution will be appreciated."

"I can't give the church money," said Eugene on the way home. "I can't give him one red cent. I cannot imagine that any other farmer can either."

"I can bake some bread for him and give him some of the preserves from the cellar."

"That would help, but it's not enough."

They drove without speaking, each lost in their thoughts. Then, finally, Eugene said, "I could give him my trumpet. He goes into St. Paul frequently, where he could sell it. I know there's a demand for musical instruments right now."

"Are you certain about that, Eugene? I mean, are you certain you want to part with it?"

Often when there was a dialogue with emotion, both Eugene and Elizabeth returned to their mother tongue.

"*Ocht, ya!*" he replied in German. "Wenig Konsequenzen"

His thoughts reverted to the past. In his mind's eye, he could still see that big freight train he had jumped on when he left Ontario. He thought about the daring leap he had made to get into the boxcar. He thought about how he tossed his duffle bag ahead. The duffle bag that held his trumpet securely in its core.

He raised the reins with a firm grip, snapped them, and, clicking his tongue, brought his horse to a gallop. Elizabeth would have been sad indeed had she noticed the tears forming in Eugene's eyes.

Chapter Twelve

Eugene heard a broadcast on the barn radio when he was milking the cows. It immediately captured his attention! King George V announced that Canada had entered the war. Mackenzie King, Prime Minister of Canada, followed with the same proclamation. The year was September 10th, 1939. A few days earlier, Eugene had read in the *Edmonton Journal* that Germany had invaded Poland; that hadn't overly concerned him, but this latest broadcast made him sit up and take notice. What would it mean to Canada? What effects would it have on his family?

The mass exodus of men to fight in the war created an abundance of part-time jobs for the farmers in Canada, and jobs were available for women in the plants and factories. The continuance of the war created a shortage of many commodities, such as coffee and tea. It became necessary to ration sugar, the one item taken for granted in the kitchen. It was sorely missed. 'There is a simple solution for this,' thought Eugene. 'I will raise some bees.' With this thought foremost in his mind, he ordered a Bee Book and waited for it to arrive. It contained instructions on how to tend the bees. He marveled at what unique and organized little creatures they were and noted what he needed to get started.

All three beehives sat amongst the wildflowers that grew behind the barn. Eugene kept the bees at bay when he collected the honeycombs with a hat and veil perched squarely on his head and a puffing smoker in hand. Before long, there were two cream cans filled with honey.

'Who misses sugar when one has honeybees?' thought Eugene.

Elizabeth didn't miss it one iota. She used honey instead of sugar for all her baking and canning. It provided a tasty treat for the children when spread on a piece of buttered bread hot out of the oven. And they loved to spoon it on their porridge. On one rare occasion, a can of peanut butter came into the house, and, to extend it, Elizabeth mixed it with honey.

***

The days were warm, and the nights were cool. The leaves were turning to a buttery yellow; Fall had arrived. The kitchen cookstove burned continuously as Elizabeth canned the last of the garden produce and made pickles of every description: mustard, sweet, carrot and of course, dill.

"Look, Eugene, I have eight two-quart sealers of dill pickles, three mustard, and eleven jars of other kinds."

She stood proudly by the table, wiping the sealers with a damp cloth before taking them down to the cellar. Eugene smiled. He enjoyed seeing the pleasure his wife took in the activity that was so very necessary. He drew a long and slow puff on the cigarette he'd just rolled. He been busy repairing the corral around the haystack and had come back to the house for a drink of water.

"Good for you, sweetheart! Why don't you take a break and have me a game of rummy?" said Eugene, reaching for the cards on the windowsill.

"Are sure you want to lose again," laughed Elizabeth. She sat down at the table and wiped her hands on her apron. They were halfway through the game when nine-year-old Mervin came running into the house.

"Why aren't you going outside?" he asked. His eyebrows were knit together in earnest.

"Because we are sitting here out of the sun," said his father.

"But you should be outside," Mervin continued. "You always told us when the house is on fire, we should go outside."

"That's true, son."

"Then why aren't you outside? The house is on fire!" His voice had reached a high pitch.

Eugene jumped to his feet. "Where?"

"On the roof, come and see." Mervin had started to whimper.

Eugene and Elizabeth hurried out the door, and, sure enough, there was smoke and a small flame by the stovepipe that came out on top of the roof.

"Get me a long-handled pot," hollered Eugene. Elizabeth scampered to fetch him one. He grabbed a ladder that lay beside the woodpile and with the pot full of water from the nearest rain barrel that cornered the house. It was a frantic joint effort! He climbed up and down, up and down and Elizabeth kept filling the pot for him.

Finally, after much effort, Eugene declared. "The fire is out and just in time. It hadn't spread!"

He tussled Mervin's hair and said, "Thanks to you son!" Later, after dousing the fire in the kitchen stove out, Eugene went up on the roof with a creosote brush on a chain to clean out the pipes. The wood wasn't always dry, and more than half was filled with sap. Thus, creosote gathered along the insides of the pipes. He scolded himself several times for not cleaning out the lines regularly and vowed he would be more attentive. Finally, he carefully replaced the burned shingles.

'But what would I have done if not for those water barrels?' The very thought made him shudder.

Young Mervin received an abundance of praise from his parents. He became the family hero and was immensely proud of himself. The family would talk about this episode during the upcoming winter and for years to come, and it would become a measure in time–before Mervin saved the house and after Mervin saved the house.

While Mervin enjoyed his notoriety, Milton, a genuine little woodsman, followed his father's instructions on trapping, learning what bait to use, removing the hide, and building the stretcher frames. Milton spent long hours checking his trap lines. The fur trade in Alberta was active, and there was a market for most animals. The pelt of smaller ones such as weasels and muskrats always brought in a few dollars. They were used to trim gloves, purses, boots, and collars.

***

"Come in," said Elizabeth in response to the knock on the door. She was shocked at the sight of the stranger who crossed the threshold. He was disheveled, and his tattered clothes hung upon a frail body. The dark circles beneath his eyes accentuated his gaunt, unshaven face and spoke loudly of his weak condition. He shifted a duffle bag from his back and set it on the floor, creating a poof of dust.

Elizabeth could not speak as she attempted to get over the shock at her sight. The stranger spoke first. "Hello, Ma'am, my name is Marcel Jodoin.

"You have to come to the Waechter farm," said Elizabeth

"I've walked from Lac La Biche." He caught his breath and continued, "Could I have a glass of water, please?"

"But of course," replied Elizabeth as she moved to fill a cup of water from the pail that stood on the washstand. He accepted it with a trembling hand.

"Lac La Biche, my, oh, my, that's a long way to come. Where are you headed?" she asked.

"I want to make it to St. Lina. I have a brother there. He has property behind the co-op store. Is it far from here?"

"Two and a half miles north up the road, give or take," replied Elizabeth. "Are you hungry?"

He nodded and gazed longingly at the chair by the table.

"Please sit down. I can fry up some spuds and a couple of eggs. And I have some fresh bread; it just came out of the oven."

"Thank you, Ma'am, I sure do appreciate it," he stammered as he sat down with eyes glossing over.

The eggs began to sizzle in the frying pan when the children came in from school. They were startled to see a stranger seated at their table and couldn't stop looking at him. Georgina looked at her mother and rolled her eyes. All the while, Rolly sat on the staircase with his arm protectively around Marie.

"If you are tired, Mr. Jodoin, and need to rest, there's fresh hay in the loft," said Elizabeth. He seemed to inhale the food; it disappeared so quickly. He wiped his mouth on his sleeve. "Yes, thank you. I sure could use a rest before I trek out again," said Marcel.

After he had left for the barn, Elizabeth gathered the children around the table.

"We must always be kind to other people. There are people in the world that are not as lucky as we are. These are hard times. Some people are poor and need help from others. You must never forget to give support to others when they need it. One must always be kind and thoughtful."

"But he was so dirty looking," said Georgina.

"That doesn't matter, not even a little. The man is a human being with a heart and a soul. You must be kind. Did you all hear me?" She softly spoke their names aloud: "Georgina? Milton? Mervin? Alvin? Celine? Rolly and Marie? Did you all hear me?" The murmuring of 'yes' harmonized around the table, even down to the soft voice of the youngest, two-year-old Marie.

A short while later, Eugene came in from the field where he worked on fencing. When he entered the house, there was a hush in the room. Milton spoke up first, "Dad, a man is sleeping in the hayloft. He is poor and needed help from us. Mom fed him. We are always supposed to be kind to others."

"That's right, son," said Eugene. Then, smiling, he turned to Elizabeth and winked.

***

The seasons floated by in slowly, one after the other, but it seemed once gone their passing was in a flash. Each day began with chores and ended the same way, with everyday life stuck in between.

"There are some white clouds in the sky," said Eugene, hanging his cap on a hook. "And it's cold for August, feels more like November . . . strange weather for this time of the year!"

"I noticed quite a strong wind had picked up when I brought the clothes in," said Elizabeth.

Eugene and Elizabeth spoke no more about the weather when the children had settled down for the night, despite the anxiety they both were feeling. A loud pounding on the rooftop awoke them in the middle of the night. The crash of broken glass and chards hitting the floor added to the noise. Eugene jumped out of bed and stepped into his shoes.

"It's a hailstorm, a granddaddy of all hailstorms!" he declared.

Carrying the coal-oil lamp he'd lit, he hurried to check on the children. They all were sleeping soundly. They would sleep through anything!

"Stay in bed, Lizzie, I'm going downstairs to get the broom and dustpan. I don't know where all this glass has flown. Are your slippers nearby?"

"They're under the bed,"

"Wait, don't get up until I sweep," said Eugene.

After Eugene had swept, Elizabeth found her slippers. She tried looking out the window, but all she could see in the darkness was a maze of white on the ground while the brisk cold breeze blew her hair back. Then suddenly, it stopped. Eugene quickly stuffed a pillow in the broken window to keep the cold out, and they went back to bed, listening to the thundering noise on the roof.

Elizabeth began to cry. "I, I, know what hail does. You've worked so hard getting the crops in just to have them destroyed in a couple of hours! It's not fair!"

"There now, Lizzie dear, dry up those tears. I'll find a way. There are a lot of jobs in construction right now. I always have that to fall back on. We'll get by. I know we'll get by."

Wrapped in each other's arms, they went back to sleep.

The following morning the late summer sun beamed down on flattened fields covered with melting ice pellets. A swath three miles wide ran for twenty-five miles across the farmland in the St. Lina area, bringing morning heartache.

The struggle to keep staple items on the shelves and the family fed continued, but unfortunately, the little cream cheque was not enough to cover all else.

Eugene had just returned from the post office with a letter in hand from the Wainwright Army Camp offering him work. He had applied ten days earlier. The salary offered was more than anyone could ever hope for, including free room and board on the base.

It's an Army Camp Eugene. With a German name like Waechter, do you think you will run into prejudice?" asked Lizzie.

"Good heavens no. I better not. I'm a third-generation Canadian. And the American General who has the German name of Eisenhour is running the military show overseas, so I've read." His response quieted her concern.

Eugene approached the Tremblays, knowing they delivered lumber in that Wainwright area.

"But of course, we'll give you a lift to Wainwright. We have been supplying dem with lumber for some time and expect to continue. Dey are building barracks and a new hospital. Every ten days, we deliver a new load. So, we would be able to give you a ride der and back home again. We haul lumber der regularly," said Leo Tremblay.

Eugene, overcome with gratitude, reached out to shake Leo's hand.

'Now that the problem of travel is solved. I couldn't be luckier. The Tremblays have been wonderful friends. I don't think I will ever be able to repay them.'

Sadly, he left Elizabeth alone on the farm with the children, only returning every ten days for three days, at which time he was able to catch up on jobs around the farm. The older children could manage the animals' milking and feed under Elizabeth's guidance when he was away. But the loneliness was something Elizabeth had to deal with on her own. She put the rosary that hung on her headboard in use every night; it was her solace. Having a strong faith gave her the strength needed to carry on. And the thought Eugene would always come home in a few days was the extra consolation she needed.

***

The weeks and months peeled away, ending winter and Eugene's absence. When he came home in early spring, he was busy. Gardens needed planting, and Eugene needed to rototill fields in preparation for seeding. All took considerable work, but the spring sunshine warming their shoulders made it a pleasure. After last season's disaster, they hoped for a better year.

News from the outside world came to them via radio. When the batteries were low, the children would lay on the floor, covering themselves with a blanket, and listen to the radio. On this particular day, they had a specific interest. Celine had entered a contest that the radio station had sponsored. Today, they will announce the winner. It was a special event in the Waechter children's life, and just as they had feared, the battery was running low with no replacements in the house. They huddled together beneath the blanket, quietly waiting for the announcement, barely being able to hear.

Eugene and Elizabeth sat at the kitchen table, chuckling. The antics of the children amused them.

"Look at those silly kids!" remarked Eugene.

"They're just having fun," said Elizabeth.

Before they could say anymore, there was a squeal of delight, the children threw the blanket off, and Celine emerged shouting, "I won, I won!"

"Good for you!" said Eugene, patting her head.

"What did you win?" asked Elizabeth, smiling broadly.

"I don't know. I heard my name announced, and then the radio faded out completely. We couldn't hear anything more."

"You'll find out when it arrives. It will be a pleasant surprise."

Whenever the family went into St. Lina, they always checked at the post office for mail. Of course, now there was a particular reason to check. But much to the disappointment of this little girl called Celine, every time they checked there wasn't any parcel addressed to her. She was beginning to think that she wouldn't get her surprise.

. Two days later, Eugene rode Silver into town to check once more. Low and behold, a parcel addressed to Ms. Celine Waechter with the Edmonton Radio Station, CFRN return address was waiting at the post office. Joyfully, he rode Silver home in a fast gallop. He tied his horse, went into the house, and laid the parcel on the table.

"At last, it's come," laughed Elizabeth.

"Where are the kids?" asked Eugene.

"They're playing a game behind the barn. If you call, I'm sure the kids will hear you."

Eugene stepped out the door and, raising his voice to the top octave, hollered: "Yahoo, parcel has arrived."

Like a flock of sheep hurrying to the feed trough, the children came running with excitement on their faces; Celine led the pack.

`They entered the house and surrounded the kitchen table. A small, mysterious package lay in the middle. Elizabeth gave Celine scissors to open it. Within was a small, blue velvet box. Celine paused as though afraid to open it.

"Hurry up and open it. We can't wait all day," said Alvin.

Her other siblings were also egging her on to open it. Finally, she did. Everyone gasped! Within, nestled against blue velvet, a beautiful diamond ring sparkled beneath the light of the kitchen window.

"Ah, it's so pretty!" exclaimed Celine. "I love it!" She took it out of the case and put it on her middle finger, and it fit perfectly. She looked at Georgina and said, "You can wear it sometimes."

"Thanks, but my fingers are five years bigger than yours. There's no point in trying it on. It probably won't even fit my baby finger. It'll be too small, sister, dear." They both went upstairs with the new treasure.

The boys had laughed at this before going back outside.

Elizabeth turned to Eugene beaming, "I'm pleased that Celine offered to share her new ring with Georgina. It tells me she has a kind heart, and I'm glad."

Eugene, smiled then stretching the words said, "So sweet!"

Chapter Thirteen

St Paul, Alberta, twenty-two miles from St. Lina, had the nearest doctors and hospital. However, it would take three hours to get there with a trotting horse; this posed a problem should any of the families in St. Lina become ill. Elizabeth's mother taught her well. She taught her how to treat colds in children using the products from a Watkin's man who drove his Model T Ford through the countryside selling his wares. Her instruction was to rub the chest with his camphor salve he sold, and also rub the bottoms of a baby's feet. Her mother also emphasized the importance of a balanced diet, especially the benefits of eating plenty of fruit and vegetables. Elizabeth followed her instruction by canning many quarts of wild berries and all the vegetables from the garden.

All the training, however, could not prepare Eugene and Elizabeth for the worry and exhaustion they were experiencing when the children came down with the childhood diseases. They came knocking on their door early in the spring, .one after the other: chickenpox, measles, tonsilitis and mumps. Georgina became ill first, then it went down the line, and when the first disease had finished, it had weakened the children for the next bout. Eugene and Elizabeth had little or no sleep for days. In addition, Elizabeth had to deal with a nagging toothache that just wouldn't cease.

Filled with worry, Eugene looked at her tired face, "We should do something about that toothache, Lizzie. I should take you to St. Paul." She sat across the table from him, holding a warm cloth to her cheek.

"I can't leave the children. I just can't. They're still not well, but they're getting better. Just a few more days, and they will be. She left the table and went upstairs to check on them. The next day when he saw her swollen cheek, he broached the subject again but got the same response. So, what on God's green earth was he to do? He was in a quandary!

Finally, two days later the children were on the mend, the nightmare was over, but not for Elizabeth. Her toothache persisted. Having no doctors nearby proved difficult, equally so not to have a dentist. Elizabeth had gone for several days with that horrible toothache. She treated it with cloves to no avail. Then her right thumb started to ache. She suffered immeasurably for three days but, at last, could take the pain no longer. She sobbed to Eugene:

"I must go to the hospital. This pain isn't getting any better. First my tooth and now my thumb as well." She covered her face with both hands and sobbed.

"I'll ride over to Tremblays right away and fetch Yvette to watch the children then we'll go to St. Paul as fast as Silver can take us there."

Oh, how she dreaded the long, bumpy ride!

Three hours later, with Eugene's arm around her, a sobbing Elizabeth with her arm in a sling she'd made with a tea towel, walked through the doors of St. Therese Hospital in St. Paul.

"My wife has had a toothache for a few days and now a very sore thumb. I would have brought her in sooner, but our seven children have been sick for days now. First with the mumps, then the measles and chickenpox and tonsilitis. It has been one hell of a nightmare!"

The Triage Nurse took one look at her thumb and quickly summoned the doctor. She repeated what Eugene had told her.

He took a look at her swollen thumb and said in a louder than usual voice, "This is a severe infection that needs immediate surgery. Take her directly to the operating room. "

Elizabeth, her face ashen and with dark circles beneath her eyes was seated in a wheelchair.

Eugene bent down and kissed her. "I'll be waiting here, Lizzie dear. It will all be better soon. You'll see, my darling!"

When they left, Eugene went outside to check on Silver. His body was dripping wet with sweat. Eugene wiped him down and gave him some water from a barrel nearby and some feed he'd brought along. He patted his head. "You're a good horse, Silver."

All kinds of scenarios were going through his mind when he was back in the waiting room.

'Poor Lizzie, she's suffered so much! I pray they can help her! I cannot understand how her thumb became so infected. What possibly could have caused it?'

St Therese Hospital, operated by the Grey Nuns, served the community within sixty miles. When a haggard Eugene walked into the waiting room, five people sat waiting for family members with different medical issues, but only one was waiting for a child to be born. The first hour passed with conversation and witnessing the joy the birth of a healthy baby brought to the father. But slowly, the room emptied. There was no one to talk to, only the tiny room's four walls to see. He could hear horses whinnying outside making him grateful he'd attended to Silver. With a heart filled with worry, he listened to a chime clock echoing through the halls. It mixed in with the hurried footsteps of the nuns and their swishing habits.

'What is taking so long? My poor Lizzie!'

Finally, at long last, the doctor walked into the room. Eugene was on his feet!

"Your wife, Mr. Waechter, has just come through a successful, tedious operation. She has suffered from septicemia, which is blood poisoning of the bone. Poison from the tooth ran down her bloodstream into the bone of her thumb. I first had to extract the back, left molar, and then her left thumb's first digit. The operation took longer as there was much bleeding, but we got it all in time. Had it been much longer, it might have been a different outcome."

"Oh, thank you, Doctor. I've been so worried! Can I see her now?"

"You can look in on her. She has just awakened from the anesthetic and will be going back to sleep. We have heavily sedated her, so she'll have a good night's rest. We need to keep her overnight. There's a boarding house and stable directly across the street where you can stay. I want to see her again in two weeks to take out the stitches. I suggest she keep her arm in a sling to aid healing for as long as possible. I'm also going to give you fresh bandages that will need changing at least once before returning. If there are any problems whatsoever, bring her back to see me. But I don't anticipate any. She's a healthy woman and should heal quickly."

Eugene shook the doctor's hand vigorously. There were no more words to express his gratitude. Walking up the long hallway, he passed several nuns scurrying about, wooden beads swinging against their grey habits. Lizzie lay behind a cloth screen in a room with three other women. A large crucifix hung overhead on the wall. She was sleeping peacefully. 'She is so beautiful,' thought Eugene as he gazed upon his sleeping wife, 'and she has suffered so much!' Her sweet, round face was slightly flushed, and her auburn hair was spread fan-like against the white pillow.

Then, a thought crept into his mind. His mother had died at the age of thirty-three from the very same thing. 'Thank God Elizabeth is still alive!' He bent down, kissed her cheek, and whispered, "It's all over, darling. You're on the mend. I'll see you in the morning." It was barely audible, but he heard her say, "Uh-huh." He crossed himself, then left her bedside.

One month later, the morning sun was bouncing off all corners of the yard as Eugene walked out to do the morning chores. It slanted across the wheatfield, touched on half the woodpile, and glinted off the axe stuck precariously on the chopping block. Euphoria swept over Eugene as he surveyed the beauty of the morning. He felt good. His Lizzie was healthy once again, and so were his children. Life was finally back to normal.

The next day, Elizabeth awakened early, thinking about the day ahead. A soft breeze blowing through the open window across her face felt invigorating. Her thumb had healed but a little itchiness remained. The chatter of children, when they arose, would soon fill the house, but now all was silent, except for the rhythmic breathing of Eugene, who lay beside her. Her heart was heavy despite the moment's tranquility since receiving a letter from her sister in Heisler that said their beloved mother was very ill. Her mother hadn't been well for several weeks and had recently been diagnosed with cancer; this explained why Elizabeth hadn't heard from her mother for some time, which was unusual as they frequently exchanged letters. When she received the news from her sister, Elizabeth was shocked and filled with sorrow. She paid a quick visit to Heisler. Her mother was lying in a hospital bed. Elizabeth's father, always loving and supportive, sat in a chair at her bedside, grief-stricken.

It was a tearful visit. It was shocking to see the once energetic little woman now reduced to frailty. Her mother said, "It's God's will, Elizabeth dear. Be strong. Above all, keep your faith."

Two weeks later, she passed away at the age of sixty-four. Elizabeth was heartbroken! Every morning since, upon awakening, she'd think of her mother without fail.

'My dear mother, who helped so many, her life cut short! It just isn't fair!'

Today she was thinking about her mother's life. She thought about how people in the Heisler area would tell her what a wonderful mother she had. It was all due to her mother's kindness and generous heart. She would deliver babies for free when a family couldn't pay for her service. Other times, she accepted a chicken or sealers of canned goods. And when there was no clothes or layette ready for the newborn, she would quickly hand-sew little shirts and nightgowns from second-hand material she'd brought along. On two heart-wrenching occasions, she miscarried her own child which blamed on the jostling on the horse she'd ridden to deliver a baby. In the end, she had raised eight children and lost six babies.

Elizabeth thought about how when she was eight years old how her family had immigrated from White Lake, South Dakota. It must have been a tedious trip to take with such a large family!

Elizabeth thought about how her mother had trained to be a midwife in California when she and her husband, Frank, went there to seek a fortune following the economic boom of the gold rush. After five years, they had returned to Heisler, not wealthier but wiser, and with a new midwife's occupation.

Elizabeth also recalled how she came riding over the night before they left Heisler to St. Lina. She had been concerned that Elizabeth would have to give birth in Alberta's North, where no hospital was nearby. She had given Eugene and her explicit instructions on what to do if that were to happen. And she was right; it did happen when Rolly and Marie were born, for then her instructions were a godsend!

Elizabeth wished she could wake up without the constriction of sorrow in her throat. She wished she could stop thinking about her mother like this each morning. Just then, a white dove perched in the open window space and made its regular call. Three times it warbled. It was as if her mother was speaking to her through the dove. Then, finally, she heard her mother's words: "It's God's will, Elizabeth dear. Be strong, and above all, keep your faith." It was like a miracle! At that precise moment, the sad feeling lifted.

Eugene stirred in bed beside her. He glanced toward the window. "Good morning, Lizzie dear," he said. "It looks like a lovely day out there. That's good. I have a lot of fencing to put up. I have to finish that area behind the granary, so the cattle don't get into the alfalfa."

"The first thing I'm going to do today is set some yeast," said Elizabeth. "I'm going to bake some cinnamon buns today. I have a new can of cinnamon from the Watkins Man."

They heard the pitter-patter of little footsteps in the hallway and two-year-old Marie pushed the bedroom door open. She scampered up onto the bed between her parents and snuggled under her mother's chin. Then, just as quickly, she slithered back off the bed

"Where are you going so soon?" asked Eugene.

"I have to go, potty," she replied, holding her flannelette nightgown high up over her little knees as she hurried out into the hall.

"It didn't take much to train that child," commented Elizabeth. "Not like some of her brothers. I thought they'd never get there."

Arising, they dressed, anxious and happy to start their day, Eugene with the chores and fencing, and Elizabeth with the baking of cinnamon buns and all the many things a mother had to accomplish.

***

The scenario of Eugene working off the farm six months of the year during the winter continued and, as the years rolled by, the social life in St. Lina continued to center around the church. Every Sunday after the service, parishioners assembled in the front yard, where conversations in both French and English abounded and where the people honed new friendships. The parishioners also readily shared invitations for Sunday dinners with a potential for card games afterward. There was no talk about the war raging in Europe, despite some farmers having relatives fighting there. It was it was an unwritten philosophy to keep things light and upbeat to combat the struggle they all had within. Eugene and Elizabeth did express concerns to one another privately about the effect the war might have on Canadians and the future of their children.

Being an observant man, Eugene noticed that Jake Curling, a middle-aged bachelor who lived on the other side of town, and a non-parishioner, was always hanging around the fringe of the crowd outside the church on Sundays. He also noticed something that gave him concern. In her thirteenth year, Georgina had developed into an attractive young lady and. Jake Curling kept eyeing her up and down with a lustful leer on his face, which turned into a satisfied smile as if he were mentally undressing her. This gave Eugene an uneasy feeling right in the pit of his stomach. I'll have to keep an eye on that creep, he thought.

This Sunday, they invited a new couple Raymond and Blanche Jodoin over to play a game of cards. Usually, they would have played cards with the Tremblays, but Leo was out of town. It was a warm summer day with daylight stretching well past early evening, in which case all the children would have a high old time playing outside. They played hide-and-seek, and chased each other around the yard, playing tag. Eugene stopped them from playing the game of Annie-High-Over when they broke a window.

The evening with the Jodoins was going happily by playing a game called five hundred when the evening took a sharp turn; Blanche broke out in tears right out of the blue. It was shocking to everyone, including her husband.

"Whatever is the matter?" asked Elizabeth, offering her a hanky.

Looking stunned, Blanche's husband put his arm around her shoulders in consolation. But unfortunately, he knocked over a cup of coffee on the table in the process. Elizabeth quickly wiped it up.

"Did we offend you in some way?" asked Eugene.

"No, no, you didn't," sobbed Blanche. "It's just that I'm worried about something. She turned to her husband, "I haven't even told you, dear,"

"Please, Blanche, tell me, tell me now, tell us all. There's nothing so bad or wrong that cannot be fixed, *mon cheri*."

"I, I think I'm going to have a baby."

"Why are you crying? That's wonderful news!" exclaimed Elizabeth before anyone else could say anything.

"We've always wanted a son, Blanche. Maybe now we'll have one," said her husband, laughing aloud, albeit nervously. Their two daughters were outside playing with the Waechter children.

"But, but I'm over forty years old; it can be dangerous at this age. I'm so worried." She took the hanky from her sleeve and wiped her eyes.

"Now, you listen to me, Blanche," Lizzie said. "My mother was a midwife in Heisler, and she delivered many a baby from mothers older than forty. Why there even was one that was fifty years old! They all turned out to be beautiful, big healthy babies. So having this baby is a blessing, a gift from God above. Yesiree, a blessing!"

Blanche gazed gratefully at Elizabeth. "You've made me feel better, Elizabeth. Thanks for that."

"You're more than welcome. It brings to mind my last son, Alvin, was born, my mother was the midwife. When my labor started, Eugene still had to milk three cows. He was hesitating to leave the house. I told him to go. He milked one, then came back in to check on me. I said: 'I'm just fine, nothing to worry about.' He did this again for the second time. I told him to go back out and finish the milking. He was barely out the door when the pains became stronger and closer. When he came back in, we said the Litany of the Blessed Virgin together, and when we finished, Alvin was born. He was small and weighed only five pounds, but he was filled out. His head was the size of a teacup. He was perfect! What a joy it is to have a baby! You are lucky Blanche. Uh-huh, you are so lucky!"

Blanche thanked Lizzie again, dried her tears, and turned to her husband, "I'm sorry, dear, I should have told you privately."

"Don't worry about that. I'm delighted to have a wee one in the house again!"

The following day, Eugene was chopping wood and lining cords up along the side of the house for the extra insulation. He was taking a break from the laborious job when he saw a figure of someone walking up the road in the direction of his farm. 'I wonder who can be walking afoot?' He continued chopping for a few minutes, then glanced up the road again. This time he saw a man walking slowly through his gate. As he approached closer, he recognized him. It was, of all people, Jake Curling!

He walked over towards Eugene, who had planted his axe into the chopping block.

"And why am I honored with this visit?" asked Eugene with raised eyebrows.

Jake took a few seconds to reply, and his voice was hoarse when he did.

"I just decided to take a stroll. It was further than I anticipated."

"Then you must have had a destination in mind," chided Eugene.

"No, not really. Well, kind of."

"It has to be one or the other." Eugene was beginning to lose his patience.

"I've come to do you a favor. Something that I think is a big favor that will please you immensely."

"And what might that be, I dare ask?"

"I know you have a big family, a big family to feed and clothe. So, I've come to help. I could do something for you, which will make a big difference with your food and clothing costs. I know how expensive a big family can be."

"And how exactly could you be helping me?"

While ignoring Eugene's question, Curling continued, "People should be helping each other, stepping in when needed, being observant to see where they can help, and doing all they can.

"And how, exactly would you be helping me? Eugene repeated feeling his dander rising and his face flush.

"I could take your oldest daughter off your hands."

His offer did not take Eugene by surprise. He had been expecting something from this reprobate since seeing him ogling Georgina all these past Sundays. However, he didn't expect to see him walk the distance and make his plea so obviously practiced.

"Did I hear correctly? You want me to give you, my Georgina. My beautiful, first-born child?" He raised his voice to a shout. "You want me to give you, my Georgina?"

He picked up his axe and hollered at the top of his voice, "You get the hell off my property, you bucket of horse manure! If you ever show your face around here again or at the church, I'll have the R.C.M.P. on your tail so fast that you won't know which end is up!"

Eugene shouted a few more choice words, then held the axe up over his head. He continued, "Get out of my sight, before I, before I . . ."

"I'm leaving, I'm leaving, don't hit me," said Jake Curling in a panic. He whirled round, and his straw hat fell to the ground. He snatched it up, then scurried up the path, through the gate, and down the road as fast as his legs would carry him. The loud swearing uproar brought Elizabeth out of the house. She was shocked! It was the first time she had ever heard Eugene swear! She saw him sitting on the chopping block with his hands covering his face. She went to him.

"Eugene, such language! The air is blue with it! I'm glad the children weren't around to hear their father curse as you just did! Whatever is going on? Whatever is the matter?"

He removed his hands; his face was ashen.

"You'll never believe this, Lizzie. Remember when I told you how uncomfortable that man, Curling, made me feel. You know, the one with the big straw hat who was always lurking around the church. He was just here and, get this, he asked me to give him Georgina. He asked me to give him Georgina! I lost my temper and nearly took the axe to him. I can't remember when I've been so angry! Can you believe it?"

"But did you have to swear like that?"

"He made me swear! Don't you understand that Lizzie?"

She looked at his pleading, sad face. "Yes, I do!" replied Elizabeth. "Who could think of such a thing, giving up a child?"

"He must be off his rocker," said Eugene. "You can bet your bottom dollar he won't show his face around here again."

"We mustn't tell the children, Eugene. The boys will tease the living daylights out of Georgina. It's a good thing Rolly and Marie are having their nap, and the others are in school."

"No, mums, the word."

Several weeks had passed since the Curling incident. Eugene and Elizabeth were in bed in the evening and were about to go to sleep when Eugene said, "I haven't seen old man, Curling around the outside of the church lately. Maybe the old critter croaked!"

"Eugene, that's no way to talk," Lizzie murmured.

If he had seen her face, though, he would have noticed a smile was sneaking around the corners of her mouth.

As the weeks continued without incident, not even a small one, which was remarkable for a family with seven children. Eugene remarked to Lizzie how tranquil life had become that Saturday morning. However, they were expecting a calf to be born, which was always fun and exciting for the children. It was Alvin's turn to name this calf. He was anxiously waiting. Although he had a name picked out, he wasn't about to tell anyone until it was born.

Eugene was walking back from doing the evening chores when he saw smoke billowing out over the brush across the road. What the Sam Hell was burning?'

He hurried into the house. "Lizzie," he called out. "I'm going to check our land across the road. I can see smoke over there."

Eugene crossed over to the property known as Pancha Place, Pancha, being the previous owner's name.

He ran to the site. Sure enough, the old barn he used to store extra hay was beginning to burn. He was helpless with no water source nearby. The dry timbers were engulfed right before his eyes. The heat was so intense that he had to stand several feet away. All he could do was watch it burn.

'It's a good thing I didn't have hay in there! There's been no thunder and lightning on this sunny day.' How on earth did that ever get started?

He returned to the house to an anxious Elizabeth.

"It's our barn on the Pancha Place. It's a mystery as to how it started. So much for a tranquil day. Where are the kids? I don't want them to go anywhere near the fire; beams will be falling."

"Georgina and Celine are upstairs. Rolly and Marie were playing behind the house. I don't know where the boys are. Your face is awfully red, Eugene," said Elizabeth.

A horse galloping into the yard bought their attention to the window. Abe Asselstine, the neighbor to the north, sat atop his horse, steadying the reins. Eugene went out to greet him.

"Hello Eugene, I was just passing by when I saw the smoke billowing up in the direction of your property. So, I've come to see if I can be of any help."

"Thank you for your concern," said Eugene. "It's just an old barn on my property across the road. I've no idea how it started. It's a good thing there are no trees nearby."

"I was wondering if you were having trouble. I'm glad to hear it was nothing serious. Let me know if that changes." He tipped his hat and rode out of the yard.

As Eugene walked back into the house, he thought that was mighty nice of him.

Rolly and Marie came running in. "Hey, Dad, I think there's a fire. I see smoke across the road," said Rolly.

"We know, son, the old Pancha barn is burning. You must not go there as it's very dangerous. Where are your brothers?"

"They're pouring water into gopher holes again."

"If you see them, tell them Dad wants to talk to them."

In the meantime, Eugene hollered out the front door. Then, finally, he had all the children gathered before him.

"The old barn on the Pancha Place has caught fire and is burning down. I want you all to go nowhere near the fire. Then, once all the wood and coals have burned away in a couple of days, we can look. Do any of you know how the fire got started?"

They all shook their head," no."

"Okay, I believe you, go back and play outside. The children returned to what they were doing before their dad called them in.

Eugene turned to Elizabeth. "That fire sure is a puzzle. I wonder if we will ever find out."

There was one person who knew. Georgina, their eldest, ran upstairs and flung herself on the bed. She felt terrible because she knew she had sinned. She had lied to her father. She just couldn't admit how it happened. She felt so bad. It made her throat tighten. She had taken a lantern into the old barn; it was dark inside, and she had wanted to look around. She had tripped after crossing the threshold, and the coal oil lantern went flying. When it landed, it hit a rock and burst into flames. Frightened, she ran home as fast as her legs could carry her and went upstairs. Celine was there sitting on the bed looking through the Eaton's catalogue.

The next evening at supper time, Eugene came in after doing the evening chores.

Eugene turned to Alvin at the supper table, "The calf is born now, son. What are you naming it?

Alvin was quiet for a few seconds, then, much to Georgina's dismay, he said, "Smokey," then he laughed and said, "I bet you can't guess why."

"That's appropriate," said Eugene. "By the way, the lantern that hangs in the barn is missing. Has anybody seen it?"

No one responded. "Oh, well," he said. "I suppose it will turn up sooner or later."

Georgina was silent. She wanted to say. 'It won't turn up, Dad. It burned in the fire.' But she didn't; this just added to her feeling of guilt.

***

Life went on in the Waechter family. The episode of the fire melted into the past. Remorse, however, kept hold of Georgina. Whenever she passed the burned rubble of the old barn, she would cross herself. And if she felt particularly guilty, she would genuflect as well. The following year Eugene used the ashes from the fire to spread on the garden area and the fields. He said ashes added nutrients to the soil. And Eugene was right. The following year the wheat crop was the best it had ever been. At that same time, Elizabeth and the older children had planted an enormous amount of seed potatoes simply because she had so many on hand, and she wanted to fill the half-acre of land that Eugene had tilled and added ashes. The multitude of potatoes that grew astonished everyone. Hill upon hill sprouted up, and when they leafed out and blossomed, it was a sea of white. Growing them was one thing. Digging them up, bagging them in gunny sacks, and hauling them to the house on a stone boat pulled by Silver, the good old horse, was another. It took several days to harvest all those potatoes. The cellar was packed floor to ceiling. After reading a note in the co-op store advertising their sale, people flocked by droves to buy them. Ashes enrich the soil. Eugene knew that. But he never understood how much until he had that bumper crop.

Knowing something good had come from that fateful incident she had caused brought an end to Georgina's remorse. She couldn't find the words to tell her parents about what had happened, but she vowed she would let them know one day. But not just yet, no, not just yet.

When the month of May arrived in St. Lina, it came with the promise of summer ahead, so welcome after the harsh winters. But it was the coldest months, December, January, and February falling well below zero, that gave a measure of difficulty keeping the children warm when being transported to school. Despite warm, woolen socks, the youngest, Marie, often had her heels frozen, making her cry from pain when circulation returned.

Eugene eyed the left-over lumber he had that lay behind the granary. He would see it every day when he went out to do the chores. On this day, the idea struck him to build a covered caboose. The children would be warmer when going to school.

"Lizzie, I'm going to build a caboose to transport the children to school on the cold winter days. I have all the lumber, nails, and screws I need." He had just finished the chores, and they were having their breakfast.

"A caboose? What will it look like?" Will it be safe for the children?" asked Elizabeth.

"Well, much like a large wooden box with a door on it and benches inside where they can sit. It can even have a stove with a stovepipe going through the roof. There will be a small opening at the front to see the road ahead and hold the reigns. Silver can pull it. Milton could drive it and be in charge as he's the eldest son and very capable. But more importantly, the children will be warm. I know we are only two miles from the school, but that's a fair distance when it's thirty below." Eugene nodded his head to punctuate what he said.

"I don't know, Eugene. I have bad feelings about it. All our children are going down the road to school in a box pulled by a horse. What if it tips over and catches on fire?"

"For heaven's sake, Lizzie, why are you always seeing the worst of everything? It would be difficult to tip over; it's low to the ground and wide at the bottom. Yes, it would definitely be difficult for it to tip over."

"What if there was a run-a-way? Horses can get spooked, you know!"

"I'm sick and tired of all your prattle. Don't you want the children to stay warm? I'm building this caboose, and that's the end of it! I have all summer to work on it, and by the time the cold weather is here, I'll have it finished."

He slammed his cup down on the table, spilling coffee onto the oilcloth. Then, he slammed the door on his way out, making the mirror over the adjacent washstand jiggle.

Startled by the noise and shocked at his show of temper, Lizzie climbed the stairs to their bedroom and laid down. Since his shouting at old man Curling, she had not witnessed Eugene's temper, but now when it was directed at her, it took on a whole new meaning. She felt hurt and began to sob. She quickly chastised herself as she recalled their wedding vows: 'through good times and bad,' and then gave her thoughts to the meal she would prepare for supper that night.

The strained relationship remained during the summer months. Every time she heard the rat-a-tat of a hammer across the yard while working in her vegetable garden, she knew he was building 'it.' Although enough time had passed to have dissolved the incident, the hammering brought it back. She had expected him to apologize, but he never did.

Lizzie dreaded the cold weather for more reasons than one. Now the children would ride to school in the caboose. Each day she said a prayer as they all piled into the wooden box with grey-blue smoke coming out of the stovepipe while Silver nonchalantly trotted down the road to the school. Each day, they returned warm and happy just as they had left. Each day when Elizabeth saw them return, she felt a flush of relief.

It was a Friday in the middle of January; Eugene was busy stacking wood against the wall behind the Quebec Heater; the Tremblays were expected for dinner. Elizabeth was busy all of the day and early in the afternoon. She baked fifteen loaves of bread and three caramel pies and had cream chilling on the back steps to whip before serving it. She looked out the kitchen window to see a light snow falling; then she saw something that made her scream, "Eugeeeeeeene!"

He ran across the room to her. She pointed out the window, and then he saw it. Silver came galloping into the yard dragging a broken hitch behind him without the caboose, without the children!

Eugene flew out the door, grabbed the halter to steady the horse, took his harness off, then mounted and galloped out the yard. Elizabeth fell to her knees by the kitchen bench and prayed, "Oh Lord, please let the children be alright. Please, Lord, don't let anything happen to my children! Sobbing, she left the kitchen, went upstairs, and retrieved her rosary from under her pillow. She sat by the kitchen window back downstairs, praying while waiting for Eugene's return. With relief, she saw him trot back into the yard. Rolly sat on the horse behind him, and Marie sat in the front. She opened the door. Eugene called to her, "Everyone is fine! I'll get the others. No one is hurt."

'Mommy, I'm so scared," said Marie. "Me too," said Rolly. "It was a big truck." Trembling, that was all they said.

"Come, sit at the table, and have a cup of cocoa. It will make you feel better.

"Georgina, Celine, and Alvin were galloped in next, followed by Milton and Mervin. They all sat around the table having cocoa.

"Tell me, son, what exactly happened?" queried Eugene.

Milton stammered before speaking.

"Dad, a big truck came towards us and hogged the road. I had to hold a tight rein on Silver. He was scared of the big truck, then the caboose slipped into a ditch, and Silver reared up and lurched forward. He pulled the reins right out of my hands. I think that's when the hitch broke, and he galloped away. The stove didn't tip over. I told the kids to stay in the caboose so they would stay warm.

"We were packed in there against the wall like dill pickles in a jar," laughed Mervin.

"Thank God you all are home safe and sound," said Elizabeth.

"Well, that certainly was an experience!" stated Eugene, avoiding eye contact with Elizabeth." You did an excellent job Milt. It was not your fault. We all have to remember, boys, that the reins are the only control we have over horses. And something else, we must always double-check harnesses on horses that they are well attached. If not, they will come loose, and the horse will gallop away. The children listened bright-eyed and intent.

Chapter Fourteen

As time goes by, incidents in life have a way of repeating themselves. It seemed only yesterday when Elizabeth told Blanch Jodoin: 'A child is a blessing, a gift from God.'

Lying in bed, Elizabeth whispered, "Eugene!"

"Yes, Lizzie," he replied, not yet asleep.

"Remember some time back when the Jodoins came over, and Blanche broke into tears."

"You mean when she blubbered at the dinner table."

"She cried Eugene because she was worried. She was having a baby at the age of forty-two. And she feared the baby might not be normal."

"Just joking, Lizzie. I knew she was worried. So, what's brought that up?"

"Well, I'm forty-two."

"And?'

"We're expecting another baby."

He turned over quickly towards her. "That's good news, Lizzie. Marie starts school soon. I'll miss not having a little one in the house. Yes, good news. When do you think this will happen?"

"I figure it will be in November sometime, six months from now. But we don't have to tell the other children just yet."

"Okay. It'll be our big secret! I have some lumber in the shed. I can build a new crib."

"That would be nice, Eugene."

A few moments passed, and they were both silent. Eugene thought they would have to throw another spud in the pot as he tried to take the edge off his worry of another responsibility and concern for a healthy child. He thought about his Lizzie and how she had to endure another pregnancy and childbirth. Then, finally, he spoke, this time in German, "*Ich Liebe dich*, Lizzie Waechter."

"And I love *you*, Eugene Waechter."

He leaned over and kissed her, and then they both turned over and went to sleep.

The days passed uneventfully until one day, Georgina said to her mother, "Mom, your stomach looks big. You can't be expecting a baby, can you?"

Elizabeth pretended she didn't hear the comment and just kept on stirring the gravy. She decided then and there it was high time to break the news to the children, but she first spoke to Eugene privately. "Eugene, I think it's time to tell the children about the baby. Georgina commented today about my stomach.'

"Yes, Lizzie, I think we should. It's time."

"Let's do it at the supper table tonight. Could you do it, Eugene?

"But of course, Lizzie.

Steam rising from the large pot of stew and dumplings so expertly prepared by Elizabeth made the stove's overhead warming oven moist. The children were taking their places at the table, but Mervin was missing. Elizabeth called out the door, "Mervin, Mervin! Supper!" He came running in and quickly washed his hands at the washstand before taking his place at the table. Elizabeth then spooned out the food on each plate while the slabs of homemade bread quickly disappeared off the center plate. Everyone was hungry. There was no time to talk. Forks clicking against plates broke the silence of the meal.

Although satiated with the thick, delicious stew, there was always room for dessert. After supper, Elizabeth served a decadent chocolate pie topped with whipped cream, then Eugene spoke. It was July 1944.

"We have some wonderful news to tell you. Our family will be welcoming a baby in November!" He quickly glanced at Elizabeth. Her eyes were moist.

"I knew it," laughed Georgina. "I knew it. I could tell."

"No, you didn't, smarty-pants," said Milton, laughing at his sister.

"I hope it's a boy," said Mervin, taking another bite of his pie.

"I'll teach him how to fish if we ever get close to a lake," said Rolly.

"What do *you* know about fishing?" said Alvin. He laughed, making his face turn red.

Celine smiled and said, "Good news! A baby. I can hardly wait!"

After the banter, Elizabeth said, "A child is a gift from God! Therefore, we must give thanks and pray for a healthy child."

Little Marie sat listening to her brothers and sisters' banter, but all she heard was 'a child is a gift from God.'

"Mommy, will the gift be wrapped with a ribbon?"

Everyone broke out into laughter, laughing at Marie and happy there would be a baby in the house come fall. Marie didn't know why they laughed, but she decided to laugh with them, drowning out all others with her high-pitched giggles.

Now, the wonderful news was out. The Wachter family had enjoyed a delicious dinner, and everything ended on a cheerful note.

Eugene smiled at his Lizzie and winked.

They decided this baby would be born in a hospital as time drew near, unlike the last two. Elizabeth calculated it would be around the middle of November when the baby would be delivered, but they weren't taking any chances. Eugene drove her to the St. Paul hospital ten days ahead. Again, he saw the grey nuns bustling around the hospital when he admitted Elizabeth. It brought back memories of her sore thumb just a few years earlier. Now she's back for a much different and more profound reason.

He kissed her goodbye at the admitting office, where a nurse took her to the maternity ward. He left immediately to head back to St. Lina and brought Silver to a fast trot. 'Please, Lord, let Elizabeth deliver a healthy baby!'

When he arrived in St. Lina, he dropped into Lozeau's store and spoke directly to Joe Lozeau.

"I just took Elizabeth to the hospital in St. Paul. Our baby is not expected until the middle of the month, but I wasn't taking any chances. You know how that goes. It could be any day. They will be phoning you when our baby is born. I knew you wouldn't mind taking the message for me. I'll come around frequently to check on any news."

"I'm more than happy to do that, Eugene, and I'll tell the Mrs."

The shout rang through the house, 'Daddy's home,' when Eugene pulled up into the yard. The kids ran out to meet him.

"There's no news today," he told them solemnly.

Meanwhile, back at the store, Joe Lozeau spoke to his wife. "Eugene Waechter was here today. He's taken Elizabeth to St. Paul's hospital to have her baby. The hospital will phone us when the baby is born."

His wife smiled for now she had juicy news to tell every customer that came into the store.

St. Lina was a cohesive, neighborly community. It didn't take long before friends from the church sent food items to the Waechter farm; not the least was bread, the most needed. They received several loaves and a variety of cakes and pies. Georgina, now sixteen, was set to bake bread as Elizabeth had taught her, but now it wasn't necessary. She was busy making lunches for school and keeping meals on the table the best she could. She and Celine kept the dishes clean, washed all the discs of the cream separator, and swept the floor after each meal. The boys kept the wood boxes behind the cookstove and Quebec heater full.

Eugene and the boys attended to the chores and kept the wood-burning stove in the supply of its fodder. Keeping busy helped to pass the time.

But not for little Marie, who missed her mother more than words could express. The house seemed hollow without her. She sat in a corner holding her teddy bear, watching her siblings, and waiting for her mother to walk through the door. She didn't even feel like playing with Rolly, which was highly unusual. He tried coaching her to go outside but to no avail. "It's too cold outside," she had said, and he replied, "We can play in the hayloft." Rolly, a sensitive boy, could see his sister was sad, and he wanted to fix her, but she wouldn't budge.

Each day, Eugene rode into town to Lozeau's store to see if there was a message from the hospital, but he had to ride back repeatedly with no good news to tell the children. Eugene was worried!

On November 11th, 1944, Eugene brought Silver to a gallop when he rode once again into St. Lina to see if the word had come. Light snow was falling, adding to the thin layer already on the ground.

When Eugene walked into the store, Joe Lozeau smiled broadly. "I just hung up the phone," he said, picking up his notepad. "I have a message for you." It was music to Eugene's ears. He'd walked over to the Quebec heater to warm up when he'd entered. With hopeful anticipation, he quickly closed the distance between him and Joe, who was standing at the counter.

Joe read from the notepad he held in his hand: "Elizabeth Waechter delivered a healthy baby boy at 2:00 A.M. this morning. He weighed eight pounds, three ounces. Mother and baby are doing fine. Both mother and baby will be released from the hospital in five days." The message came from Sister St. Augustine of the Grey Nuns at St. Theresa Hospital, St. Paul, Alberta.

Relief mixed with joy washed over Eugene. Grown men don't cry, but he indeed felt like it. *So now I have five sons! So now I have eight children! I can hardly believe I actually have eight children!*

"Thank you so much, Joe. It's been tough without Lizzie in the house. The kids have been waiting patiently. We just don't realize how much a woman does in the home until they're gone. I want to buy seven chocolate bars to give the kids to celebrate the birth of their new little brother!" He walked over to the shelf that held the chocolate bars.

When he mounted Silver and headed home, he said aloud, *Wunderbar*! And, as the horse's hooves clacked rhythmically against the frozen ground, he gave prayers of thanks all the way home and vowed he would help Elizabeth in the house when he could.

Just as they had done every time he'd returned from St. Lina, the children came running out to meet him.

Still astride, he shouted, "A big, strapping baby boy, and he weighs over eight pounds. I'll bring Mom and the baby home in five days."

"Hurray!" the children shouted. "Hurray!" They jumped up and down.

"Come on, let's go into the house. I've brought you a treat!" said Eugene tethering the horse.

They sat around the table eating their bars. Finally, Mervin asked, "What will his name be?"

"Well, your mom and I decided that we would call him Dennis if the baby were to be a boy."

"If you guys don't know, it is spelled D E NN I S," stated Georgina.

"I love the name. It sounds nice," said Celine.

Alvin said, "I like the name Alvin better." Then, he went into a fit of giggles.

"I think it's a fine name," said Mervin.

Milton just stood by smiling.

Rolly turned to Marie at his side and said, "Just five more sleeps, and Mom will be home." Marie started to cry with joy. Rolly put his arm around her.

In St. Lina, there were two Model T Ford cars. Eugene arranged the use of one to bring Elizabeth home from the hospital. It was far too cold to be traveling with a horse and buggy, especially with a new baby.

Jauntily Eugene walked into the hospital with a new spring to each step. He passed the nursery on his way to Elizabeth's room and looked through the window, but he did not see his baby. Finally, however, he did see him in Lizzie's room.

She sat all smiles, proudly holding him, and dressed, ready to go home. In her arms, she held baby Dennis. He was wearing the sweater, bonnet, and booties she had knit for him. His long sleeper was drawn together with a ribbon at his ankles. A blanket to wrap him in and a white lacy shawl as his final covering were on the bed.

Eugene bent down and kissed Elizabeth's forehead. "Hello, darling." He took the baby from her arms and kissed its forehead as well.

"My, oh, my Dennis! Aren't you a fine young man!

He carried him over to the window to have a better look. "He looks different than the other children when they were born. His face is round and filled out."

"His body is nicely filled out too," said Elizabeth, "We have to remember, Eugene. He weighs over eight pounds. It makes quite a difference in appearance."

When the parents brought Dennis home, the other children's fuss over him differed from the family's last additions. The older siblings took a more practical viewpoint on this new baby except for Celine. Of course, she was all set to be the primary caregiver after her mother.

Rolly and Marie thought their new little brother was ever so cute! Marie thought, 'I have older brothers and now a younger one.' She wondered if he would be called Baby instead of Dennis like she had been. She had thought her name was Baby until she became older and realized it was Marie And now that Mom was back home, the lump in her throat had gone, and she could enjoy life playing with Rolly once again. Oh, how she loved Rolly!

Father Berube baptized Dennis during Sunday Mass. It was a bright, sunny day with the snow sparkling on the ground like a thousand diamonds. Elizabeth made a roast beef dinner that day and a unique, tall, white cake she'd made with thick cream. She finished it with a boiled caramel icing that cracked ever so slightly when one bit into it. Father Berube and the entire

Tremblay family came to enjoy it with them. The house was packed, noisy, and filled with camaraderie. Elizabeth had to steal away upstairs to check on Baby Dennis, who lay in Eugene's new crib. He was a contented baby and only fussed when he wanted his mother's milk.

***

Rolly and Marie grew incredibly fast. Soon it was time for Marie to start school. After her first week of school passed, Elizabeth remarked to Eugene.

"I didn't know Marie had become so attached to Rolly. When he started school last year ahead of her, she was lost. Rolly told me she ran out to meet him when he came home that first school day. She was so happy to see him, she cried. Rolly said it made him feel both sad and happy at the same time. Oh, well, now she's in school too and doing well. Georgina was a big help to Marie, teaching her how to read, which put her ahead of the game. Our once baby in the family is fairing well, Eugene. "

An important event in the Waechter children's lives was receiving the Catholic Church's sacraments. It was time for Rolly and Marie to receive their first Holy Communion and

Confirmation, just as all the others had done. And it was customary for young girls to wear a white dress and veil and for the boys to wear a white ribbon on their sleeve. Both children were excited about this event. Rolly was incredibly proud of it. He was a sensitive, bright boy, and, even at the tender age of eight, he could look at the bright side of everything. If there was a cloud in his sky, he always found the silver lining.

On the other hand, Marie was a dreamer and ever so emotional at times. She felt intimidated by her older siblings even though they coddled her. Georgina had taught her how to read before starting school. When she did, she excelled because she knew phonetics.

Elizabeth did not have a white dress for Marie to wear. She didn't have the one Celine had worn five years earlier because it had been on loan. Luckily, she had the long, white stockings to go with it, and the nuns would provide the veil. So, after giving it much thought, Elizabeth decided to sew the dress herself. She worked long and hard and was pleased with the finished product. Very happy, indeed! After the First Communion Mass, Marie tried in vain to brush off the spring mud clinging to her white stockings from kneeling in the pew before Georgina snapped their picture.

As usual, the people congregated outside after Mass. Eugene and Elizabeth had spent a few moments with the Tremblays before they had to leave. Raymond and Blanche Jodoin quickly replaced them with their three-year-old son, Pierre. Blanche's concern about her pregnancy was unfounded. Pierre was a normal, healthy, smart little boy and a delight to his parents and sisters.

Eugene patted his head and said, "You're a fine-looking young man, and how you've grown!"

Much to everyone's surprise, the little lad declared in a loud voice, "Thank you." It drew laughter all around. It was clear he had received compliments before, and his parents had coached him on how to respond; it was delightful!

"He's a bright boy," said Elizabeth, chuckling.

"I know," replied Blanche with pride. "And to think I was worried about having him."

"Children are a gift from God. There is nothing in this whole wide world more beautiful than a child. I should say. And to think, some people can't have any. I feel sorry for them."

She gazed toward Rolly and Marie. They had climbed up into their wagon ahead of their siblings. Those two, she was thinking are always together; many people thought they were twins despite Rolly being eighteen months older. They were laughing about something while patiently waiting to go home.

"I feel the same way, Elizabeth. Especially now after having Pierre. Raymond and I were talking about it this morning at breakfast. Of course, the girls will be grown up and gone, but we'll still have our Pierre."

"Would you folks like to come for Sunday dinner?" asked Elizabeth. "I don't know what I'll cook, but I'll rustle something up. After, we can have a game of whist."

"We would love to," replied Blanche happily. "I can speak for Raymond and the girls. I know they'll agree."

On the way home, Elizabeth announced, "The Jodoins are coming over for dinner today."

There was a hurrah from the children at the back of the wagon. Georgina said, "We can play ball. I'll be the pitcher."

"No, you won't. I want to pitch," said Milton in a loud voice.

"We can take turns, then," Georgina replied, grimacing.

Eugene was smiling as they rode along. He was also smiling as he sat at the kitchen table, enjoying a cigarette he'd just rolled. Watching Elizabeth work in the kitchen always brought a smile to his face. He thought about the excellent pie crust she made from rendered pork fat and how she could turn out beautiful cakes without a recipe, using the extra cream they had. And no one on the face of the planet could make gravy as good as hers.

Today, she had peeled and sliced several large potatoes and several onions; all went to the large rectangle pan she used for baking loaves of bread. Next, she sprinkled flour over the lot, shook in some salt and pepper followed by chunks of butter, then covered it all with milk and put it in the oven. Scalloped potatoes were everyone's favourite. Therefore, she needed to make a lot.

"Georgina, please, I want you to get some lettuce, carrots, and peas from the garden. Celine, you can help to shuck the peas. "

Her little helpers hurried out the door to fill their mother's request.

Elizabeth turned to Eugene as she began to trim the ham for baking.

"These hams that you cured are so tasty. This one looks excellent and will go great with the spuds in the oven. I'm going to make a brown sugar paste to put onto this little bit of fat on the top, and then I stud it with some cloves, which always give it great flavour. I'm glad we have the hams and don't have to kill a chicken for this Sunday's dinner."

"Yeah, and they keep so well. I'll have some of the leftovers with eggs in the morning," replied Eugene.

With the produce from the garden now ready, the girls went back outside. A cry of, "They're here," could be heard in a few moments. Elizabeth gazed through the window and saw the children running out to the road to greet the Jodoins. Naturally, they were anxious to have little Pierre in their midst.

Life was good!

The dinner was exceptional, and now, with all the dishes washed and the children playing outside, Elizabeth showed Blanche the first communion dress she had sewn for Marie.

"It's beautiful!" said Blanche. "Elizabeth, it's really quite beautiful!" I noticed it at Mass today.

"It was a challenge as I did not have new material to work with, so I had to compromise. I used an old white shirt of Eugene's for the bodice, which I had almost thrown out. And for the skirt, I bleached out a flour sack in the sun and, as you can see, I added some white lace I happened to have to the bottom and embroidered white daisies here and there." Pridefully, she added, "I did it all without a pattern."

The little, white dress drew raves from the nuns when Marie had gathered with other first communicants at the convent. The children had marched in single file from the convent to the church. Some had their veils. Others, like Marie, received one from the nuns. The front pews were marked with big, white, satin bows and reserved solely for the children. The congregation had enjoyed watching the little children of the parish lined up the aisle. They were dressed in their finery, girls in white veils, boys with white bows on their sleeves, all had genuflected in unison when the nun activated the hand-held clicker.

To receive First Holy Communion was a special time for the children. Receiving the host, they were taught, brought Jesus into their hearts. Therefore, it was a special time for them, indeed! The nuns instilled faith in them to know and believe that the Holy Eucharist Sacrament is what Jesus had instructed his apostles at the last supper, the night before He died. He told them to do it in his memory as he handed out bread and wine, representing His body and blood that He was going to shed for the world's sins.

Additionally, before receiving communion, they were taught by the nuns the importance of the sacrament of Penance, whereby they learned to examine their life for sins and make a confession in preparation to receive the host. This sacrament also helped them to develop a conscience.

It was also a joyous and prideful time for the congregation to see these pious little children, well trained by the nuns and dressed in their finery, receiving their first Holy Communion. Elizabeth and Eugene were incredibly proud. Rolly and Marie were treated like royals the rest of the day. And they felt especially important, indeed. Rolly told Marie he could feel Jesus in his heart.

Chapter Fifteen

Eugene kept abreast of world news and the war raging in Europe by reading *the Edmonton Journal* he'd picked up at the post office. The most recent information to read was that the Americans had dropped an atomic bomb on Hiroshima and Nagasaki, Japan, on August 6th, 1945, killing upwards of 150,000 people. Eugene was shocked! How could such a thing happen? He tried to imagine what it would be like to have a bomb dropped on St. Lina, but he couldn't. Fraught with help-lessness, he pushed the war thoughts out of his mind, focussing on his family instead.

Baby Dennis seemed to grow more quickly than the others. The little guy walked before his first year and talked at eighteen months. Perhaps it was the stimulation all around him.

In his mind's eye, Eugene could see Celine holding him and singing the old song by Albert Von Tilzer, one he used to play on the trumpet: "Put your arms around me, honey, hold me tight. Huddle up and cuddle up with all your might."

And Dennis would hug her. So sweet! And he surprised Mrs. Lozeau at the store when she gave him an apple, and to her delight, he said, "Thank you." Unlike most other little ones his age, there was no 'tata' in his vocabulary.

Eugene was very proud of all his children, but little Dennis, the baby in the family, born to them when they were at an older age, and who gave them concern during the pregnancy, now brought delight to everyone in the family.

Eugene sat on a stump at the pasture's edge with thoughts in turmoil contemplating his family's future. Several cows grazed and contentedly chewed their cud. He did not register the smell of their manure mixed with the clay earth as it wafted through the air. Beyond the pasture was the acreage he had sown with wheat in the spring. Across the distant expanse of the field, he saw wheat sprouting up sparsely. Oh, how he loved to see things grow. Witnessing the magic of a tiny seed reaching up out of the ground to grab the sunlight and flourish amazed him. But this wasn't the case here. What Eugene saw saddened him. *Scheisse*, he thought, noting how difficult it was for grain to emerge successfully from clay-ridden soil.

'If the soil had been good, I can only imagine what a dandy of a crop I would've had. But unfortunately, I will never see it here. I will never get ahead here in St. Lina. Life here these past eleven years has always been in tiny pieces. Lizzie has no life with me going to work and leaving her alone with the children. They are growing up so fast. There is no future for any of us here. I need to move the family to a better place. Many fellow workers have said that the West Coast of British Columbia is an ideal place to live. I've heard it repeatedly. The climate is mild, and fruit grows in abundance. And there are no harsh winters there. In fact, I've heard there are no winters at all, so to speak. How wonderful that would be! But a move takes money, lots of money. A farm sale could make some to help with the train fare. But where would we all live once we got there? I won't mention it to Lizzie just yet. I can hear her say that moving takes money, Eugene. No, I won't tell her until I get all my chickens lined up.

He thought about all the attempts he'd made trying to get ahead. Finally, his last-ditch effort had been raising sheep. He recalled hauling them home in the wagon two years back. He had hoped to make money selling the wool. The purchase was sixty breed ewes, for which he paid a fair price. It was early spring when their lambs were born, and the weather hadn't warmed. It had taken all his effort to keep them alive, some he had to bring into the house. Then, when all was said and done, he had realized only a small profit, merely enough to buy flour for bread, wool to use for a couple quilts and a few socks.

He stood up, dropped his spent cigarette to the ground, and crushed it with his heel. Then, overcome with despair, he gritted his teeth and pounded his fist hard on his left hand. He looked down at his left hand, sore from the hard punch, but it was a good hurt. It exposed the epiphany of the moment. His thoughts were circular in a swirl of German and English.

"I'll talk it over with Lizzie tonight," he said aloud.

"I'm going to move my family," he whispered. 'I'll check *the Edmonton Journal.* Maybe there will be jobs advertised for carpenters in British Columbia. If there are, I can apply, and once there, I'll be able to check things out.'

Eugene felt a certain resolve with his decision. He felt better, a whole lot better. The dark clouds covering his sky disappeared. There was a new spring in his step as he walked back to the house.

A light rain had fallen, and the air was fresh. It was a warm summer day when Eugene rode into St. Lina two weeks later. Halfway there, above the clap of Silver's hoofs on the hardpan, he heard church bells ringing like they were beckoning to him. Something must have happened. The bells never rang on a Tuesday afternoon.

As he rode into town, he was further surprised to see a small crowd gathering in front of Lozeau's store, and more were arriving. They had responded to the bell. Father Berube and several nuns were amongst the crowd, mixing and conversing with the group. Curious, Eugene dismounted, scattering magpies out of his way. He tethered his horse. Then he saw it. Joe Lozeau had raised a Canadian flag on a pole high over his store. It was flapping in the breeze, creating a snapping sound. As he approached, he heard shouting.

"The war is over! Hurrah! The war is over!"

Father Berube moved slowly to the front of the gathering and called out over the din, "Ladies and Gentlemen, please give me your attention."

A hush fell over the crowd.

"It has been a long war, and many Canadians have lost their lives. Our hearts go out to St. Lina's Belliveau family, who lost their eldest son. And we all have been through some hard times. But now, at long last, World War II is over. Things will change. Things will get better. It will be a new beginning for us all. So, let us all thank God by saying the Lord's prayer."

The irony of the term 'new beginnings' struck Eugene full force. A new beginning for his family was precisely what he had been planning for the past two weeks.

The priest made the sign of the cross and led the prayer.

When the prayer concluded, Father Berube added, "Tomorrow morning at ten, there will be a special Mass of gratitude. So please pass the word around. The church bells will be ringing tomorrow before Mass as well."

Then Mother Superior, who had organized students to be the tollers of the church bell, walked gingerly over to him and whispered something in his ear.

"Oh, yes, after Mass, there will be a luncheon served in the hall to celebrate this momentous occasion. So please bring your addition to the food table, whatever you can manage."

The audience clapped their approval, and the shouts continued, "Hurrah, the war is over!" There was a joyous cacophony peeling through the tiny hamlet of St. Lina, Alberta: people shouting, the church bell continuously ringing, the flag making its snapping sound, and several dogs, excited by the noise, barking in the background.

World War II, which had been raging on for the past six years, finally ended. It was September 2, 1945, and it would be two years later before Eugene managed to move his family to Abbotsford, British Columbia, the town his fellow construction workers had raved about so often.

Chapter Sixteen

Abbotsford, B.C., the hub of the Fraser Valley and the berry capital of British Columbia., was a progressive community. It was also the home of a sizeable Mennonite settlement of German/Russian descent. Both Eugene and Elizabeth enjoyed conversing in German with these fantastic folk who had their private school called the Mennonite Educational Institute commonly known as the M.E.I. It was located within a section of Abbotsford called Clearbrook. It was 1947 when the Waechter family moved to B.C. Eugene rented an old Japanese house for ten dollars a month on Marshal Road Extension where Mennonite families dwelled namely, Krauses and Driediger's. .

It is here we find Eugene and Elizabeth drinking coffee at the kitchen table, eighteen months later, reminiscing.

"Well Lizzie, we've been in B.C. three years now. My, how time does fly!" said Eugene.

"I know it just seems like yesterday when I had the farm sale in St. Lina! I remember feeling nervous doing it, but I managed. Uh huh, I did.

"And I was lucky to have found jobs for Mervin and Alvin as carpenter helpers with Marvel Construction in Vancouver, kind of young, but it's the best that could have happened for them. I knew Milton would go off logging. Ever since his trapping days, he loved the woods!"

"And Georgina now in Normal School studying to be a teacher. I also knew she was cut out for something important; such a great help with the younger kids she always was, uh huh! I always knew it. She has quite the load with her studies and working for her room and board at Paxtons! Oh well hard work never hurt anyone, I say," proclaimed Elizabeth.

She moved to the stove for the coffee pot and while refilling their cups said, "Only four children at home now, half have flown the coup."

Her voice had a melancholy tone that did not go by unnoticed by Eugene, so he quickly changed the subject.

"Well Lizzie," he said again. "What do you think of this house now that you've been here a while. It's a far cry better than the log house, don't you think?"

" Yes Eugene, it sure is great having electricity, just have to pull a little chain and the light comes on like a miracle. No more coal oil lamps to deal with."

"Too bad there's no running water but that's why the rent is so cheap, gives me a chance to save, stated Eugene.

"I was really surprised when owner, Johnny Malloy said he only wanted ten dollars a month for this place. I expected more. He also told me Japanese had built this house, but unfortunately, they were forced to vacate when, during the war, Canada forced Japanese people into internment camps in B.C.'s interior.

"How sad for the Japanese," declared Elizabeth. "Do you think they might come back?"

"Ah, no Lizzie, the war is long over."

The house had three bedrooms, a living room, a kitchen, a cultivated patch in the backyard ideal for a garden, and a sizeable prune-plum tree behind the outhouse. The house had electricity but no running water hence the cheap rent; however, there was a well with a pump outside the back door. An extra shed on the property had housed a large, Japanese-style wooden bathtub. Also on the property was an outside toilet. Near the back steps of the house was a pump providing fresh water. The large plum tree on the property delighted Elizabeth. She quickly took advantage of it by canning fruit and making jam and jellies. She also preserved other fruits which were readily available in the area. The place, so cheaply attained, was adequate for the family and much superior to the log house in St. Lina, Alberta. How could anyone trying to save money say 'no' to this ideal arrangement?

"And you do have some kinfolk nearby, said Eugene.

Elizabeth was delighted to be near an aunt and uncle Henry and Mary Thomas, who lived only nineteen miles away in a small town called Chilliwack. Many years earlier, when the Thomas family immigrated from Germany to White Lake, South Dakota, U.S.A., two of the Thomas brothers had married two Schroeder sisters, one being Elizabeth's mother. Uncle Henry and Aunt Mary, who were childless, were doubly related to Elizabeth, making their relationship special, indeed! Eugene had suggested that Christmas and other special holidays, he would drive to Chilliwack to pick up Aunt Mary and Uncle Henry to join in the family celebration. He knew it would make both of them happy, and especially, Elizabeth.

***

As Eugene was driving back to Vancouver the next evening to return to the room he was renting. He thought about their life in St. Lina, which now all seemed like a dream. The move to Abbotsford had gone smoother than he could ever have anticipated. First, upon arrival, the family had moved directly into cabins provided for pickers, at the Baker Raspberry Farm where they earned a few dollars.

Then, after the raspberry season, he saw a basement suite advertised in the local paper, at the home of Jacob Rempel. He had driven to the Rempel farm on the outskirts of Abbotsford and knocked on the door. Mr. Rempel had answered the door. He remembered their conversation verbatim.

"My name is Eugene Waechter. I read you have a basement suite to rent. I've relocated my family from Alberta, and we need a place to live," Eugene had asked.

Jacob Rempel had replied, "Yes, I do have a furnished suite to rent. It has three bedrooms and a large kitchen completely equipped right down to the last pot."

He spoke in a soft voice and smiled which had quickly put Eugene at ease.

"How much are you charging?"

"I was thinking forty dollars a month would be a fair price."

Now as Eugene drove along, he told himself he would never forget what a kind man Jacob had been. He had refused to accept any rent at all. That generosity afforded Eugene a chance to get on his feet financially that first year in B.C .and bank a little money.

During that time, Eugene injured his hand on the construction site in Vancouver. He was using a whipsaw when it happened. To this day, when using that hand to steady a piece of lumber, an ache runs across his fingers, triggering memories of that painful accident. He had sliced two fingers near the bone and spent several days in the hospital while they grafted skin from his abdomen. It healed nicely, but much to Eugene's chagrin, it prevented him from playing the violin, which he thoroughly enjoyed. His memory of living at Rempel's was two-fold: kindness and pain.

***

Two years later, at dusk on Friday night, Eugene drove his 1927 Star Truck across the plank-covered culvert onto the property. He parked it under the shade of two trees to the left of the house. Elizabeth watched from the window, always happy to see Eugene back home from his workweek in Vancouver, but she was surprised to see where he had parked the truck.

"Hi, Eugene. Why did you park there? Usually, you park across the road." She motioned towards the vehicle.

He was expecting her question. "The brakes need repair, Lizzie. I don't feel safe driving to and from Vancouver every week in the old truck. So, I bought a 1938 Plymouth from a dealer in Langley on the way home. I got an excellent deal on it. There're delivering it tomorrow."

"I guess it's better to be safe than sorry!" she replied. 'Even if you didn't discuss it with your wife first."

"I'm sorry, Lizzie, I was impulsive when I saw the car in the dealer's parking lot." He gave her an affectionate pat on the back.

"I didn't feel safe anymore in the old Star truck. The brakes were acting up."

***

Eugene longed to be doing what all the farmers around the Abbotsford area in British Columbia's Fraser Valley were doing, growing fruit and vegetables for market. But first, he needed land, which would take money enough of which he didn't have but what he was saving for these past few years. He was lucky to be working steadily in construction and saving every penny, but he needed more. Fortunately, household expenses had diminished considerably, with half his family now out on their own.

Georgina, attending normal school, came home to visit. Before she left to go back to Vancouver, she sat on a chair by her parents.

"I have something to tell you," said Georgina, struggling to get the words out, "I was the one that started that fire in the Pancha Place."

"Oh, so that's what happened," declared Elizabeth

"How did it start, and why did it take you so long to tell us?" asked Eugene.

"At first, I was too frightened to tell anyone. I was playing outside and decided to look inside the barn, but it was dark there, so I took a lantern. When I walked in, I tripped over a board on the ground, and the lantern went flying. The flames shot up so quickly that I couldn't pick it back up. I ran as fast as I could back to the house, scared out of my wits, and there were so many people asking about it. Then as time went by, the fire episode faded into the background. It has bothered me all these years, so I decided to tell you now that I've left home."

"Accidents will happen. As I said, it was an old barn, and no one was hurt. And remember, I did get to use the ashes on the potato patch, and we had a bumper crop that year," smiled Eugene. He reached for his eldest daughter and hugged her.

Her confession cleared the little black smudge off her conscience that she'd harboured all those years.

Eugene was pleased his children lived their early life on the farm, where there was much to learn. They knew the cycle of the farm animals' lives. They witnessed their procreation and birth. They had watched the butchering of an animal. They had learned how to milk a cow, clean out the stalls, plant a garden, and preserve the produce. Even though they were away from the farm and working in different industries, they carried two most valuable assets: responsibility and the ability to work.

Milton had joined a logging company in Northern British Columbia. Working in the woods was what he loved most. He had trapped in the woods at St. Lina at an early age. Back then, when he'd come home singing from checking his trap lines, the family knew his trapping that day had been successful. He would dry the skins behind the stove on wooden stretchers. He quietly stashed away the money he earned from selling the pelts to the Hudson Bay Company. It also wasn't long before the logging company promoted Milton to the position of faller. Now he didn't have to look further. He'd found his niche.

The other two brothers, Mervin, and Alvin, only thirteen months apart in age, roomed together in Burnaby. Like their father, they worked in construction. Both worked as laborers. There was no shortage of employment because of the postwar boom. They were thrifty young men and saved their money.

The four children remaining at home: Celine, Roland, Marie, and Dennis attended school and made a few dollars picking berries in the summer. They blackened their hands, picking hops in the Rosedale area near Chilliwack one season. Then, because Roland was an ambitious lad, he found a market for bark peeled off the cascara tree. So, he filled gunny sacks with the bark which he sold to the company that gathered them for medicinal purposes.

Located in Abbotsford's town center was the Catholic Church. The congregation comprised mainly of Hungarian people who had immigrated from Hungary during the revolution. Father Csakic, also a Hungarian Immigrant came to Abbotsford to serve the Hungarian population. He gave lengthy sermons in Hungarian, followed by a short one in broken English.

It was a test of patience for the Waechter family to sit through these long sermons not understanding a word. The similarity between the sermons in Abbotsford and the French sermons in St. Lina was uncanny. After Mass on Sunday, Eugene would treat the family with ice cream cones from the local Milk Bar café, an ice cream parlor that offered a variety of flavors.

***

There were four children in the Paxton family where Georgina worked. Each day, she had to pack their lunches, give them their breakfast, and get them off to school before she left to go to Normal School herself, and at day's end prepare the meals and perform other duties for several hours before studying for her exams.

One day while Georgina was working for the Paxtons, a tall, dark-haired man appeared in the dining room doorway. At first, she didn't see him when she ran across the room to answer the phone that hung on the wall.

"Hello there," said the stranger in the room, "And who might you be?"

Startled, Georgina laughed, showing a flash of perfect, white teeth. At a glance, he could see she was a beautiful girl.

"I'm Georgina. I work here. And who just might you be if I may ask?"

Before he could answer, Mr. Paxton, who'd walked into the room, quickly responded, "Georgina, I'd like you to meet Lloyd Gropp. He is a fellow Knight of Columbus and is going to the meeting with me tonight. Lloyd, I like you to meet Georgina. She's helping out with the family for the missus. And she's going to Normal School to become a teacher."

"Pleased to meet you, Georgina," said Lloyd, admiring the attractive woman who stood smiling in front of him.

"Pleased to meet you too," said Georgina, noticing his tall stature, dark, curly hair, and soft voice. She felt a hot blush creep up over her cheeks.

The mutual attraction was instant, but Georgina had other things on her mind at this moment. She had written the final exam for Normal School yesterday and had felt she didn't study enough. After tending to the family's needs, studying was difficult in the evening. Most nights, she would fall asleep before giving it the full attention needed. Tomorrow the successful students will have their names published in *the Vancouver Sun*. She spent a restless night, finally falling asleep only to be awakened, not by the children who usually demanded her attention, but by the newspaper making a whacking sound as it was tossed it against the front door. She ran down to retrieve it and hurried back upstairs to her room. Nervously, she scanned the long list looking for her name. Then, there it was: *Georgina Pauline Waechter*. She fell across her bed and sobbed with relief.

Later, excitement overtook her fatigue as she began the day. After Georgina washed the dinner dishes and cleaned the kitchen, the telephone rang. Mr. Paxton called out, "Georgina, you're wanted on the phone." Georgina hurried into the dining room, wondering who would be calling her.

"Hello," she said breathlessly.

"Hi Georgina, this is Lloyd Gropp. I hear you passed your course at Normal School. I wondered if I could take you to dinner tomorrow night to celebrate. Generally speaking, it's great to celebrate when there's something that important to celebrate."

His voice was music to her ears. "I'd love that. What time will you be coming by?"

"Does seven work for you?

"I'll be ready. See you then."

It wasn't long after that that Georgina and Lloyd were going steady and speaking of marriage.

Georgina landed her first teaching position in a small community called Hatzic in the district of Mission. It was a small, one-room schoolhouse with a cabin in the back, ideally for the teacher to live.

***

Living off the farm was an adjustment for the remaining family. There was no demand to attend to animals, and it seemed strange to see a neighbor's home from the front porch. Playmates came from Krause's, the nearest family. There were girls Marie's age and a little boy named Frankie, age four, the same age as Dennis. The boys played together congenially every day, until one day when they had a or disagreement. Elizabeth overheard it. She had to hold back her laughter, but the next day when they were playing together again, she told them about the importance of getting along with each other. When Eugene came home, she was anxious to relate the incident.

"That youngest child of ours, Eugene, is very witty."

"What makes you say that Lizzie?"

"Well, Frankie Krause was over, and they were playing in the backyard when I was hanging the clothes out. I don't know what happened, but Frankie became angry and said he was going home. Just as he was leaving, he turned and said, 'I'm going to chop your head off.' Dennis hollered back, 'Well, you're not going to use our axe!"

Eugene threw his head back and laughed. "That's my boy,"

"The next day, they were back playing together again as though nothing happened," stated Elizabeth.

The passing of time snuck by like a shadow crossing the floor. The eldest four children were now on their own, and the last four were growing rapidly. Rolly, now fourteen, had made friends with Ralph Carter, a neighbor boy who lived a quarter of a mile up the road. Both had practiced the Tarzan call they'd heard on the radio and in the movies. Often, one would call out to the other at a predetermined time, and a few seconds later, the other would respond. This exchange of puberty-cracking voices, carrying through the night air, amused the neighbors as they sat on their back porches.

Clouds had formed in the Fraser Valley Sky, and rain was threatening. This afternoon, Rolly kept eyeing the old Star truck that Eugene had parked by the house. When he saw the keys in the ignition, temptation overcame him.

"How would you like to go for a little ride?" he asked his younger brother, Dennis, who at the age of seven, had become an avid fisherman just returning from the local creek. He laid his catch down by the well, a row of trout strung through the gullet on a stick, ready to be cleaned.

"Where are you going, Rolly? Are you taking the truck?" He pointed at the vehicle.

"Yes," replied Rolly. "I'm going to pick up some gravel up the road by the Pouche's home to spread around the front door that's always muddy. Jump in the back and let's go."

Surprised that Rolly was taking the truck, Dennis jumped in the back of the old Star truck. Rolly turned the key; the motor started. He backed it up a little too fast, slammed the brakes, jammed it into first gear and stepped on the gas. He crossed over the wood-covered culvert, made a sharp left turn and sped down the road leaving a cloud of dust in his wake. Proceeding up the road, he sailed down a hill and stopped at the bottom beside a pile of gravel at the roadside. He spaded some into a box he had in the truck. Happily, he saw Ralph Carter in his yard when he drove by and proudly gave him a wave.

"This will save Mom from always having to wipe the mud up from the floor," said Rolly, thinking Dennis could hear him from the back, "She'll be pleased!"

He turned the truck around in the nearby driveway and headed back up the hill on his way home. Halfway up the hill, the truck's gear jumped into neutral, and the vehicle started to roll back down the hill. Rolly slammed his foot on the break but to no avail.

"Oh no!" said Rolly as he kept trying the brakes. "Dennis," he shouted, looking in the reverse mirror, but in horror, couldn't see him. He glanced out the passenger window and saw him standing on the road just as the vehicle landed in the ditch bending the back fender.

Quick to see what was happening, Dennis had jumped out the back, landing unhurt on the gravel road.

"Goodness gracious, Rolly, you shouldn't have taken the old truck!" Elizabeth cried. "The brakes don't work! That's why your father bought a different car! You both could have been killed if the truck had rolled! We can thank God, we have you both still with us! I saw you leaving and shouted after you, but you were speeding down the road so fast, you didn't hear me."

Looking sheepish and exhausted from the mile walk back home, Rolly responded, "I just wanted to get some gravel to put by the front door to cover up the mud that you're always cleaning when it gets dragged into the house."

"I know your heart was in a good place, Rolly." She was thinking of the compassion he'd displayed in so many ways.

"What will I tell Dad?" asked Rolly with his lip quivering. Dennis stood quietly alongside, listening intently.

"Don't worry about it, I'll tell him. First, we have to get the truck back in the yard."

"I'll walk up to the top of Mt. Lehman to the garage and order a tow truck. I can pay for it, Mom, from my paper route and cascara money."

"Just a minute Rolly, what have you done to your hand. That's a nasty cut.! I'll have to put a bandage on it!"

"Thanks, Mom. I cut it when the window broke in the truck."

Rolly turned to Marie who was standing by looking distraught. "Marie, would you please do my paper route for me today, my hand is too sore to do it myself. I will make you a list of customers.

"Sure, I can do that" responded Marie.

Rolly rode back in the tow truck with the driver, and they returned the damaged vehicle to it's parking spot in the yard. A while later, Marie returned from delivering the papers soaking wet. The rain was coming down in torrents. All the names of the customers on the list Rolly given were washed off.

"I didn't know what to do Rolly, so I gave a paper to every other home. What else could I have done?"

"You did just fine Marie, don't worry about it. Get yourself dried off."

That Friday, when Eugene came home, he didn't notice the bent fender because of the truck's angle; it was out of sight. But he did see the graveled walkway outside the front door.

Later, when Eugene and Elizabeth engaged in their pillow talk like they always did before going to sleep, Elizabeth asked him a question she'd been rehearsing in her mind all day. "Eugene, you have often spoken of your childhood as I have, and there were some funny minor incidents. Did you ever take your father's tractor for a spin when you were about fourteen?"

Eugene thought for a moment, then chuckled. "Oh, yes, I took the old Rumley down the road a half-mile and stalled it. My dad came after me and was he ever angry! I was out of his good favor for over a week."

"Oh, well, Eugene, boys will be boys!"

He was quiet, then he asked, "Tell me, Lizzie, what happened this week while I was away? There must have been something for all this psychology you're employing."

She giggled and said, "Yes, there was one minor incident. Rolly wanted to put some gravel by the front door. He was worried that the mud everyone tracked into the house was causing me a heap of work, having to wipe it up every day."

"And?" asked Eugene.

"Well, he knew where he could get the gravel. You know up past the Caldwell's. There was a pile up by the Pouche's house."

"And?" repeated Eugene.

"He took the old Star and, and its brakes failed. It rolled back down a little hill and landed in a ditch, denting one back fender. Dennis was in the back, but he jumped out before hitting the ditch. We can thank the good Lord our boys weren't hurt!"

The thought of Dennis jumping out of the moving vehicle reminded him of when he jumped onto the moving train all those years earlier. "Yes, we can. I don't give a damn about that useless, antiquated old truck. How did Rolly get the vehicle back to the house?"

"Rolly walked up to the garage at the top of Mt. Lehman Road and organized and paid for a tow truck," continued Elizabeth."

"How could he pay for the tow truck?" asked Eugene with a hint of sarcasm in his voice.

"You know, Rolly. He knows how to make a buck. He has his paper route, and he's been selling cascara bark," replied Elizabeth.

"I see. Do you know what it cost him?"

"I think it was five dollars."

"That's a lot of papers to deliver!" said Eugene.

The following day as Eugene passed Rolly at the breakfast table, he patted Rolly's head and said, "Good job with gravel out front. That'll make a big difference in keeping the mud out. It was thoughtful of you. But in the future, wait until I'm home before driving any vehicle so I can go with you. And I daresay when you have a driver's license.

"Yes, Dad," said Rolly hanging his head and staring down at his plate.

Then Eugene reached into his pocket and gave Rolly a five-dollar bill.

"Thanks, Dad," said Rolly brightening. He turned to look at his mother's nodding smile.

***

Marie sat on the bed watching her sister getting dressed for the Abbotsford Legion dance. The news around town and high school was that American men from across the nearby border of Washington State in recent weeks regularly attended the dances held at this Abbotsford Legion. Celine was putting on the new dress she'd purchased with money she'd earned working as a secretary at the Abbotsford Airforce Base. It was a pale-yellow, waffle-pique fabric in an A-line style with a zipper up the front and two patch pockets. Celine was pleased with her reflection in the mirror. She wanted to look her best.

"Can I go too?" asked Marie

"You're too young," replied Celine, smiling at the thought of her barely thirteen-year-old sister going to the dance.

"I could wear one of your dresses. No one will know my age."

"No, Marie, you're way too young, besides Mom would never let you!"

Marie sat forlornly, her big green eyes moist with disappointment.

"You look pretty, she finally ventured. "I like your dress."

"I like it too," said Celine, pivoting in front of the mirror and looking over her shoulder at the back. "I'm going to meet an American tonight."

The Legion dancehall was filling up quickly. Celine and her friends entered the hall and joined the ladies on one side; some were seated; others were standing. Across the room, at the opposite wall, men stood chatting while stealing furtive glances at the bevy of prospective partners. Amongst the handful of strangers, Americans were on a quest to find a suitable wife. Celine stood facing the wall with her back to the men, visiting with her friends.

On the stage, the musicians were tuning up their instruments. The singer walked over to the microphone, and the music began. The lilting notes of the Tennessee Waltz filled the room, and the purpose of the gathering swung into action. Men quickly walked across the room to choose their partners.

Celine turned and first saw a hand stretched out to her. She raised her eyes to a stranger with laughing brown eyes and dark brown curly hair. He whispered the two words, "May I?" with a smile as big as Texas. Celine was captivated. She took his hand. They walked out to the dance floor and slipped into the rhythm of the music. It was the most exciting waltz Celine ever had!

His name was Johnny Zender, and he was from Deming, Washington, USA. He had eight brothers and two sisters, making eleven in the family. His family owned and operated a logging company called The Z Brothers Logging, where all the boys worked.

What Celine found most amusing of all, the nine boys in the family formed a ball team called The Deming Loggers, competing with other western and up-state teams. Johnny had come to the dance with two of his brothers.

They danced with no others and never missed a dance. At evening's end, Johnny looked at Celine with a serious face and asked, "Can I drive you home."

Celine responded, "Sorry, but I won't ride in a car with three strange men."

Johnny was quick to ask, "Well, then, can I make a date with you then next Saturday night?"

"I'd like that," said Celine trying not to appear too anxious. She gave him her address, and they bid farewell.

There was no stopping that romance. It was in full swing. Within the year, Johnny and Celine were married. Marie and Johnny's youngest sister were precisely the same age to the month, so they became junior bridesmaids. Marie had written the following poem for her sister. She stood on a table at the wedding reception held in Mission, a town nearby, and recited the following poem to a crowd of over one hundred:

'A handsome young Yankee came a rolling on his way

To the Legion dance that was not far away.

He met a pretty, dark-haired gal dressed in soft yellow

She thought he was, without a doubt, quite the fellow.

He dated her a year, then popped the little question

She said "Yes" with no objection.

A cute, little house they both picked out,

and they are fixing it all around and about

Celine was a master painter from the faraway hills.

She painted the bedroom, the bathroom, and windowsills

And Johnny was doing things mighty fine.

He fixed the living room walls with knotty pine.

They are fixing and fixing and doing their best.

They are going to have a cozy little nest.

In November, the wedding bells will be a-ringing.

And the choir will be a-merrily singing.

The bridesmaids and best men are in their places

Celine is smiling, is all decked out in satin and laces.

Johnny is handsome too and just couldn't wait to say, I do

An anxious, little couple standing patiently in the aisle

Father Csakic receives them with a winning smile.

"Will you take this man to be your lawfully

wedded husband?"

Said the priest with admiration for the two, but

before he could finish the question, Celine had said, *"I do."*

Marie enjoyed reciting her poem. She was proud of what she'd

written. She did, however, feel silly standing on top of a table.

Chapter Seventeen

Eugene and Lizzie sat together enjoying their breakfast, both sipping on their second cup of coffee. It was 9.00 A.M. on a Friday.

"Mighty fine breakfast, Lizzie dear!"

He had eaten three hotcakes, two fried eggs, and three rashers of bacon like he used to cure in the smokehouse in St. Lina; this was Eugene's favorite breakfast, although he did enjoy a bowl of oatmeal porridge now and then.

"I cannot believe it, Lizzie. We have only two children left under our roof, Marie, and Dennis. Rolly was mighty young to be leaving."

He took a long draw of his coffee, draining the cup. He placed it back on the table with an unintended thump.

"He'll do fine, Eugene. He's always been ever so good with people! I think he's cut out to be a salesman! Uh-huh, I do. And he's very fussy about his appearance. That's a good thing for a salesman."

"And with his ambition as high as Mt. Baker, he's bound to do well in this world," replied Eugene, smiling at his analogy.

They sat quietly at the table, lost in their thoughts. Finally, Eugene broke the silence.

"Time has gone by so quickly! It's like the children came in the front door and left out the back. Time has gone by so quickly!" he reiterated. Melancholy showed on his face.

"You know what I think, Eugene, the best time of all was when the children were little. It seemed hard at the time, but now, as I look back, it was beautiful! I wish all young mothers could know this."

Elizabeth sat pensively, pondering her statement. Finally, she spoke again, "I pray and hope Eugene that our children will always keep their faith. It means so much in creating a happy life! It gives them the courage to weather the storms. Yesiree! If only they could know all that above all else."

She stood up and began clearing the breakfast dishes. As she walked to the counter with a stack, she kept repeating, "If only they could know all that. If only they could know all that!"

Eugene remained at the table, listening to the clanking of dishes as Lizzie washed up after breakfast. He glanced out the window. The kitchen noise faded into the background as his thoughts took over.

It was a godsend going to Skelly's tomato cannery in Kamloops. Good money was made with Lizzie cooking for the bunkhouse crew, assisted by Marie at mealtime. I can still hear Lizzie's response when I asked her if she'd be all right doing that job.

She had laughed and said, "Eugene, how can you ask me that after all those years cooking for the threshing crew on the farm?"

And she was amazing! She took over the kitchen in the bunkhouse and fed all the workers who stayed there three meals a day. It was her first job away from home, and she stepped up to the job like a pro. He thought about how when Marie wasn't helping Lizzie, she worked in the tomato cannery, and because she was fast at stacking tomatoes in cans, she earned piecework wages.

Both kitchen and cannery wages gave Marie a healthy paycheque. And I earned a fair wage hauling tomatoes.

He thought about the wages earned by all three, when all pooled together it gave a healthy sum towards buying the land, he needed to grow the berries he was dreaming about. Now he had enough saved for a healthy down payment on land. He purchased a 28-acre parcel directly behind the Abbotsford Airbase. First, he had to plow and prepare the soil on the five acres he had just cleared. He needed to buy canes and hire help to put them and the posts in the ground. All of that took more money, more than what he had. Oh, he hated to borrow money, but there was no recourse. The time had come to pay a visit to the community's credit union office, and Lizzie agreed wholeheartedly.

When Eugene walked into the credit union's office, he was shown into a small side room and invited to sit down in front of a desk. The desk held a telephone, a desk calendar, a writing pad, and a ballpoint pen. The clerk told him someone would be with him shortly. He glanced around the room. His eyes rested on a slogan on the back wall that faced his chair:

NOT FOR PROFIT, NOT FOR CHARITY, BUT FOR SERVICE

Eugene hung on the word 'service' and wondered what kind of service he would get this day. As he waited for the agent to come in, he hoped he'd be successful in his quest for a loan. It was his only hope to keep him from having to go back to work in Vancouver. It wasn't fair for Lizzie to be alone all week stuck in the house. She was always so sad when he had to leave on a Sunday afternoon to go back to Vancouver to his construction job after spending only a couple of days at home every week. Lizzie had been such a brick in St. Lina when he had left for employment off the farm for weeks at a time. She had been alone with the children, the chores, and stoking the fires during the bitterly cold weather. Not many women would have been able to handle all that.

"Now is the time for us to build up a raspberry farm and have you home twenty-four seven," she had said, "Now is the time, Eugene!

She was right. Her words resonated in his head for days. It was all he could think and dream about lately. He recalled when he had to ask the municipality in St. Lina for money to pay for Lizzie's medicine after Marie had been born and how it had ripped a corner off his pride. Back then, he had been asking for a handout. Today was different. Today was all about business. He was asking for a loan yet asking for a loan also niggled his craw.

His thoughts were interrupted when the agent walked brusquely into the room. "Mr. Waechter, how do you do? I hope you haven't been waiting too long. My name is Abe Doerksen. Shaking Eugene's hand vigorously, he continued, "What can I do for you today, sir?" His voice was melodious like he spoke the phrase frequently. As well, Abe's smile was broad and brightened his entire face. He was a middle-aged man with receding gray hair and a rotund body that left little space. There was a swoosh of air when he lowered himself into his armchair.

"I need financing for my farm project," stated Eugene, coming right to the point.

"Where is your farm, and how many acres do you have?"

"I purchased eighteen acres behind the Abbotsford Airforce Base."

"How much of the land is cleared? What is your intent?"

Eugene perked. He was anxious to tell his plan.

"I have five acres cleared and intend to clear more. I want to build a raspberry farm by increasing the planting each year with the growth of canes from the previous crop. The soil is rock-free and rich, unlike the pitiful land I homesteaded in Alberta. When walking, one could step from one rock to the other without touching the ground. I know the difference between good land and poor."

Listening intently, Abe smiled as he tried to shift in his chair.

Eugene continued. "The beauty of this land is the creek that runs through the property. I have applied for water rights and just found out yesterday I was successful. Furthermore, because I am the first person to do so, the creek will be named after me. Henceforth it will be called Waechter Creek. And should there ever be a drought, I will be able to irrigate. I also have the 'Right to Purchase' of a ten-acre parcel on the other side of the creek, which has a home on it. I plan to build cabins there to house pickers outside of the community."

"It appears you have a well-thought-out plan, Mr. Waechter. As you probably know, the Fraser Valley has proven to be the perfect climate for growing raspberries amongst other vine fruits and vegetables. I know you have farmed, but what do you know about growing raspberries? Have you researched?"

"Indeed, I've read up on growing raspberries and have spoken to several growers here. My conclusion is that the Willamette berry is the best. It is a large berry and very prolific. I have a keen interest in growing it. That berry is precisely what I intend to sow."

Abe was smiling and, while being very impressed with Eugene's plans, he was thinking: 'One sows wheat, and one plants berries; typical farmer!'

"As I said before, you have a well-thought-out plan. The credit union will be happy to give you a line of credit to help you establish your berry farm. Your land will be the collateral."

"I appreciate that," said Eugene feeling a ton of bricks lifted from his shoulders. An exhilaration engulfed him, the likes of which he'd never experienced before. Smiling broadly, he stood up and began to leave, but he quickly turned around before walking through the doorway.

"You have more collateral than that, Mr. Doerksen," said Eugene.

"What would that be?" asked Abe, scratching his head in puzzlement.

Eugene was silent, then, squaring his shoulders and leveling his gaze, said in the deepest tone he could muster, "My determination!"

***

The Abbotsford Airport officially opened in 1943 as the Royal Canadian Air Force (RCAF) Station Abbotsford. This airport was constructed on land expropriated from fourteen farmers to strengthen Allied defenses on the West Coast, which was considered in danger following the catastrophic events of Pearl Harbour. Subsequently, this base became invaluable as a training center for airmen locally and abroad. Following the 1948 flooding of the Fraser River, the airport served as a shelter for people and livestock. It also served as a temporary school for Abbotsford School District 34.

After visiting the employment office in downtown Abbotsford, Eugene was anxious to talk to Elizabeth. When he walked through the door, she was mixing a batch of bread. The smell of yeast lay heavy in the air.

"I found out today that the Abbotsford Airbase will be hosting a cadet training camp all summer and will be hiring workers for the mess hall.

"What's the mess hall?" asked Elizabeth as she stripped the dough from her fingers.

"It's where they eat," replied Eugene with a half-smile. "Sounds funny, I know. I inquired at the employment office. They told me the Dept. of National Defence only hires people with kitchen experience. So, Lizzie, my dear, what do you think? I can put your name down along with Marie's because of your experience in the bunkhouse at Skelly's Canning Co. in Kamloops."

"That sounds great, Eugene, and I know Marie will be happy. We can walk there too as it's not that far. When do we start?

"I'll head back to the employment office and sign you up, then take you both there next Monday at 10:00 AM for indoctrination. I hear there is a squadron of cadets coming in soon. They must have a few cadets there now because I caught some yesterday sneaking through the backwoods stealing some of our strawberries, the scallywags."

"They probably are from the prairies and just haven't seen strawberries growing as they do here in B.C. Lordy knows they have only seen the little wild ones I canned in St. Lina. Anyway, Eugene, it's good to know we will have work all summer."

On June 30, 1954, Eugene worked diligently expanding the raspberry farm, and Lizzie and Marie began work in the mess hall while Dennis, now ten years old, spent his days fishing for trout at a nearby creek. He had grown into a strong, handsome lad with curly, brown hair and soft, brown eyes. Marie would tell her girlfriends, "You have to come over and see my cute little brother!"

The mess hall was a hive of activity. Many tables filled the dining area while steam tables holding hot and cold food lined up against the wall to serve two hundred young Airforce Cadets, ages twelve to eighteen, who filed by the steam table three times a day. They banged their cutlery on the edge of the steam table to express their hunger as they jostled along. Behind the table were the servers, local girls, giving them scoops of food as they filed by.

Regular airmen worked in the Headquarters Building, and others worked here in the kitchen, organizing the food service, cooking, and directing the staff; most were married men, which did not stop them from using suggestive language to watch the girls blush.

After noticing Marie was sullen during dinner, Lizzie spoke to Eugene, "Marie has been acting strange. It's not like her to be that quiet. I think there's something wrong. We're going to have to talk to her."

They had just finished breakfast on a Saturday when Marie was about to leave the table when Eugene quickly spoke to her.

"You seem to be upset lately, Marie. Is something the matter?"

"I don't like working on the Airforce Base."

"Why not? The pay is good, and I don't think the work is too hard. Is it?"

"It's not that, Dad. It's the Airmen. They are always talking dirty."

"Talking dirty? What are they saying?"

When Marie told her father some of the things they were saying, he put his fork down, stood up, and said, "I'm going up to that damn airbase!" He was out the door before Elizabeth could stop him.

Eugene drove up to the gate of the Abbotsford R.C.A.F. station and rolled down his car window while the Canadian flag fluttered in the wind above the guardhouse. An airman dressed in a blue uniform came out and greeted him.

"Can I help you, sir?"

"I want to see the commanding officer," said Eugene.

The airman pointed Eugene towards the headquarters building. Eugene walked into the front door of the headquarters building and passed several astonished personnel who looked up from their desks, astonished to see a farmer passing their desks in dusty overalls, their base where deportment was all important.

Eugene walked directly to the door marked *Commanding Officer.* When his door burst open, the officer sitting at his desk was quick to his feet. A wooden plaque on his desk read: *Wing Commander Shanks.*

"Are you the commanding officer?" Eugene asked with a snarl in his voice, knowing full well he was.

"Yes, I am, sir," replied the officer standing tall and straight with ribbons ablaze on his uniform and yellow cresting across the front of his officer's hat that sat on his desk. He had just returned to his office from an all-ranks parade held on the tarmac. Puzzled, he looked at the angry, unshaven farmer in front of him, standing in his dusty overalls.

Eugene continued, "What kind of a joint are you running here?"

The officer blanched and said, "What can I do for you, sir?"

"You can train your men to have respect for women; that's what you can do. I've had strawberries stolen out of my yard by your cadets, and I haven't complained, but I'll not have it when it comes to disrespecting my women. Do you hear me? I'll not have it. Both my wife and my daughter work in the mess hall. Your staff there have filthy mouths, and you better do something about it."

"Are you lodging a formal complaint?" Mr., Mr . . ."

"Waechter," replied Eugene, unabashed, "Eugene Waechter, and yes, I am lodging a complaint. That's precisely why I'm here!"

The officer reached into his desk, drew out a notepad and pen, and then set them on the desk in front of Eugene.

"I'm sorry about that, Mr. Waechter. I can see how distressed you are. I certainly will look into this. Please offer my apologies to your wife and daughter. I would like you to list on this notepad what was said and when and where it occurred. Please sign and date the bottom."

Eugene nodded and began writing. When he'd finished, his anger had subsided; standing up, he said, "Thank you for your time," then walked swiftly out the door. There were some barely audible snickers as he walked past the staff in the outer office.

Immediately after his departure, the commanding officer picked up his phone and called the mess hall.

"I would like all regular staff in charge of the mess hall to meet in my office at 1:00 P.M. sharp."

Elizabeth and Marie were happy to see Eugene return. They had been anxiously waiting to hear what he had to say.

"Well," he said. "I hope that visit with the commanding officer puts a stop to that nasty little piece of business. Now those degenerates should get the comeuppance they deserve."

His ladies looked at one another and smiled. Elizabeth gave him the plate of food he left behind. She had kept it warm in the warming oven. He ate it with gusto.

"Thank you, Lizzie. That little episode has made me hungry." While he finished his breakfast, he'd started an hour earlier, for some strange reason, his thoughts reverted back to St. Lina all those years earlier when Mr. Curling had the nerve to ask for Georgina. He was a degenerate, too, albeit a different kind. He pushed those thoughts aside and concentrated on developing his raspberry farm, anxious to acquire the adjacent ten acres with a suitable home.

Following the obvious reprimand, those Airman received, there was over politeness in the mess hall, almost to the point of mockery. Marie was aware of it but she paid no heed. because there was something brewing on the horizon; something of much greater importance in life! He was an Airman working in the headquarters building. His name was Randy Rickwood. He was from Edmonton, Alberta's One Tack Air Command, and he had captured her eye, and her heart.

Chapter Eighteen

Six months later, when Eugene picked up the mail, there was a letter from Marie. This letter explained why they hadn't heard from her for some time. She had left Abbotsford at the end of that summer and went to Vancouver to visit her sister, Georgina, and she had never returned. Marie was with Georgina for a short while, and then she boarded a train to Edmonton, Alberta. She had made arrangements to board with her Aunt Mary, Elizabeth's older sister, who welcomed her with open arms. And there, Marie quickly obtained an office job with the Wawanesa Insurance Company in downtown Edmonton. But more importantly, she now was close to Randy, who was posted there with the Royal Canadian Airforce, only two miles from Aunt Mary's home.

'And Mom and Dad, I told the man interviewing me that I was an excellent typist, the best in high school. And that the principal

asked me to come to the office to type for him whenever the school secretary was away. The man at Wawanesa hired me right on the spot. Also, Mom and Dad, I want you to know that I plan to go to night school to get my shorthand, then I'll be a full-fledged secretary. And eventually, I plan to go to college, so please don't worry about my education. And the big scoop is that Randy and I plan to get married sometime soon before he gets posted to another place.'

After reading Marie's letter over twice, Eugene and Elizabeth looked at each other with a measure of shock. They were dismayed their youngest daughter was no longer under their roof but more so to hear she planned to marry at such a young age.

After a few silent moments, Eugene broke the silence, "She's a little go-getter. We have to hand her that! Your sister, Mary will be good to her."

"All we can do now is pray for her," said Elizabeth, reaching for her rosary "We know nothing about this Randy Rickwood guy other than he's from Ontario," said Elizabeth.

"Well, now, that's not so bad!" Eugene smiled. Elizabeth caught his drift.

"We knew nothing about the mates our of other children chose," continued Elizabeth. "Georgina and Celine are happily married.

As you know, Eugene, Alvin introduced Mervin to Margaret Muir, and I think wedding bells will be ringing down the road for him. And Alvin has been seeing a lot of Theresa Veldkamp. Both those girls are lovely and will make good wives. And if nature has its way, there will be grandchildren coming. I hope its not too long before Milton and Rolly find their mates.

Milton is up in the interior slugging it out in the woods, but he's happy, I'm glad he visited us when we were working in Kamloops. And Rolly is traveling all over the place. He sounds happy, too, in his letters. And doing well as a salesman. I wish we saw more of them. I hope they all stay safe. That's all we can ask for, eh, Eugene?"

Elizabeth sat in the living room, thinking, and reminiscing about the children. She covered her face with both hands. When she removed them, she continued,

"Uh-huh, Yesiree, that's all we can ask for. I pray our good Lord will take care of them all."

"Now, we only have Dennis under our roof," declared Eugene, somberly.

Then, sitting side by side on the sofa, they prayed the rosary together.

The next day, Eugene was notified that the Right to Purchase the ten acres that adjoined the property they now owned was in effect. All he had to do was sign the papers. And, after signing the documents, he could move his family into the residence there. The home had a kitchen, dining room, living room, two bedrooms, and a bathroom, just what they needed. Elizabeth was delighted because now, she would have running water and a flush toilet for the first time in her married life.

The move was quick. Eugene hired a truck, and, with the help of a neighbor lad, he was able to load up their belongings and deliver them to the new home. They settled in quickly.

Now all their attention was placed on expanding the raspberries. Eugene planted more canes when the land was cleared to receive them. Each year that passed saw more berries being produced. which necessitated more pickers. The raspberry plantation had now grown to almost fifteen acres.

Dennis, now a young teenager, became invaluable to Eugene. He helped around the farm by weighing in the berries each picker brought to the weigh scale at the end of the day. Dennis also rototilled and disced between the rows to loosen the soil for air absorption. At the same time, Eugene devised a system of driving between the rows with his tractor, pulling a metal wagon behind. In this wagon, he burned all the dead vines as he went along and deposited their ash back in the ground; this enriched the soil while cleaning up the vines, leaving space for the new growth to form the next crop. When doing this, he recalled how, back in St. Lina, he had grown a bumper crop of potatoes by putting ash on the ground.

The cabins Mervin helped build now, during the berry-picking season, were occupied by families from Alberta who came to the coast to pick. In addition, there were the locals who showed up every day. Elizabeth was the field boss, making sure the pickers stripped the vines of their ripe fruit, leaving none behind to fall to the ground, while Dennis did the weigh-in at the end of each day. The pickers were paid five cents per pound and received an extra cent if they stayed through to the end. Many did.

On this bright spring day, Eugene arose early, pulled on his overalls, and went outside. Daylight was breaking through the morning mist. He walked over the culvert and surveyed the raspberries that grew in abundance, this being something he frequently did in the early morning hours. He loved the sight of them! He loved the white blossoms that grew on every inch of the vines even more!

"It's going to be a bumper crop," he said aloud.

A bird chirped in the nearby woods as if to agree. Then, a thought threw a cloud over his joy. 'What if we don't get the rain needed to change those blossoms into berries. Past years there was sufficient rain, but that wasn't a given. What if there was a drought this year? What then? All would be wasted. Many of the blossoms would dry up and fall off, and what fruit there was, would be stunted and dried up on the vines. I need to invest in an irrigation system. Yes, I need to irrigate. I'm lucky to have the creek right near with water rights. All I need now is a pump to suck the water out of the creek and spray the crop.'

As he walked back to the house, he thought about his finances and how he had cleared his line of credit and now had money in the bank. After struggling for so many years trying to make a go of it, he could finally say he was comfortable financially.

When he walked back into the house, the tantalizing aroma of bacon hit his nostrils, awakening his appetite. Lizzie hummed as she flipped it over in the big, cast-iron frying pan. Dennis had just come to the table.

"Two eggs, please, Mom," he said. "Same for me," said Eugene. When they were all seated, he asked them to bow their heads for grace:

"Bless us, oh Lord, and these thy gifts which we are about to receive through the bounty of Christ, our Lord, Amen."

Before the fork hit their mouths, Elizabeth quickly spoke: "May the souls of the faithful departed through the mercy of God rest in peace."

Conversation continued around the table.

"I'm happy Milton has now found a wife. I think Kathy is lovely girl and I feel the same about Rolly's Molly, whose ever so smart. Both these ladies were good choices for our sons. Don't you think so too, Eugene?

"Most certainly, he replied, they couldn't be better!

At this moment, Eugene's thoughts were centered elsewhere.

When they had finished eating, Eugene told them about his plan to install an irrigation system. He told them he'd read up on it and that it was the only way to go. Elizabeth nodded in agreement. She knew how important water was for growing things.

After Mass the next day outside the church, where many of the congregation's chins wagged, Eugene had the perfect opportunity to talk to the other growers about irrigation. The growers didn't daunt Eugene when the talking circle poo-pooed irrigation. Some broke into laughter, saying British Columbia never lacks rain. Then, as luck would have it, Abe Doerksen, whose farm was on the other side of the airport, spoke up.

"I have all the pipes. They lay at the edge of the field and are in the way. I'll give them to whoever will haul them away. I never did buy the pump, just never needed to irrigate. There was always enough rain."

"I'd be interested in taking them off your hands," said Eugene, thinking that was a stroke of luck. "Whereabouts is your place?" Abe gave him the directions.

"My son, Dennis, and I will come by tomorrow when he gets home from school."

"Great, see you then," replied Abe watching Eugene depart.

The following year, the berries needed sunshine. The cloudy skies and persistent rain hindered the ripening process. When the sun finally showed its face and ripened the berries, the collective produce was more than the previous year. Eugene's crop, albeit less, remained sufficient for winter's sustenance. Every time he passed the stack of irrigation pipes down by the creek, he found that they gave him a measure of comfort, though he didn't need them yet. He told himself, 'If we have a year with too much rain, we can have one with too little, and that, without irrigation, would be a fine, how do you do!'

There was a change the next year. After several days without rain, Eugene decided to set up the pipes and started watering. Dennis was a big help setting up the pipes, watering, and then moving them throughout the fifteen acres of berries, especially now when rain was badly needed.

He called out to Eugene this day, who was heading back to the house.

"Dad, come and see the rainbow." Eugene turned to see a kaleidoscope of color above the raspberries through the irrigated sprinkles. Mt. Baker in the background added to the vista. Wow!

I wish I had a camera. I should carry one in my pocket for situations just like this.

***

Dennis was smiling when he came home from school the following week. He was anxious to tell his parents the good news. Eugene and Elizabeth were sitting in lawn chairs at the back of the house, relaxing and talking about the great summer. Now, with all the older children married, the main subject of their many conversations was the grandchildren coming one after another.

"They all are so sweet!" said Eugene.

"Uh-huh," I loved them as soon as I laid eyes on them, and I know there'll be more to come. I know I've said this many times before:

: *"There's nothing more beautiful in this whole, wide world than a child!"*

"Last Sunday, when they all came home with their families, the sawhorses and sheet of plywood was a great table for the gaggle of little ones to have their meal outside. The benches I built sure came in handy too," declared Eugene.

Dennis walked to the back of the house and sat down on the grass in front of them. "The principal called me into the office today and told me the teaching staff selected me as the best all-around student of School District 63.

"That's wonderful, son!" said Eugene.

Dennis continued. "There's more. The Rotary Club sponsors the selected student with all expenses paid for one week's visit to Ottawa. I will be billeted there by a Rotarian family and join around one hundred other students from all around B.C. He told me there is a program of activities planned, including a trip to the parliament buildings."

"Now that's something to toot your horn about," smiled Eugene.

"I should say," said Elizabeth clapping her hands and chuckling.

"I think it's time we talk about your future," said Eugene. You will be graduating soon. Have you thought about what you want to do with your life?"

"I've been thinking about medicine," said Dennis. "The principal told me because of my high average in math, I shouldn't have any trouble being accepted into the medical program at UBC. I'm interested in helping the sick, but I don't know the cost."

"You don't have to worry about that," said Eugene. "I can afford to help you. You have been an invaluable help here with the berries. Lord knows you've more than earned it.

Later in bed that night, Eugene said to Elizabeth, "Remember how worried we were when you were giving birth to him at the age of forty-two, and now he's going to be a doctor! Just think we will have a doctor in the family!"

"It's simply wonderful, Eugene. I should say!"

Chapter Nineteen

Days melted one season into the other, and the vines kept producing, averaging up to two and a half tons a day in peak season. Some years necessitated little irrigation, and other years none at all. Then, unexpectedly, there came a severe drought. Berries were drying up on the vine for the farmers in the Abbotsford area as the sun kept blazing day in and day out. Only a few growers had irrigation. Eugene was one of the lucky ones. Moving the pipes across the fifteen-acre growth kept him and Dennis busy every day. Their effort produced a bumper crop, the best they ever had. Some days at the peak of the season, Eugene made two truckloads to the cannery with a total daily weight of four thousand pounds. Knowing Mr. Waechter was coming back with a second load, the men at the cannery's weigh-in section allowed him to drive to the front of the line.

And, because of the shortage of berries from other growers that year, Eugene's price per pound was sky-high. Eugene felt like the Raspberry King of Abbotsford, all because of irrigation!

After many years of struggling, living hand to mouth, Hope Road, where they lived, should now be renamed, *Easy Street*. Eugene and Elizabeth couldn't be happier!

The other growers didn't stop after Mass to visit during this period; they were too depressed.

At the end of that summer, in 1963, Dennis left for medical school making it necessary for Eugene and Elizabeth to replace him with hired help. But how does one replace a dutiful son who has his heart and energy on the job of helping his father grow raspberries? They did manage to get part-time help and continued to produce bountiful crops over the next few years by continuing the irrigation, until one morning after another successful season, they decided, over breakfast, enough was enough! The decision was made to retire. Their success over the past few years enabled them to stop working, live in comfort and take life easy. They were ready! They more than deserved it!

When their property came on the market, there were many buyers who'd heard of the farm that boasted the highest production in the Fraser Valley. They finally sold to a young East Indian couple who were recently married and anxious to get started. They engaged the same realtor, that sold their property, to find them a home in town. He was happy to get both ends of the deal.

"It has to be a home within walking distance to our church," said Eugene.

"What church is that?" asked the realtor.

"St. Ann's Catholic Church."

"Oh, I know which one that is. I'll check it out when I get back to the office. I believe some homes nearby have recently come on the market.

"I might just like to go to Mass every day," said Elizabeth, looking at Eugene gratefully.

"But of course, my dear," replied Eugene, knowing how important it was to her.

The home finally selected was a rancher on a corner lot at 1949 Horizon Street. It was a modern, two-level, three-bedroom rancher with a cathedral entrance and, most importantly, only a five-minute walk to church.

It was 1965 when Eugene and Elizabeth moved into their new, modern home.

The children were happy, too, when hearing about the purchase. They knew the sacrifices their parents had made over the years.

Dennis paid a visit to his parents when passing through Abbotsford. He had returned from the Deaconess Hospital in Spokane, Washington, where he was working on his internship. He was on his way to Vancouver to marry his beautiful sweetheart, Jacqueline Rein, whom he had met at the University of British Columbia. The wedding celebration was going to be held the next week in the faculty room of U.B.C. on August 23, 1969. After which, he would take his bride back to Spokane to complete his internship. And subsequently, he would begin a position as a family physician with the Delta Clinic in Delta, B.C.

"This is quite the house you have here!" stated Dennis. "I'm happy for you Mom and Dad!" They discussed his upcoming wedding for a few moments then the conversation switched to his internship.

"Have you delivered any babies?" queried Eugene.

"I've helped deliver many babies since I began my internship," declared Dennis.

"Can you deliver a baby all on your own now, son?" asked Eugene.

"Of course, I can Dad," said Dennis."

"So can I, son," replied Eugene, with a proud smile. "As a matter of fact, as you probably know, I delivered Rolly and Marie. I told Marie she had the nicest little belly button in town."

He laughed heartily at his own words! Dennis laughed too, then said, "That would be mighty hard to prove, Dad!"

Elizabeth was sitting in the easy chair across the room, listening. She was crocheting a doily for under the lamp on the end table beside her. She was chuckling to herself, and her eyes were twinkling. She thought, *Silly men, I know exactly who did the 'delivering'*

Dennis was also chuckling as he drove to Vancouver. He was thinking about the visit he just had with his parents. Then, he thought about Jacquie, his beautiful Jacquie, and stepped on the gas. He was so very anxious to see her and hold her in his arms.

***

The following month, Eugene and Elizabeth had said their morning prayers and were now enjoying their breakfast and their usual small talk. The aroma of scrambled eggs and bacon permeated throughout the kitchen. The late summer sun streaming through the window glinted off the corner of the toaster as Eugene popped in another slice.

"Your homemade bread sure makes good toast," he declared.

"I like it too," said Elizabeth. "So nice and crispy."

"Well, Lizzie, now that Dennis is married, all our children have found their mates. I guess we can expect more grandchildren."

"As I said before, Eugene if nature has its way."

"When Dennis and Jacquie last visited, I regretted something that I asked her."

"And what was that?"

"I asked her if she was with child."

"You did what? You must have embarrassed the living daylights out of her."

"Well, she did blush a little. Did you know Lizzie, her mother, Claire, speaks several languages?"

"So, I've heard."

"Including German," said Eugene, in a tone that made his statement one of utmost importance.

"I think Jacquie is a lovely girl and has such beautiful brown eyes! We have been blessed with eight wonderful children and the sweet little ones that have come into their lives! And we mustn't forget the great daughters-in-law and sons-in-law we've been given! Uh-huh, I should say! We have been truly blessed!" She folded her hands and looked upward.

"Yes, we certainly have," declared Eugene.

They were quiet for a short time, lost in their thoughts. Adding to the moment's tranquility, in the background playing softly on the radio, Elvis Presley was singing; *It's Now or Never*. Eugene was tapping his foot under the table. Age had placed several inches to his girth, but ironically, there was nary a gray hair on his head. On the other hand, Elizabeth had to lend half her auburn hair to different shades of gray, but the sparkle remained in her eyes.

She glanced around the kitchen, finished her coffee, and then stood up to clear the table, but Eugene beat her to it. He placed the dishes in the sink pridefully, for it was something he seldom did, then sat back down. His eyes were upon her as she moved about the kitchen, putting the dishes in the dishwasher, then wiping the counters and stove while humming. He couldn't tell if she was humming along with Elvis or if the tune was one of her own. He watched her leave the kitchen.

He stood up and poured himself another coffee draining the pot. He turned off the radio and sat back down. His thoughts were filled with Lizzie and with all the years they had spent together. What an amazing and wonderful wife she has been! He couldn't have asked for anyone better than his Lizzie. Joy filled his heart, knowing that now they could retire in comfort.

Elizabeth had walked over to the living- room window and gazed out. Thoughts of the past came rushing in. She thought about the birthing of their beautiful children and how she worried when they were all sick at the same time in St. Lina. She thought about the beautiful grandchildren now in her life, whom she loved the moment she saw them. She remembered how sad she felt when her mother, who helped so many, passed away at only sixty-four years old. She also recalled the vision she had when they were about to lose their first farm and how it gave her strength to survive the cold, lonely winter months when Eugene had to work away from the farm,

She turned from the window and ambled around the house from room to room, admiring her new home: the two fireplaces, one up and one down: the cathedral entrance; the plush carpeting; the ensuite plumbing in the master bedroom, and the fully equipped laundry room that made her remember how she toiled for a family of ten with a washtub and scrub board. She admired the paintings and new furniture—especially the large burl coffee table they couldn't resist buying—and then she whispered into the room's silence, "Is this all really mine?"

She walked back to the window and gazed out once more. This time, she saw something just over the rooftops peeking between the trees that brought her into the full realization of something she had known all along, something that had sustained her. Material things are of little consequence; they are just that, material things! There is something fundamentally much more critical in this life, and she knows what it is. Her eyes were focusing on the cross atop the steeple of her nearby church.

Yes, she knows what it is! SHE KNOWS!

Overcome with happiness, she walked back into the kitchen to where Eugene was sitting.

"I just cannot tell you, Eugene, how much I love this home. Everything about living here is wonderful! I feel so lucky to have such a beautiful place! Uh-huh, I do!"

Her bottom lip was quivering as if about to cry.

Eugene smiled at his Lizzie and stood up and embracing her said,

"*Lizzie, Liebling, ich bin fest entschlossen, das fur dich zu erreiche.*"

He said it once more in English, "I was *determined* you should have it, Lizzie dear!"

The End

Glossary of Definitions

Disc – a machine to cultivate earth after plowing

Harrow – machine to refine soil after discing before seeding

Summer follow - growing clover and plowing under to nourish the land.

Two bits – 25 cents.

Four bits – fifty cents.

Rosary – prayer beads with the Hail Mary and other prayers repeated.

A decade on the rosary – ten Hail Mary's prayed on ten beads.

Democrat – a four-wheeled, open wagon

Plough – pulled by a horse to turn over the soil

Stoneboat – a flat box built on wooden runners to carry stones, etc.

Stook – stacking wheat bundles into a small hill for pitching into a wagon.

Genuflect – bending a knee to honor the Host in the tabernacle on the altar

before entering the pew.

The Marriages Of Eugene And Elizabeth's Eight Children And The Birth Of Subsequent Grandchildren:

Georgina married Lloyd Gropp on April 18, 1949. They had six children: Celia, born July 11, 1951; Janice, born July 20, 1953; Randy, born October 10, 1954; Catherine, born February 24, 1956; Annette, born February 28, 1960; and David, June 11th, 1957.

Milton married Kathy Danes on July 1st, 1957. They had three children: Cheryl Laverne, born June 16, 1960; Martin Anthony, born July 18, 1961; Shane Travis, born April 17; 1970.

Mervin married Margaret Muri on December 28, 1954. They had three girls: Sandra Pauline, born Dec. 3, 1957; Maureen Elizabeth, born Oct. 29, 1959; Donna May, born June 12, 1964.

Alvin Married Therese Veldkamp on July 2, 1955. They had two children: Brenda Louise, born May 24th, 1957; Bruce Alvin, born Sept. 24th, 1959.

Celine married John Zender on November 17, 1951. They had six children: Dorie Jean, born July 22, 1952; Patrick John, born December 17, 1954; Dale Jacob, born February 10, 1956; Diane Marie, born January 24, 1957; Perry Robert, born Sept. 17th, 1958; Donald Duane, born October 28, 1961.

Rolly married Molly Baker on May 30th, 1958. Their children were those within Christ the Redeemer Catholic Parish, North Vancouver, where they taught religious education and trained altar boys. For their many years of service, a hall in the church was named after them.

Marie married Randy Rickwood on May 14, 1955. They had six children: Rory Robert, born March 4, 1956; Michelle Marie, born March 16, 1957; Derek David, born Oct. 3, 1958; Kellee

Kathleen, born Dec. 7, 1959; Roanne Ruth, born Oct. 4, 1963; Jill Jennifer October 20, 1971.

Dennis married Jacqueline Rein on August 23, 1969.

They had four children: Jason Eugene, born May 8th, 1971; Ryan Burke, born June 3rd, 1972; Warren Patrick, born May 20, 1980; Maria Elizabeth Claire, born December 18th, 1982.

In loving memory of our beloved
Husband, Father, Grandfather,
Great Grandfather and Brother

EUGENE PETER WAECHTER

who passed away into the presence of his Lord
at Abbotsford, B.C.
on Friday, March 27, 1981
age 78 years
late of 1949 Horizon Street, Abbotsford, B.C.
born at Formosa, Ontario, August 9, 1902

PRAYERS:
Sunday, March 29, 1981 at 4:30 p.m.
at Saint Ann's Catholic Church

MASS OF THE RESURRECTION:
Monday, March 30, 1981 at 10:30 a.m.
at Saint Ann's Catholic Church
Abbotsford, B.C.

CELEBRANT: Father Nicholas J. Boomars

SOLOIST: Donald Zender
accompanied by Pat, Dale, Perry and Diane

PALLBEARERS:

Milton Waechter	Roland Waechter
Mervin Waechter	Dennis Waechter
Alvin Waechter	David Gropp

INTERMENT:
Aberdeen Cemetery

Elizabeth Catherine Waechter

Elizabeth Catherine in her 101st year, beloved wife, devoted mother, and grandmother passed away peacefully on Oct. 13, 2004. Predeceased by her loving husband Eugene on March 27, 1981, her grandson Bruce Waechter on April 29, 1995, and her son-in-law, Lloyd Gropp on Nov. 9, 1997.

She leaves to mourn her passing eight loving children: Georgina Gropp of New Westminster, BC, Milton Waechter (Dawn) of Coombs, B.C., Mervin Waechter (Margaret) and Alvin Waechter (Terry) both of Aldergrove, B.C., Celine Zender (John) of Deming, Washington, USA Roland Waechter (Molly) of North Vancouver, B.C., Marie Rickwood (Randy) of Nanaimo, B.C. and Dr. Dennis Waechter of Armstrong, B.C.

Elizabeth, who often said, "There's nothing more beautiful than a child" dearly loved her eight children, 30 grandchildren, 68 great grandchildren and seven great, great grandchildren. On May 26, of this year she welcomed them and their spouses to her amazing, centennial birthday celebration in Aldergrove, B.C.

Elizabeth was born in Parkston, Aurora County in South Dakota on May 26, 1904. At the age of nine her family moved to the Camrose area of Alberta where they farmed for many years. She married Eugene Waechter in 1926 and they lived in the same area until taking up residence in St. Lina, Alberta as homesteaders. In 1947 they relocated to the Abbotsford area where Elizabeth and her husband managed their raspberry farm until retirement in 1965. The last few years of her life were spent with her son Alvin and daughter-in-law Terry in Aldergrove, and the Cartier House in Coquitlam.

Elizabeth, an inspiration to all her family, was a woman of sterling Christian character and for many years faithfully attended St. Ann's Catholic Church in Abbotsford, B.C. and more recently Saints Joachim and Ann's Catholic Church in Aldergrove, B.C.

Other Family Members who have passed away.

Marie E. Rickwood

Waechter Family Photos

Eugene's parents: John Waechter and Cecelia Fischer

Thomas Family 1908. Elizabeth is seated between her parents.

STEPHEN WAECHTER FAMILY
early 1800's — Carrick's oldest citizen, Lot 23, Concession 9
Back row, left to right: Louis, Caroline (Mrs. Knapp), Pauline (Mrs. J. Weber), Mary (Mrs. Simon Hergott), Barbara (Mrs. A. Weber), John.
Seated, left to right: Annie (Mrs. B. Rich), Father and Mother, Matilda (Mrs. Reid).

278

Eugene's father, Johannes (John) Waechter is standing
on the right. His father is seated in the front row. His father's
father was Laurent Waechter who came to Canada from
Alsace-Lorraine, France. His father's mother was
Anne Marie Lacroix, also from Alsace-Lorraine.

Eugene Peter Waechter & Elizabeth Catherine Thomas Wedding Day

NOVEMBER 1926

The Waechter Gang

Taken on Homestead Farm in St. Lina, Alberta.
Back row: Elizabeth;
Front row: Georgina, Milton, Mervin, Alvin,
Celine, Roland & Marie

Alvin's first communion picture taken with cousin
Ronnie Thomas on the left, he is the son of Nick Thomas

Rolly and Marie's First Holy Communion just as all the other
siblings ahead had celebrated. It was the Spring of 1945, and the
pews were muddy causing Marie to be upset over the
soiled stockings.

Hello Dennis

He was the last child born to the Waechter's on Nov.
11th, 1945.

Dennis not yet two yars old with pet lamb called Bunky.

Riding a bike at four years old.   Dressed for St. Lina's
cold weather

Back row L-R: Dennis, Roland, Milton,
Georgina, Mervin and Alvin.
Front row: Celine, Eugene, Elizabeth, and Marie.

Standing in the garage in their new home in 1967.

Lloyd Gropp and Georgina Waechter April 18th, 1949.

Milton Waechter married Kathy Danes on July 1st, 1957.

Dec. 28/54 - from left to right, Marie Waechter, Shirley Muri, Margaret Muri, Mervin Waechter, Alvin Waechter, Randy Rickwood

50 Years

Alvin Waechter and Theresa Veldkamp
July 2, 1955, wedding picture as it appeared
on the invitation to their golden anniversary.

John Zener and Celine Waechter November 17, 1951

Roland Waechter and Molly Baker – May 30th, 1958

Marie Waechter & Randy Rickwood, May 14/55

The wedding day of Dennis Waechter and Jacqueline Rein
On Aug. 23, 1969

1949 Horizon Street, Abbotsford, B.C.
This is the home where Eugene and Elizabeth retired in 1965

Figure 3 This is the church Elizabeth attended every day after Eugene passed away.

Elizabeth prayed her rosary every day.

At home on the raspberry farm.

Georgina 60, Celine 55, Marie 50

45th Wedding Anniversary

50TH ANNIVERSARY

From L-R – Eugene's sister, Sr. St. Antonio
Bernetta Freiberger, Eugene's sister-in-law
The second nun is a niece, daughter of sister Nora.

This Last Supper picture was given to Eugene and Elizabeth by her parents as a wedding gift and hung over their kitchen table in St. Lina, AB. Today it adorns the kitchen wall in Alvin and Terry's home. the home where Elizabeth spent the last five years of her life before going to the senior's residence.

Back row: Alvin, Milton, Georgina, Marie, Celine & Dennis
Front row: Mervin. Elizabeth and Roland.
A family get-to-gether at Dennis' home in Armstrong.
B.C. to celebrate Elizabeth's 95th birthday.

Marie, the youngest daughter of
Eugene and Elizabeth. at the age 16

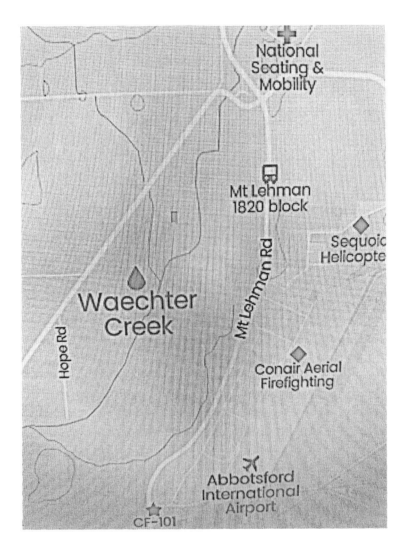

Eugene was first to get water rights for his berries
thus the creek was named after him.

Georgina, at age 20.

Georgina was the eldest of the Waechter children. She became a Schoolteacher. While studying for this profession, she worked for her room and board in Vancouver with a family of four children.

Georgina was an excellent teacher and loved by all who knew her. She also raised six great children of her own.

Happy 100th Birthday Elizabeth!

Born on May 26th, 1904

Ancestors of Eugene Peter Waechter

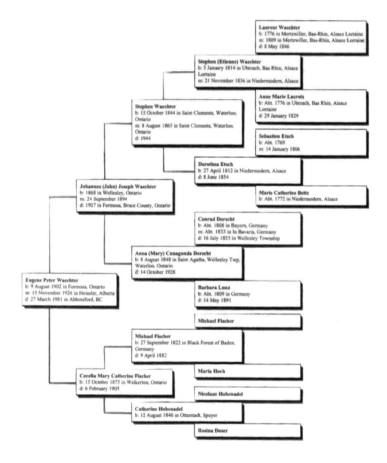

Laurent Waechter
b: 1776 in Mertzwiller, Bas-Rhin, Alsace Lorraine
m: 1809 in Mertzwiller, Bas-Rhin, Alsace Lorraine
d: 8 May 1846

Stephen (Etienne) Waechter
b: 3 January 1814 in Uberach, Bas Rhin, Alsace Lorraine
m: 21 November 1836 in Niedermodern, Alsace

Stephen Waechter
b: 15 October 1844 in Saint Clements, Waterloo, Ontario
m: 8 August 1865 in Saint Clements, Waterloo, Ontario
d: 1944

Anne Marie Lacroix
b: Abt. 1776 in Uberach, Bas Rhin, Alsace Lorraine
d: 29 January 1829

Sebastien Etsch
b: Abt. 1769
m: 14 January 1806

Dorothea Etsch
b: 27 April 1812 in Niedermodern, Alsace
d: 8 June 1854

Johannes (John) Joseph Waechter
b: 1868 in Wellesley, Ontario
m: 24 September 1894
d: 1927 in Formosa, Bruce County, Ontario

Marie Catherine Beitz
b: Abt. 1772 in Niedermodern, Alsace

Conrad Dorscht
b: Abt. 1808 in Bayern, Germany
m: Abt. 1833 in In Bavaria, Germany
d: 16 July 1853 in Wellesley Township

Anna (Mary) Cunagunda Dorscht
b: 8 August 1848 in Saint Agatha, Wellesley Twp, Waterloo, Ontario
d: 14 October 1928

Eugene Peter Waechter
b: 9 August 1902 in Formosa, Ontario
m: 15 November 1926 in Heissler, Alberta
d: 27 March 1981 in Abbotsford, BC

Barbara Lunz
b: Abt. 1809 in Germany
d: 14 May 1891

Michael Fischer

Michael Fischer
b: 27 September 1822 in Black Forest of Baden, Germany
d: 9 April 1882

Maria Hoch

Cecelia Mary Catherine Fischer
b: 15 October 1875 in Walkerton, Ontario
d: 6 February 1905

Nicolaus Hohenadel

Catherine Hohenadel
b: 12 August 1840 in Otterstadt, Speyer

Rosina Doser

Ancestors of Elizabeth Catherine Waechter

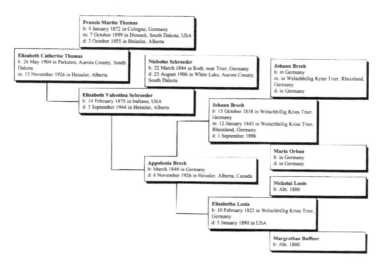

Francis Martin Thomas
b: 4 January 1872 in Cologne, Germany
m: 7 October 1899 in Dimock, South Dakota, USA
d: 3 October 1955 in Heissler, Alberta

Elizabeth Catherine Thomas
b: 26 May 1904 in Parkston, Aurora County, South Dakota
m: 15 November 1926 in Heissler, Alberta

Nicholas Schroeder
b: 22 March 1844 in Rodt, near Trier, Germany
d: 25 August 1906 in White Lake, Aurora County, South Dakota

Elizabeth Valentina Schroeder
b: 14 February 1875 in Indiana, USA
d: 3 September 1944 in Heissler, Alberta

Johann Brech
b: in Germany
m: in Welschbillig Kries Trier, Rheinland, Germany
d: in Germany

Johann Brech
b: 15 October 1818 in Welschbillig Kries Trier, Germany
m: 12 January 1843 in Welschbillig Kries Trier, Rheinland, Germany
d: 1 September 1898

Maria Orban
b: in Germany
d: in Germany

Appolonia Brech
b: March 1849 in Germany
d: 6 November 1926 in Heissler, Alberta, Canada

Nickolai Louis
b: Abt. 1800

Elisabetha Louis
b: 10 February 1822 in Welschbillig Kries Trier, Germany
d: 5 January 1890 in USA

Margrethae Buffner
b: Abt. 1800

About the Author

Marie Elizabeth Rickwood lives in Nanaimo, B.C., Canada with her husband, Val Fenton. She is proud to say she has raised six wonderful children and today enjoys her many grandchildren.

Writing and painting have always been part of her life. More recently she has painted portraits of her children which are on display in her home.

Together with her husband, Val Fenton, they are part of Nanaimo's dance society and go dancing once or twice a week. They also belong to the Nanaimo North Probus Club.

Prior to her retirement in the year 2000, Marie was an Office Administrator/Accountant in Nanaimo for 30 years, and she also, during that time, owned and operated a catering business called, Maria's Catering Food and Bar Service. She catered many banquets in the Nanaimo area, and with great success catered a political convention in Victoria, B.C. for a crowd of 400 which included the Premier of the province.

Marie's slogan for her catering business was: 'Pleasing Palate and Pocketbook'.

Other books Marie has written, are **Hornets In The Office; Behind the Smoke** - co-authored with her husband, Val Fenton, retired District Fire Chief, and her most recent novel, **Rules For Living On Earth,** of which she has a sequel in progress.

Marie welcomes any comments you may have by emailing: marierickwood@shaw.ca.